Sleeping Tom

E.V. Fairfall

Book design/Illustration by Kendall Roderick (RMind-Design.com)

The text of this book was set in Adobe Devanagari
Manufactured in the United States of America

ISBN: 978-0-9912832-2-4

To Ronnie,
"Folders and cotton balls."

&

To Michelle,
Black is the only color worth wearing.

The two of you inspire me!

Rebecca shut her eyes and leaned over the edge of the bridge. The rain was smothering her, pulling her in the direction it wanted her to go: down.

Jump, it seemed to say.

Weak, pathetic, Rebecca. Damaged, broken, Rebecca.

That was what she was.

Her tears came again, mixing with the rain, each breath stinging her lungs with the cold.

Sean.

He'd left her. Just like Mom had said he would.

Jump.

Rebecca whimpered as she opened her eyes. The drop off the bridge looked dire enough to end her suffering, but Sean wasn't worth it. Rebecca pushed her body, heavy with rain, away from the edge.

No, Sean isn't worth it.

Asshole. That was all he would ever be. Over months he had molded her into a pliable substance, a submissive helpless girl. He broke her down so that he could be her crutch, and then he left her.

Another wave of crying tore through her, causing her body to shake. Her eyes burned from her running mascara. Sean always insisted she wear it.

Rebecca shook her head. *I can be strong. I have to be strong.*

Of course, that wasn't what he'd said. Sean had told her she was used up, worthless, and "just not good enough."

A burning sensation filled her body like a scream.

I can be strong, I can do this. I just can't be Rebecca. I can't be what he's turned me—her—into.

Straightening her shoulders, she looked down at the mist-covered road. Trees hovered above the black pavement, overgrown and feverishly green. *I can be someone else. I can be...Caden.* Emotions streamed through her like a poison, dissolving her confidence; deep down she didn't really believe it. Could she do that? Become someone else?

The rain beat down on her, pounding her new name into her skull. *Caden, Caden, Caden.* It fit her better. It had to. She would make it fit; she would change into a new girl. This time she would do things right. She wouldn't mess everything up.

Caden peered into a puddle and watched as droplets drowned in its mass, ringlets echoing their lost life. Her head tilted up toward the sky; beautiful swirls of thin purple clouds curled like snakes, choking the blue and swallowing the sun as if devouring a meal. The raindrops continued to dive for her eyes.

Oregon could get cold—not Michigan cold, but it was unpleasant all the same. The rain always found a way to seep under any jacket. Her teeth chattered painfully. She didn't even have a jacket for the rain to seep into. Her arms shook, but she refused to wrap them around herself. Caden didn't need comfort like Rebecca did.

She saw two faint dots of light hovering over the road in the distance. She crossed her fingers at her side, cursing herself for wishing it would be Sean. Her body stopped shaking momentarily, her hope growing with the lights as they got brighter, bigger. Just a faint outline of the car was now visible in the distance, still too far for her to identify any definite color. Sean's truck was dark green. He always insisted it was black, but it wasn't; green could never be black. She lifted her arm from her side and turned her hand to the rain, letting a few drops collect in her palm before she closed it and put out her thumb. Shivers ran through her, reminding her just how much she needed whoever it was in that car to give her a ride. She could freeze out here. Even in a small town, storeowners didn't let young girls sleep in the vegetable aisle; no, they would call her mother.

Love isn't real. That was what her mother had said to her the night she left to go live with Sean. There was no way she would prove her mother right, but there was also no way to prove her mother wrong. Avoidance was the answer, for now.

The lights ahead seared into her eyes and made her blink. Luminescence reflected off the shower of water tossed out by the purple clouds. The innocent, ever-growing puddle lapped at her ankles. Ahead of her the lights flashed, and she waved back. She bit back her disappointment, knowing it wasn't Sean; he would never flash his headlights. He'd swerve close as if to hit her just to get a good laugh.

The car that pulled up was much newer than Sean's car, and it wasn't a truck, but a mid-sized sedan. It was black; not green, but black. Caden looked at the car with its windows rolled up and its doors shut, sitting in front of her like a gift: her ticket out of the rain. She grabbed the handle on the car door. Her thoughts briefly ventured to the question of safety. Hitchhiking was a bad idea, but sitting out in the rain without a jacket wasn't exactly a good one. Caden thought of her mother and all the times she'd scolded her about the decisions she made. Her mother had been right about a lot of things, maybe everything; still, she wouldn't turn back now. *I'm a new person, confident and strong.* Caden's fingers wrapped around the handle. She counted silently to three and pulled.

"Get in." The top of the car hid the driver's face. His harsh voice cut through her self-loathing.

She stared blankly at his midsection and upper legs as heat rushed out around her. *It's now or never.* Her feet stepped onto the beige carpet and smeared dark mud into its roots, creating a stain the driver would never be rid of. The smell of cinnamon and leather lingered in the air. The leather seat felt warm against the cold chill of her wet clothes, and for once she was glad she didn't have a jacket on; she didn't need to bring more water into the car than she already had.

"Don't…" The driver made a strange hand movement, as though to scold a two-year-old for touching something expensive with sticky fingers. "Just try not to move too much." The man leaned over to the back seat and grabbed a gray shirt. "Put this behind you or something. I don't want you destroying my heated seats."

"Sorry, I…"

"It's fine. Close the door, close the door. You're letting out all the heat."

"Sorry." Caden quickly shut the door. *It will be okay, I'll make it okay.*

Her eyes ventured to the man. He was younger than she'd originally thought, probably about her age. His skin was tan for Oregon standards, as if he had just returned from some exotic vacation. His hair was blacker than all of her black clothing and swept to the side in messy strands.

"Alright, where do you want to go?" His voice was deep. The set of his mouth looked deadly.

"Go?"

"Yeah, isn't that how this stuff works?" the driver asked.

Caden looked at him questioningly. "Pick up a hitchhiker, drop them off?" He put the car into drive, and soon the bridge disappeared in the distance behind them.

"I don't know." Caden hadn't put much thought into hitchhiking. Aside from turning up her thumb, her only thought had been to get out of the rain. "Don't you do this often?"

"No. Do you?"

"No." Caden grabbed her hair, twisting it nervously. An uncomfortable atmosphere filled the car. She looked at his face through the strands of her wet hair. He was beautiful; the copper that wove through his eyes drew her in. She wanted to look closer. Instead, Caden wiggled in her seat, releasing her hair so that it covered more of her face. His handsome demeanor made her starkly aware of how much she probably resembled a half-drowned rodent. "Now what?"

The young man sighed, leaning back into his seat. The raindrops pounded harder on the car, dinging and tinging as they ricocheted off the roof. "Where do you want to go?"

"I don't have anywhere to go." Caden sank farther down in her seat. The man's annoyance was almost palpable.

The young man slapped the steering wheel. "Try to do one goddamn good thing and this is what I get? A hitchhiker with nowhere to go." His voice grew louder. Caden's heartbeat quickened. "Well, what am I going to do with you?"

"I don't know." Caden really didn't know. Her hand gripped

the door handle. "Maybe you should just drop me off here. I'll figure it out." The next driver to pick her up could be worse than this guy, but she doubted it. She wondered how long she'd have to wait for another car. It seemed like a chance worth taking. She didn't trust him.

Where would she go? She didn't have Sean anymore, she hadn't talked to her mother in a week, and her dad lived somewhere else with someone else. She couldn't remember his phone number anyway. Cell phones cost money, and money was something she didn't have. She didn't have friends either; she had given them up for Sean.

"Just relax, okay?" He exhaled and continued to speak in a rush. "Look, what's your name anyway?"

"Caden, my name is Caden."

"Alright, Caden. Well, do you have a friend who can take you in?"

"No. I told you, I don't have anywhere to go." Her knuckles turned white from her firm grip on the door handle.

"Can I drop you off at the library maybe?"

"Maybe. Where are you going? I can just go wherever that is."

"I'm on my way home."

When she didn't respond, he frowned and took his eyes off of the road to give her a quick glance. Silence refilled the car. "I have a couch in my living room that isn't half bad, but you're gone in the morning."

Rain blanketed the windshield as the wipers struggled to clear it away. Caden nodded, reluctant to the idea, but thankful for the offer. "Thank you. What's your name?"

"Gabriel, just Gabriel."

"Well…" She twisted her sleeve between her fingers and watched as drops of rainwater splashed onto the seat beside her, rolling off as if repelled by the leather. "Thanks for picking me up."

Gabriel made a grunting sound, which Caden thought could either be amusement or annoyance.

Gabriel looked over at the girl and shook his head again. He couldn't even see her face behind all that dark hair. What had he been thinking? He hadn't really wanted to stop for her, but he had, and now she was going to stay with him. It was his first night back, and already he regretted not picking a different state. Though he reminded himself that Cloverdale wasn't on his parents' radar like their condos in California and Florida. He could suffer a little bit if it meant his parents didn't notice he was off on his own again, for the second summer in a row.

It seemed to Gabriel that in providing a service to a stranger, he shouldn't have had his perfectly clean beige carpet destroyed with mud stains. He kept his Saab in mint condition; it was his car—his perfectly kept, clean car. It hadn't had a scratch or stain on it, until now. He sighed again. What had he gotten himself into? Picking up a hitchhiker in the rain should have been easy karma points. Who knew she'd be homeless?

He tensed when Caden moved in her seat, her soaked shirt squeaking against the leather material. There were two types of silences: the good kind and the unbelievably awkward, stale-air kind that choked its victims. The silence in the car was already suffocating him. He wondered if it would be as awkward back at his parents' condo. He figured it would be.

Every month his parents made a ton of money off all the properties they owned, with dozens of condos on each. It had been a matter of simple forged paperwork to put this condo out of commission, making it his second home. He'd done it last summer too. They would never know where to look for him, not that it mattered; his parents didn't care. He had picked a shitty town in Oregon where they would never visit. It surprised him that they'd bought property there to begin with, but then again they had property everywhere. If his family found land, they bought it and built condos. As long as he was at least a thousand miles away from his parents, he was happy.

"So, Gabriel..."

"Yeah?"

"Where do you live, exactly?"

"Oh, just up the hill and to the right." He tried to point, but it was impossible to see with all the rain. It wouldn't be much longer. He looked over his shoulder at her. Who was this loner? Some small-town freak no doubt; every inch of her was covered in black.

"Across from the Anderson Store or farther up by Joe's Coffee?"

"Yeah, about a mile up the road from Joe's."

"Oh, okay, I kind of know where that is."

Gabriel was sure that Caden knew exactly where it was. Small towns were like that. Gabriel's mouth went dry as he contemplated something to talk about. "So the rain, pretty nice to stand in, huh?"

Caden didn't respond, remaining quiet as she looked back out the window. Her sour mood made him anxious; he itched to get her out of the car. Her black clothes didn't help. Her body reminded him of a black hole sucking in all light and happiness, conveniently located in the passenger seat of his Saab.

"So, you a Goth or something?" he asked, hoping for any kind of response. Instead, Caden sat quietly. A flicker of irritation crawled beneath Gabriel's skin. Maybe it was because he didn't spend much time with people, not since last summer.

He wondered if his condo would be cold and hoped he had enough blankets in the closet to keep her warm.

He would probably have to lend her something dry to wear. Would a Goth wear clothes that weren't black? He didn't own anything black, except maybe a shirt he got as a gift for his eighteenth birthday last year. The leather squeaked again, breaking him from his thoughts, as Caden fidgeted back and forth in her seat.

"Will you just stop moving? You're getting my perfect car dirty. Do you know how hard it is to keep a car with a beige interior clean?" There was an edge to his voice, he could feel it; it felt good to be angry. Until later when it didn't and he felt like scum. A vicious cycle he had yet to figure out how to control. "Who wears black, anyway? I mean all black?" He looked at her again. Her eyeliner, which he imagined had once gone to a point at the end, dripped down the side of her face. Her tank top and jeans were supposed to be black but were nearly gray from being washed again and again. Worst of all were her boots; they nearly covered her whole calf and had at least fifty buckles on each side. She looked ridiculous.

"What's your problem?" she mumbled under her breath.

"My problem? I wasn't the one in the rain. I—" Gabriel pointed at his chest, "—have a car. Oh, and a home, and I want you gone in the morning. Clear?"

"Crystal." Caden crossed her arms and looked back out the window.

Gabriel refrained from saying any more. He didn't know what was stopping him. She was so annoying; her demeanor, her attitude, and her clothes all bothered him. He felt the urge to yell, but he didn't. Something about her felt different, but right. Which was wrong. He didn't need a girl in his life. Gabriel's fists clenched around the steering wheel. He didn't need anyone.

When Gabriel pulled up to his building, Caden recognized the complex. She'd had a friend back in elementary school who had lived there. The property housed almost thirty condos, and as kids they used to run around counting them. Gabriel pulled his car into a parking spot numbered twenty-five. The sound of rain on the car's roof ceased under the protection of the carport. He didn't say anything, just turned off the car and got out. Caden attempted to follow.

"I think I came here for a party last summer or something," she mumbled as she opened the door. The rain hadn't let up. If anything, it had gotten worse. Although Gabriel wasn't much for company, she was glad she wasn't still out at the bridge waiting for Sean, or gauging the distance between the bridge and the water below it.

"Probably mine."

"Your party?" Caden attempted to remember the night, but the memory was fuzzy. Sean always insisted on getting her drunk, and a few times that had resulted in her blacking out. "Gabriel, wait up."

By the time she shut the door, he was already walking between the buildings. He looked back at her as rain fell from his hair, soaking his face. It was already dark outside from the rainclouds; it would be night within a few hours. Caden couldn't help but stare back as she stood under the protection of the awning, her clothes leaving a puddle in the once-dry space beneath her feet.

"Hurry up. I'll leave the door open." Gabriel turned and continued into the labyrinth of identical buildings. "Number twenty-five," he mumbled quietly, his voice almost lost in the rain, but she still heard him.

Caden looked up from the rain-soaked sidewalk; the condos weren't cute or unique, just squares with shingled roofs and an extra overhang that traveled around the center to protect the doors. With all the rain in Oregon any extra roof was godsent.

Caden raced after Gabriel, eager for shelter from the cold. He had taken a turn to the right where the walkway led to a corner that concealed a dark gray door. As her hand reached for the slightly ajar door, her eyes glanced at the unit number: twenty-five. The five swiveled back and forth in the wind and her hands itched to stop it.

A stranger's car and a stranger's home; her mother would never forgive her. Not that it mattered. She entered the condo anticipating warmth. Instead, the chill of the unheated condo rattled her.

"It's freezing in here," Caden said.

Gabriel looked back over his shoulder for only a second. "You're welcome to leave if it doesn't suit your tastes."

"No, no it's fine." Her teeth started to chatter; she couldn't control it any longer. Even if she wanted to leave, she knew she shouldn't. She needed to get out of her wet clothes before she got sick, but she was walking on thin ice. Everything seemed to upset Gabriel; he made her mom seem like an angel. She watched as he sorted through partly empty shelves.

"I'll find you a blanket. There should be a towel in the bathroom."

Caden looked around. The walls were bare, and the ceiling was high for a condo. Spiderwebs clung between the wood beams and the popcorn ceiling. Movement caught her eye, and she looked back toward Gabriel as he tossed a blanket at her. Her hands reflexively rose, catching it in front of her wincing face.

"Condo's a one bedroom, one and a half bath. Full bath is in the corner over here." He pointed to a closed door. "Upstairs is off-limits, it's my room. See you in the morning." Gabriel turned toward the stairs on the far side of the condo and disappeared, leaving her alone.

Caden's body had begun to shake as she stood there dripping on the carpet. "Great." She looked back at the front door, still open from when she entered. With a tentative step forward she walked out of the condo. The wind hit her tired body. Her skin ached. The rain pelted her relentlessly. She looked back at the open door.

Time to choose.

There wasn't much of an option. She went back inside, closing the door behind her. It would be okay, she would make it okay.

She studied the condo. There was a bathroom on one side, a sad excuse for a couch in the middle with two haphazardly placed coffee tables nearby, a little table with four chairs in the corner, and a tiny kitchen with sparse countertops, an oven, burners, and a fridge. Having access to the kitchen, to make whatever her heart desired, would be a form of therapy she desperately wanted. She loved to cook. Would he have any pots and pans? Whisks? Caden took a step forward but stopped at the sound of a door opening. A pile of clothes flew down the stairs as the door clicked closed once again. *My knight in shining armor to the rescue*, she thought as she picked up the clothes.

After she dried off and changed into them, she took the blanket with her and got onto the couch. It reeked of alcohol and possibly old vomit, but the clothes had a sweet musty scent fused with cinnamon. She closed her eyes, breathing the smell deep into her lungs, and fell asleep.

—Night—

The sound of shattering glass broke the silence. Caden's heavy eyes popped open and took in the surroundings. It was kind of hilarious how much her life sucked. It didn't surprise her that of all the people in the world, she'd hitchhiked with a psycho.

Thump. Thump.

What the hell was that? she thought. Caden pulled the wool blanket up to her nose. Her heart echoed in her ears as

19

she strained to listen to the commotion upstairs. Caden never feared the silence. She feared the sounds that interrupted it.

She wanted to laugh or cry. Both feelings sat lodged in her chest, waiting for the sound again.

Her dad had told her once that if someone was in the house, it was best not to move quickly unless they saw you. *Someone is in the house,* Caden reminded herself, but this wasn't her house.

Thump, thump, thump.

"What the heck?" Caden sat up, dismissing the memory of her dad's warning and her lingering fear. She wasn't Rebecca anymore. Plus, she didn't think a robber would walk around like a noisy giant. Who the hell could possibly sleep through a noise like that?

Thump, thump, thump, sounded again. She could picture Gabriel as a sumo wrestler, practicing his wide-stance walk. The idea amused her. She laid her head back down. Why would anyone be up at this hour?

Thump, thump, thump. Caden sat up, again. This had to be a joke, a bad one at that. Who could make such a racket? *Thump, thump.* Caden wrapped the blanket around her shoulders and shifted her weight off of the couch. Even the carpet felt cold against her feet. Her hand searched in front of her, the unfamiliar layout hidden in darkness. Goose bumps spread out over her arm the second it touched the frigid air. The small amount of light that trailed in through the window from outside wasn't enough to see by, making only a vague shape of a table visible in front of her. Caden moved around it but hit something else. She grabbed at her shin, cursing as the throbbing pain laced up her leg; she hadn't seen the second coffee table. Placing her hand on the table, she moved away from it and continued to the stairs she had seen Gabriel climb earlier.

One stair.

Another breath, another stair.

Under the weight of her body, the third stair let out a high-pitched creaking sound that made Caden hiss a curse before continuing more quickly.

She stopped at the last step and listened. Quiet.

Damn it, this is weird.

The door was so close to her face that her lips brushed the wood. "Hello?" Silence. "Are you okay?" Again, not a word in reply. The moment seemed very long and quiet. Was he listening on the other side?

"Is something wrong in there?" she yelled through the door. Right now, she didn't feel like putting up with this horror-film crap. "God, spare me if this guy's a psycho," she whispered through clenched teeth. She knew she should turn back to the couch, that she shouldn't intrude, but what if he was hurt? Caden's hand gripped the door handle, the cold metal making her wince. She slowly let it turn until it clicked; the door creaked as she pushed it open. *This is it, Caden,* she told herself, *the moment you get kicked back out into the rain.*

Caden didn't see the figure at first, but when she did, her

21

whole body jumped. A squeal escaped her lips, and her hand darted to still her heart.

The figure sat on the bed, legs crossed, staring straight at her. A light from outside the window illuminated little more than a simple silhouette. Caden stood still, trying not to make any sudden movements. The figure remained stiff and unmoving, his hands on his knees. Was it Gabriel? She couldn't tell, but who else could it be?

"I'm sorry, I…I heard a noise." *What the heck were you doing? Hitting your head against the wall?* She waited a moment. The figure didn't move. "I wanted to make sure you were okay." The figure didn't respond. *Oh, God, I'm going to die like in those movies.* Part of her—the old Rebecca part—wanted to leave, but Caden was determined to stay. She rocked back and forth on the balls of her feet nervously, hesitating. "Are you okay?"

"I—I crushed it."

If it was Gabriel, his voice sounded different, lighter and timid, and definitely not what she remembered from earlier in the day. She looked around the floor and found glistening pieces of glass strewn all over the carpet, shining like freshly fallen snow. Their light twinkled at intervals from bright to dim as she shifted from foot to foot. "What the heck did you crush?"

Silence.

Caden rubbed her eyes, the exhaustion from the day setting back in as the novelty of her situation wore off. She felt unnerved by his stillness. *Who are you?* "Do you want help cleaning it up?" Caden asked, hoping to get away from him so she could clear her head. Even the wool blanket around her couldn't stop the chill that crept into her skin.

He didn't reply, so she turned around and went back down the stairs toward the kitchen, careful to avoid the coffee tables. After rummaging through a few cabinets, she found a dish towel and a small trash can. She turned to look back at the dark stairwell and the door at the top that now stood slightly ajar.

Damn it.

She didn't want to go back up. However, he had let her stay with him; she could afford to do him a small favor. Cursing under her breath, she grabbed the trash can and dish towel. When she got back to his room, her hand went for the light switch—

"Don't!" the boy on the bed shouted. Caden took a step back, startled. His voice wasn't unkind or demanding; it was more of a plea. It still surprised her.

Perplexed, Caden tilted her head to the side, examining the silhouette. *Was* it Gabriel? Weak and helpless didn't fit him; according to what she knew of him, he was cold and unyielding, harsh and on edge. Watching the silhouette intently, hoping the extra light would clear away any doubt, Caden brushed away her suspicion and flipped the switch anyway. Her chest tightened as the silhouette ducked behind the side of the bed. *Weirdo.*

"What is this?" Caden asked, lowering herself to her knees to pick up a piece of the fragmented object and examining it.

No answer came, not a word. She continued to analyze its shine, and the iridescence filled with blue, green, and purple with bits of orange here and there. Caden recognized the fragments as something she had seen many times before, but she couldn't quite place what it was. Whatever it had been, it was destroyed, yet parts of it had splintered with dull edges while other parts looked like glass. Caden carefully scooped up handfuls and threw them away. She imagined the glass had come from some kind of container or display case, and she didn't doubt that after it was tossed at the wall, it was stomped on. Repeatedly.

It really wasn't any of her business. "Alright." She stood up, eyeing the bed before brushing some of the iridescent dust off her legs. "I'm going back to bed." Caden began to turn toward the door when curious eyes peeped over the edge of the mattress. Her shoulders relaxed at the sight of his dark hair spilling out in every direction.

"Don't go."

He was creeping her out. She wanted to run and hide from him, but instead she held her ground and, as casually as she could, leaned into the doorframe. "It's like three in the morning," she reminded him, attempting a frown to hide her anxiety.

"Do you want to play a game?"

"What?" Caden asked, his voice once again making her unsure. A game? It sounded like something Sean would say. Caden shifted her weight, eyeing him warily. *I can handle this.*

She let out a deep breath; if nothing else she could use this as an opportunity. Cleaning at three in the morning obviously hadn't scored her enough *Good Samaritan* points.

"Sure… We can play a game." She wondered if her hesitation would make him angry, like she had when they had been in the car that afternoon.

She looked around for a weapon, anything she could use to protect herself. As her eyes scanned the room each surface was bare, aside from the bulky old alarm clock on the nightstand.

"First, you have to turn off the lights."

Caden's hand shook. This didn't feel right. "Okay," She mumbled, attempting to seem unfazed, and she turned off the lights with a flick of her wrist. It took a few seconds for her eyes to readjust, and when they did she saw the boy leap back onto the bed, light and agile. She took an uneasy step back. Her chest constricted and her breath caught in her throat. Caden couldn't deny being unsure of the situation, of this boy who somehow had to be the man she'd met earlier that day.

His head moved from side to side, watching her as intently as she watched him. "What do you want to play?" he asked.

Even then, with him in better visibility, Caden couldn't tell if the boy was really Gabriel. It was the same voice she had heard earlier, but without the rough edge of his irritation it sounded much younger and innocent, like that of a child. "I don't know…"

"Oh, come on, think of something," he said.

When he didn't move to grab her, she relaxed a little, her breath evening out once again. Caden could feel her confidence slowly building. *Maybe he really just wants to play a game.* "Aren't you tired?"

The boy's shoulders and head dropped. "So you don't want to play," he confirmed dejectedly. She watched as he turned around on the empty bed, to face the other wall.

Caden's little sister Reese always used guilt to get what she wanted. She hadn't known a guy her own age could make her feel just as guilty, if not worse. "No, no, I want to play. I do." *As long as you stay on that side of the room.* Caden moved farther into the room but stayed a good six feet away.

"What game? What game?" He bounced on the bed in his sitting position.

"Do you have any cards?" She clutched the blanket tighter around her, but tried to keep her voice light and casual.

"Cards?" The boy, who no longer seemed like Gabriel at all, stuck out his tongue. "Dumb. Something else."

Caden stood, astonished that a boy her own age could be so childish. He was super hot, too, but this behavior just seemed odd, to say the least. She crossed her arms over her chest and studied him. Now that she was closer to him, the moonlight revealed his features in a bluish tint. His eyes and hair appeared to be more like shadows than real body parts.

What would be best? She thought about the games she used to enjoy with her little sister. They hadn't played them since their world had been turned upside down by their parents' divorce. It had driven them apart, but she still remembered the good times. Reese was spending the summer with their dad this year. They used to play games in the car all the time, back when they were a family. Caden hadn't played a game in a long time.

She pushed the ache away, along with her memories of a time less complicated, as she tried to remember one of Reese's favorite games. "Alright, I'll ask you a question and you'll answer and explain why, okay?" Reese always liked this one, and Caden did too; Reese was always asking questions anyway, so Caden had decided to turn it into a game. She always found her sister's ridiculous questions endearing.

The boy's silhouette nodded up and down with vigor, his back straightening again.

"Alright." Caden wondered what she should ask; what wouldn't piss him off at three o'clock in the morning? "Are you a mountain lion or a crocodile?"

Silence resonated through the room. "Neither. I'm a boy."

He really wasn't funny. "That isn't how it works, you need to pick one."

"Oh. Well, I guess a mountain lion. No, a crocodile."

A laugh escaped her lips, but she quickly shut her mouth.

"Because a crocodile is sneaky and hides until he can come out to seize the moment," he said, rocking back and forth on his knees.

"Interesting." Caden scratched the side of her neck nervously, That sounded a little sketchy, though she reminded herself that she had asked the question. "Okay. Now you ask me the same question."

The figure moved around a little on the bed to get comfortable and then patted the comforter, motioning for Caden to sit next to him. "Are you a mountain lion or a crocodile?" he asked.

Caden slowly moved toward the bed. She tapped her finger against her lips, thinking. If she were Rebecca, she would probably say a crocodile, so she could hide in the murky water and be forgotten. Caden pushed away the thought. "I would be a mountain lion because from now on, I'm going to be the first to pounce." She giggled a little at the idea. "I guess I like cats too, so it works." Caden squeezed her hands together, anxiously. "Your turn to make up a question." She lowered herself on the far side of the bed, keeping her distance.

"Mmm, are you a grizzly bear or a fish?"

"Probably a fish," Caden answered without a second thought. A fog inside of her seemed to clear, and she remembered that only Rebecca would want to be a fish. Rebecca would follow the stream, go with the flow; she didn't like to be a leader like Caden did. "Never mind, I'm changing it. I'm a grizzly bear because I'm good at growling." She gave her best growl, and the boy laughed. It made her feel lighter, and her shoulders relaxed as she scooched farther onto the bed. "What about you? Grizzly or fish?" she asked as she brushed off the saliva that had flown from her mouth when she growled.

"Definitely a grizzly bear. I'm nocturnal and hibernate for long periods of time."

"Huh, I didn't know that grizzly bears were nocturnal."

"Yeah, not as strictly as I am, but for the most part." He shrugged and plopped back on the bed, sprawled out and looking at the ceiling.

They continued to play back and forth, the questions getting more difficult to answer with each turn. It wasn't until red and orange started to spill over the horizon that Caden realized they had played through the night.

"We should probably go to bed, huh?" The boy yawned, stretching his arms up above his head.

"Yeah, I guess." Caden got up and started for the door. "I had fun."

"Wait." Caden turned to Gabriel, who was now recognizable in a stream of morning light, creamy oranges and soft yellows dancing over his features. "Can I see you again?" he asked, his body still and unmoving, as though he held his breath.

"You don't want me to leave? I thought you said…"

"I don't remember what I said, but stay, I want to see you again."

Gabriel tossed back the sheets on his bed and got up. Halfway down the stairs he froze. Black ribbons of hair draped off the side of his dirty party couch. It was Caden. He walked down the rest of the stairs and into the kitchen, eyeing her. The curves of her face were soft and pleasant, or something he couldn't find a word for. He quickly turned away from her sleeping form and took out the coffee maker.

It was nearly two in the afternoon.

She hadn't left.

Gabriel's chest tightened at the thought of her staying, at the thought of wanting company.

He despised the feeling. Nothing good had ever come from other people. She would use him. She already was by overstaying her welcome.

Dark liquid streamed into the glass coffee pot. The smell drifted through the air with the warmth that normally accompanied a home. A home he'd never had and didn't want.

He took down a mug, unintentionally gripping it tightly.

His hand was shaking. He needed her gone. The last person he'd let into his life had made everything worse with her lies; he couldn't handle that again.

He poured himself a cup, and with a swift movement he brought the steaming mug to his lips and took a gulp of bitter liquid. The heat surprised him, and he pulled back from it as if it had bitten him. Caden wasn't even awake yet, and just being near her made him feel crazy, restless.

"I thought I told you to be gone in the morning. It's nearly two in the afternoon." He spoke loudly, not quite facing her.

Caden rotated slightly on the couch, her eyes opening only part of the way. She looked as tired as he felt.

"What?" she croaked.

"You heard me," he snarled through clenched teeth, leaning over her body. "Why are you still here?" As he'd grown up, his parents had given free rent in one of their condos to anyone who would provide childcare for him. He supposed he'd always supplied a roof to strangers in one way or another.

"You asked me to stay." Her voice echoed her helplessness and uncertainty.

"When?"

"Last night," Caden said, rubbing her eyes.

Heat was rising in Gabriel. Pain and disappointment overwhelmed his senses. She was lying. Just like everyone he'd ever know. The force of his anger was like a wrecking ball in full swing.

Ceramic exploded against the wall, fragments flying across the room. He'd done that. The brown drips of coffee streaked down the white wall by the door. Gabriel looked at his empty shaking hand and clenched his fist tightly together.

"You're lying," he said as he looked down at her. This was her fault; if only she had just left like he told her to. But he didn't want her to leave; that was the worst part. The tension came back, the numbness creeping in and propelling him forward. He couldn't be near her, not now. The only thing he could do was leave. He walked briskly to the door before he changed his mind.

Caden watched the door tremble as it was slammed closed. Gabriel was gone.

"You asked me to stay," she stammered the whisper, her heart pounding in her ears, but no one was there to hear it. She pushed herself up against the couch as if she could disappear within it. Her mind flashed back to Sean, his screaming, the way he called her names.

Caden sat in paralyzed shock, not quite comprehending what had just taken place. It seemed like the night before had been a dream; there was no other way to describe his change.

Her eyes traveled back to the coffee, the liquid having already run into the carpet to form a large, wet stain by the wall. Chunks of ceramic lay scattered across the floor in front of her.

What had gotten into him? Caden couldn't help but remember him being pleasant, more than pleasant, enjoyable, even fun.

Starving for something to eat, Caden decided to look around the kitchen. She didn't think he would be back too soon after his little episode. The fridge was empty, aside from a dozen beers and an old bag of moldy carrots. Caden picked up the bag, sniffed them, and gagged. She wasn't that desperate. Her stomach disagreed as it rumbled loudly. She quickly scanned through the rest of the drawers, cabinets, and pantries. Nothing.

Caden leaned against the counter as she rubbed at her face. Deep down she felt insane, maybe from lack of food? She couldn't explain the night before, or Gabriel's reaction this morning.

Abandoning her search for food, Caden went back to the drawer that had the cleaning products. There wasn't much— only an old dish towel and some window cleaner. It would have to do.

It took the better part of the afternoon to handpick the chips of mug out from the carpet. Every time she thought she'd finished, she found fragments of ceramic feet from where the mug had shattered. She used the coffee table as a step stool to clean the coffee off the wall. She liked messes she could see, things she could solve. People were more complicated, like Gabriel. She still couldn't wrap her head around his reaction to her staying. His copper eyes held something back, and she wanted to find out what.

In the kitchen corner the microwave clock glowed 5:05 p.m. Her body felt heavy, and an ache traveled through her bones. She lay down on the couch, looking up at the popcorn ceiling and the wood beams. She missed her old life, her clothes, her sister, and maybe even her mother. Her mother. Caden wanted to prove that love could be real, that relationships could be fixed. She began to bite at her nails, thinking of her parents, her broken home. She didn't want that kind of life.

Her thoughts were lost at the sound of a key in the door. Caden let her shoulders nestle under the wool blanket, and she closed her eyes. She pretended to be asleep, hoping that she was convincing enough to at least fool Gabriel. She couldn't leave, not yet; she still hadn't found anywhere else to go, and something about the Gabriel she'd spent time with the night before made her want to stay.

The door opened, and her stomach gurgled. She cursed herself for not eating the moldy carrots.

"I know you're awake," said Gabriel. The door shut and a dead bolt slid into place. He was fumbling around with something, probably hanging up his coat in the closet. "You realize I could go to the police?" His voice sounded close, and she must have reacted with a wince. "Ha, knew you were awake. No one could sleep through a hungry stomach." His voice was resigned and carried a sarcastic but subdued tone, and she wondered if he had already called the police; if they were on their way, it wouldn't be long until she was home.

Home, the thought, sounded nice at the moment. In reality home was the last thing she wanted. Her room had probably already been turned into an office, her things packed away in a storage unit, or worse: thrown out. Something soft smacked the table and caused her to jump, but she kept her eyes closed and attempted to stay still.

"I want you gone by the morning. I'm not kidding this time."

Caden waited for the sound of Gabriel's door to shut behind him before she opened her eyes. A brown paper bag sat scrunched up on the table. Like a starving dog she ripped into the bag. A sandwich was carefully wrapped with a sticker sealing it closed. It was from the coffee shop down the road; she could tell from the sticker. There was even a cookie in the bag labeled *Chocolate, Almond Cookie Delight*. Her teeth sank into the soft, foamy cookie; the crumbs fell on her lap. In a second she had eaten it, with the sandwich following close behind. She licked the pads of her fingers as she lay back down, grateful he hadn't forgotten her. Her eyes became heavy as she wished for more food, and she soon fell asleep.

—*Night*—

"Wake up."

Caden groaned something incomprehensible and swatted

at the arm nudging her. "Go away," she managed to say as she buried her face farther into the couch's armrest.

"Wake up, I want to play," the voice echoed again, soft and deep.

The voice registered. Her eyes shot open. *Gabriel*. Panic instantly made her rigid. It wasn't morning yet; judging by how dark it was outside, she didn't have to leave for at least another few hours. Would he throw her out once and for all, just because he wanted to? She felt slightly deserving of that extra four hours after cleaning up his coffee mug.

The light shone through the windows, just like it had the night before. The face that returned her gaze was veiled in a net of shadows, and though they were harsh, the face looked peaceful.

"Wake up already." His hand lightly pushed her again, her body rocking slightly as the couch ate up the rest of the momentum.

"I'm up, I'm up. What is it?" Caden couldn't hide her less-than-pleasant tone. She didn't trust him, not after that morning. She didn't like the switch of nice and innocent to mean and violent. Though he had given her that sandwich…and the cookie.

"What's wrong?"

Caden rolled over onto her back and sighed. "It's nothing, I guess. What do you want?"

"I want to play," Gabriel replied, but he wasn't Gabriel; he couldn't be. Gabriel seemed like a man—he was probably over eighteen—but this person in front of her seemed to be little more than a boy.

"What if I don't want to play?"

"You will want to play this game. We're going outside."

The excitement in his voice made Caden uneasy. "What's outside?"

"You'll see, you'll see." The boy raced for the door but didn't make it far before he ran into one of the coffee tables. He let out an irritated whimper. "Where did that come from?"

Caden sat up on the couch and looked at the coffee table. She hadn't moved that one when she cleaned. She got up and grabbed his shoulders, leading him toward the couch. "You okay?"

"I think so. It hurts."

She nodded. "Yep, that's what happens when you run into a table." She heard a small laugh under his breath, a man's laugh. She couldn't seem to look at him the same way she looked at him in the morning. This nighttime version of him, sweet and childlike, was softer, even in his features. "Well, if you haven't noticed, there aren't any sharp shards of coffee mug in the carpet."

"What?" The boy looked over at her, his dark, wild hair catching the shadows and making them darker. "Why would there be coffee mug in the carpet?"

Caden's face stiffened. "I worked all afternoon cleaning

that up. How can you forget something like that?" Her voice got louder, and for a minute she feared he would snap back at her. He didn't. The anger in her voice felt better than the shaking, timidness that had accompanied her for most of her life. It made her powerful, especially when the boy beside her pushed himself farther into the couch as if he was afraid of her. What was happening to him?

He turned his back to her. "You're not nice."

"What do you mean I'm not nice? You're not nice." He didn't respond. "You're infuriating. What's wrong with you?" As the seconds ticked by, Caden regretted what she had said. "I'm sorry, okay?"

He nodded, seemingly pleased. "What's your name, anyway?"

Jerk. He remembered. He had to have remembered. He was doing this to get under her skin. She told herself she wouldn't let it happen.

"What's your name?" he asked again.

"I told you in the car. I won't tell you again." She crossed her arms over her chest. How could he have forgotten her name? It hurt knowing it wasn't important enough for him to remember. She reminded herself that she shouldn't actually care, but she did.

He looked at her quizzically. "I don't have a car."

"You're telling me the car outside isn't your car?"

"Really? There's a car outside?" He rushed to the window,

expectantly. His shoulders dropped after only a few moments. "It looks the same."

"The same as what?" Caden said.

"The cars. They look that way every night. Well, depending on where I am, but here they're the same."

"What are you talking about? Of course there are cars, but I'm talking about your car, the one we drove in."

"Do you have the keys?" He turned to her, his voice ringing with enthusiasm.

"Why the heck would I have the keys to your car? They're probably in your room or something."

"Nope, looked." He grabbed the windowsill and leaned back from it as if it were a kind of swing. When he let go, he stumbled back a few steps before landing on the couch. He turned to look at her with a goony smile before crossing his arms in front of his chest.

Caden uncrossed her arms and placed them on her hips. She watched as he did the same. She crossed them again, frustrated that he was mocking her.

"I check the room every night." He crossed his arms again. "I look for anything new, but I have never found keys."

"What is wrong with you?" Caden motioned with her hands. "Stop crossing your arms."

"You did it." He shrugged, uncrossing his arms and crossing them again over his chest.

His movements were exhausting. She felt like she was

babysitting her five-year-old cousin. At the same time she felt something else, a kind of safety or security. "No wonder you want to play games all the time. If you're this annoying, you probably don't have any friends."

Caden regretted the words the second she saw Gabriel's lip start to quiver. The light from the window streamed across his face and caught his eyes enough for her to see them, but they weren't Gabriel's, not really. She tilted her head to the side, trying to remember what Gabriel's eyes looked like. He hit the couch with his fist, startling her as he stood up and walked toward the stairs to his room. Seconds later the door slammed shut behind him.

Caden plopped back down on the couch and held her head with her hand. It felt wrong treating him with contempt. What was with him anyway?

Gabriel definitely had anger issues, he liked to play childish games, he didn't know he had a car, he didn't like the light, he didn't know where the coffee tables were, and he searched his room every night as if new things would appear. It was crazy. She needed to clear her head. Fresh air could do the brain wonders.

Caden put on her boots and turned the doorknob. Brisk night air hit her face, pushing her hair off her shoulders as she closed the door behind her. The rain had stopped, but the sidewalk was slick with its residue. She didn't have a coat, just the baggy blue T-shirt and Gabriel's boy shorts. Goose bumps prickled her skin, rising up all over her legs and arms. If she ran, she would be warmer. Crisp air filled her lungs as her feet carried her through the buildings and into the trees. She pushed harder, running faster.

After a few minutes, the fog in her mind cleared. The solution seemed obvious: to find somewhere else to live. Caden looked back for the lights from the condominium, but they were gone. Trees from the forest surrounded her, blocking the light from the moon.

"What am I going to do?" Caden lifted her head to the sky, a scream rising in her throat. She pushed it down deep inside of her before it could escape. She felt trapped. Any direction she went would lead to her failure; it had with Rebecca, so why would it change now? Panic filled her. *I have to go back, I have to. No, there has to be somewhere else to go.*

She let her mind run though her options: Sean would laugh and close the door in her face. Her mom worked night shifts and wouldn't even be home. Sarah and Lauren had probably already forgotten her name, not that it mattered since she was no longer Rebecca. She considered the nearest store, and the kind people who might let her in and keep her warm, but then she reminded herself how unlikely people were to house strangers in the first place. Plus, she looked ridiculous. Her punk-rock boots nearly reached up to her knees and Gabriel's shorts stopped right before them. Walking around in a small town in someone else's clothes would be a disaster, one her mom would surely hear about. It was also probably close to two in the morning; nothing would be open.

She stopped, turning toward a sound in the distance. A whimper? Was that a child in the forest? Deep down, whether she admitted it or not, Caden knew it wasn't a child.

She ran toward the noise.

He'd followed her into the forest.

Creepy? Maybe, but no one had gone after her before. Her father had left, and Sean had used her and kicked her out. It was something she had always wanted. A protective feeling washed over her; suddenly she wanted to be near him, to play his stupid games.

"Gabriel, Gabriel. Where are you?"

The muffled sobs continued to echo through the forest. Tree branches scraped against her skin, clinging in her hair. Her boots were heavy, sinking into the moist soil with every step.

It wasn't much farther; she could hear him better now, closer. The wind howled through the trees, and it wasn't long before the rain joined in. A few cold drops hit her face, and then it poured.

"Gabriel." In the distance she could see him, his body hunched forward. It wasn't fair; she didn't want to worry about him the way she did, but something about him pulled her in, just like a fish caught on a hook. "Gabriel." He didn't look up. "Gabriel!"

"Why are you calling me that?" he screamed. "Why does everyone think my name is Gabriel?" He stared at her, eyes wide.

What was he talking about? Caden's hands began to shake; now was not the time to get answers. They needed to get back to the condo. "I'm sorry, let's go home. We can talk about it."

The clothes draped over his body were soaked with rain. He turned and rose slowly, nodding in agreement. The rain continued to beat down on them, and his head remained slumped forward. Her eyes trailed down his body like the water rolling down his shirt. Caden couldn't help but stare. He was muscular and toned, tall and rugged. A chill ran up her spine, making her shiver. He seemed different then Sean, at least like this, at night. Gabriel lifted his head. His dark eyes pierced her soul, making her insides melt.

"My name is not Gabriel. It's Tom."

3

Caden blinked slowly, dizzily.

Tom.

His name was Tom? Now she knew Gabriel, Tom—whoever—was crazy. She thought of possible solutions; Tom could be his middle name, or maybe he had a twin. No, that couldn't be. Gabriel's room had been empty when they were in it the night before. She watched Tom with her peripheral vision as the water dripped down his frame. He looked toward her, causing her to look away as a blush crept into her cheeks. *He came after me.*

Sean had always told her she was crazy. Maybe she was imagining the whole thing. Caden bit the side of her lip as butterflies exploded inside of her. She had thought Gabriel was attractive, but he was somewhat violent and unpredictable; Tom seemed safer, and he would never hurt her like Sean had. Lightning flared in the distance, followed by a peal of thunder. Tom jumped, looking around the sky for an explanation.

"I'm Caden. Nice to meet you, Tom." She didn't know

what was going on, but she would play along as she tried to make sense of things. Standing in the rain was not a good time or place to question either of their sanities. Thunder boomed again, shaking the ground. Tom became very still, as if afraid to move. "It's okay, Tom, it's just thunder." She watched Tom shrink into himself, as if he was afraid of the sky. It was strange to see a strong, healthy guy act like a child. Instinctively, Caden wanted to protect him. She wanted to make him happy. She didn't know how to help herself, but she knew how she could help Tom. "Do you want to play a game, Tom?"

He looked at her, unsure, tentative, and slightly shivering from the cold. "I don't know."

"Come on, it will be fun." She looked at his eyes again, his dark irises indistinct from his pupils. She hoped it would make him forget about the thunder. "Alright, this is how it works. Whoever is *it* has to tag someone before the next thunder."

"What happens if you can't catch them before the next thunder?"

Caden considered the question. "Umm—if they don't get the victim before the thunder, they have to do ten push-ups, get up and go again."

"But, it's raining."

"Yep, we are going to get soaked. We *are* soaked. Tag, you're it." In a moment, she was moving, darting over fallen trees, flying through the air. Fast enough to get away, but not fast enough for him to lose her trail. She looked behind her; he stood still and unsure. "Can't catch me," she teased, trying to coax him into responding.

It worked.

He sprang into a run and was gaining on her. She looked back at his moving body. Rain spattered against her skin, making her running seem faster and more powerful. Tom came up beside her. A giggling scream escaped her lips as his fingers just missed the fabric of her shirt and thunder struck. "Ten push-ups," she called. But he was already on the ground, doing the first one. His arm muscles bulged, slightly shaking from his weight. The soft ground was pulling his hands under.

"Ten are up," he yelled, and he sprang to a running stance like he had run a hundred races. That was it; he reached out after a few strides and grabbed hold of her arm right as thunder struck again. She yelped in surprise and started laughing. He pulled her in, pinning her body against his as if he was afraid she would get away. He smiled, breathing hard. "I'm a good runner. Are you mad that I won?" He was gloating, completely unaware of how every inch of their bodies was touching. "You're it," he said, grinning, and he took off into the darkness.

They played a few rounds, Tom nearly always winning in half the time. Caden wished, after the thirtieth push-up, that she had picked a different activity to serve as penalty. However, she hadn't thought she would lose. She finished her last push-up, wiping the mud off onto the soaked fabric that hung on her body.

"Tom!" she yelled. "I'm tired, let's go back!" She was cold, too. Running kept them warm, but not nearly enough to stay out any longer. Warmth encircled her palm as Tom came up behind her, wrapping his muddy hand in hers. They didn't say a word as they continued back to Gabriel's condo.

The inside of the condo looked the same but felt different. Tom found her some dry clothes and a towel so she could shower. After, Caden sat on the couch, wet hair around her shoulders, and Tom sat down beside her.

"Tom? What are you doing in Cloverdale?"

"Is that where we are?" Tom fidgeted with the nails on her hand, not looking at her. "I didn't know. I mean, I've been here before."

He didn't even know where he was? She decided to dig a bit further. "I know, I think I've met you before. At a party, maybe? Do you remember me?" Caden asked, hoping it wasn't a bad idea to question him. If he were Gabriel, he'd probably get mad, but he wasn't; he was Tom.

"I don't think I've met you before."

"Are you sure?" She turned her body on the couch to face him.

"I don't want to talk about this." Tom got up to leave, but she pulled him back down, not letting go of his hand. "I haven't met you before, okay?" The irritation in his voice matched that of a child who wanted a second toy at a fast-food drive-through.

"That's okay, no big deal." She removed her hand from his. *Now what?* They fell silent for a few moments.

"I talked to someone," he blurted.

What did that mean? She waited for him to continue. He didn't, so she let it go, thinking it was unimportant. Caden let out the breath she was holding as she leaned against Tom's shoulder. It was peaceful around him; it made her happy. When she had left the condo earlier, she felt like she'd left a piece of her behind, and with Tom by her side, she felt as though she had reclaimed it.

Caden wasn't worried about Tom being crazy; there was a reasonable explanation. She just needed more time to figure out what it was and what to do. One thing seemed to be true: he was practically two people, and Gabriel ruled the daylight hours. She had to convince him to let her stay.

—Day—

"Morning, Gabriel," Caden said, forcing herself to keep a calm tone as she opened the door to his room. He had slept in late, really late, and Caden understood why; Tom wasn't getting much sleep either. "I made you breakfast." Her hands shook at her sides as she waited for his reply.

She hadn't cooked in a little over a month. Sean didn't like her cooking and her mother didn't want the house to smell like anything other than air freshener. Getting back into the kitchen felt good; it wasn't just something to do, it made her feel whole.

That morning had been a challenge, but Tom had figured out where Gabriel hid some money, and after putting Tom to bed she ran to the nearest store a few miles away. It felt good to stretch her legs, but not that good; she didn't want to do it again, especially in her boots.

"What? Oh, it's you. Go away already." His voice was heavy and raspy with sleep.

"You're going to be sorry you missed it," Caden said, putting her hands on her hips and attempting to look unfazed by his comment. She had already eaten while preparing his food, and with her stomach full she felt like a new person. If there was one thing she loved, it was her own cooking. "I thought we could hang out, you know, get to know each other."

"Why would I want to do that?" Gabriel mumbled into his pillow. "I don't even want you here."

"I know," Caden said. She went to the side of his bed and sat on the corner. "I wanted to talk to you about that." She hoped he couldn't hear the fear in her voice. If she pretended to be confident, and it worked, maybe she could eventually stop pretending.

A muffled growl came from Gabriel's smothered face. "Fine," he said, tossing back his covers, "I'm hungry anyway. You better not have made cereal or I'm gonna be pissed."

Caden followed him out the door and down the stairs; she definitely hadn't made cereal.

Gabriel considered licking the plate, but she was staring at him. He had eaten everything. How could he pass it up? The layout looked like the cover of a cooking magazine: fresh blueberry muffins with butter in the middle, banana waffles, bacon, and orange juice. There were many things that could have ruined it; she could have gotten the knock-off brands of orange juice or maple syrup—Gabriel hated those—but she hadn't. If she had made pancakes, he wouldn't have touched them. Yet, somehow he couldn't complain. If he'd kept a diary of his favorite foods, he would have accused her of reading it, but he kept no such thing.

Gabriel leaned back in his chair, which groaned softly in protest along with his full stomach. Caden hadn't said a word while he ate, and she hadn't eaten with him either, which was a little uncomfortable.

"Alright, you can stay," Gabriel said in a rush, licking his lips. He could tell Caden was trying to control her excitement, but she couldn't hide the smile that spread from the corner of her lips. "Under one condition: you keep cooking and cleaning. You can stay as long as you don't mess up. The second you make something I don't like—" he made a thumbs-up and tossed it over his shoulder, "—you'll be out of here."

Caden nodded. "Sounds good, I'll start cleaning the kitchen."

"Eh, leave it for now. I thought you wanted to hang out?"

His eyes lingered over her soft features, button nose and dark eyes. His baggy clothes concealed her femininity from the neck down. The last time he'd had a girl in the condo had been last summer. Angelica had crushed his pride. He wasn't sure if he was ready to trust someone again. Over the years he'd never had any real friends, which was partly his fault. He looked up at Caden's face once more, her smile wide and contagious. He fought the urge to smile in return. If she was going to stay, he needed to know more about her, the sooner the better.

"I do." Her smile grew wider. "I do want to hang out."

"Alright, we'll leave in five." Gabriel headed up to his room and shut the door.

———————————

Caden jumped up and down a few times. Her outfit from the night Gabriel picked her up was finally dry. She put it on in haste and pulled her hair back with a string she found in the kitchen. Her makeup had washed off the day before. Sean would never let her out of the house without makeup, but she had a feeling Gabriel hadn't noticed or didn't care.

Her old clothes felt strange, stiff and tight. She already missed Gabriel's soft T-shirt and shorts; his clothes seemed to always smell of cinnamon. However, she couldn't deny feeling sexier in her own clothes, ones that actually fit her body.

"You ready?"

"Yep." Caden peeked her head out from the bathroom. "Let's go."

"Do you need a jacket?"

Caden froze. "Umm, if you have an extra?"

"Yeah, hold on." Gabriel did a quick jog through the living room, coming back with a light blue hoodie. "Sorry, it isn't black."

"I don't like black anyway."

Gabriel grinned. "Yeah, right."

Of course she loved black.

Walking in the forest outside of the condominium looked different during the day. The night before, with Tom, seemed distant and dreamlike now. The wind picked up and made Caden shiver. Would Tom forgive her if she told him she had been out with Gabriel, his other half? More or less like his older brother, psychologically anyway. Caden disliked the thought. What was Tom? She felt protective of him, like a sibling, but only because he seemed so young. He wasn't really young though, because he was somehow Gabriel... Caden shook the thought free. She couldn't possibly know what would, or wouldn't, upset Tom when she didn't even know what Gabriel and Tom were.

After a long pause Gabriel broke the silence. "Are you going to tell me why you're staying with me? I sure hope you're over eighteen so I don't get in trouble with your mom or something."

She had another six months before her eighteenth birthday, but she didn't think that he had to know that, not really. He sighed, seeming irritated that she hadn't answered yet.

Had she really taken that long? "Well," Caden said, lingering on the word to buy more time. "I, umm, have this issue—"

"Issue?"

"Not like that!" Caden waved her hands back and forth, anxiously. "I broke up with my boyfriend." In reality he had broken up with her. "Yeah, I broke up with him, but after that I realized I probably shouldn't have."

"Why?" Gabriel asked, sounding intrigued.

She needed to open up to him; if she did, he might do the same. Then she could figure out what he was hiding. She could figure out what Tom was. She took a deep breath and started again. "I don't know. I guess I thought I deserved someone better. It was stupid to think I could have someone who actually loved me instead of an alcoholic rager who... Who..." Surprised and embarrassed to hear her voice crack, Caden cupped her hands over her face in an attempt to hide the tears.

Gabriel walked closer to her. "What did he do to you?" His voice echoed with bewildered sweetness. It sounded like Tom's voice.

"He hit me." Caden leaned into Gabriel a little, and soon the warmth of his arms encircled her.

"Did you tell anyone?"

Caden meant to say *no* but the word didn't leave her lips as easily as the tears left her eyes.

"It's going to be okay. Shhh, it's okay," Gabriel whispered

as he held her close. The sun came out from behind the clouds and specks of light fell through the trees. "Maybe you should tell someone. Do you have any family? Anyone to help you besides—me?"

"No." She used the back of her sleeve to wipe away the salty droplets from her cheeks. Just telling him, this stranger, lifted a weight off of her. "No one. I haven't talked to my mom in a little over a week and, well, my dad, he lives like four hours away with some woman who's probably my age." She looked up. His embrace made her feel desired. Over the previous months, Sean had made her feel like no one could ever want her, and she'd believed him. But now, in Gabriel's arms, she felt like something had clicked into place. There was a shifting inside of her that filled her up and quieted her desperation in a way that she'd no longer thought was possible. She finally felt something like home. The way he comforted her made her think that maybe he felt the same way. If he did, maybe together they wouldn't feel so empty. The light falling through the trees landed in his eyes, and copper glistened behind them.

Caden let her feet arch to tiptoe, bringing her mouth to his.

Gabriel's lips tingled from the kiss. His insides knotted with a new hunger. There was another sensation too, a calmness. He didn't say a word as they walked side by side back to his condo. He didn't want to ruin it.

When he opened the door to the condo, he let Caden walk inside but he didn't follow. He had things to do. He had run into some friends the day before, and after some convincing on their part, he'd agreed to throw a party. It had seemed like a good idea at the time, but now after kissing Caden…

"I'm having a party here tonight."

Her face said it all—she clearly didn't like the idea of a party. Neither did he, not now. Which was all because they had kissed.

This was going to bother him all night, knowing that he could have taken the time to get to know her instead of entertaining a group of drunken teens, but there was no stopping it now. He didn't even know how many people would come. Anger flicked in his throat.

"Clean up the place for me? I'll get whatever you need at the store." He told himself she would have fun once it started. He would make her happy.

Caden nodded and went to the kitchen to start a list. He watched as she bit her lip trying to think of new items, looking to the left and tapping the pencil eraser on the counter. When she finished the list, he looked it over, but his thoughts were still wrapped around how her teeth had sunk into her lip. He wanted to kiss her again. Instead he turned toward the door without a glance back. He didn't want her to know she was so close to perfect; he couldn't let her see how she broke him down.

"Can I come too?" she asked in a singsong voice that

made him wince. God, she made him feel guilty for wanting to tell her no.

"You better not." He said quickly, wishing he could come up with a good reason besides his fear of pushing her away. "I'll be back soon." He turned toward her and swiftly kissed her on her forehead.

There was something about Caden that made Gabriel feel listened to, though he couldn't figure out why since he hadn't told her a thing about himself. She seemed pleasant and sincere, and she seemed to care about what he thought. Still, she could really use something to wear besides her Goth clothes.

An idea came to him; he would buy her something that wasn't black, something that would make her feel pretty.

Gabriel stopped at a clothing store.

"A small should fit her," he told the lady who was helping him pick out shirts.

"What about pants?" The lady looked at him over her glasses, her blonde hair laced with strands of gray. She listed off a series of numbers, sizes 0–8, but he hadn't a clue. He figured she could read the expression on his face. She suggested skirts.

"Yeah, skirts and anything else with elastic or a drawstring." He ended up leaving with a few bags and was more excited than he was willing to admit. If everything went well, Caden wouldn't be leaving anytime soon.

The door swung open with a creak as Gabriel strolled in, his hands full of grocery bags. "Help me with these?"

Caden rushed over and grabbed half the bags. Her arms buckled at the weight. There was so much food. Gabriel placed his bags on the counter and turned back to the door.

"Where are you going now?" Caden asked, sad to see him leaving so soon.

"Back to the car, that's only half of it."

Caden didn't like parties. At one time she had; that was when she was with Sean. Her stomach twisted at the thought of who would come tonight. If they recognized her, would they tell her mother where she was? Caden's mind began to wander as she moved the groceries into the refrigerator.

She had nothing to wear to the party. There would be pretty girls in slutty short skirts flipping their hair, and like usual she would be covered head to toe in thick black clothes, blending in with the shadows and being ignored.

Gabriel came back in with another bunch of bags and a

few bottles of vodka.

"How many people are coming tonight, Gabriel?"

He shrugged. "I don't know, like thirty maybe. There is a keg coming soon. Why don't you go get ready? People should be here in an hour."

"This early?" Caden looked over at the clock. "It's only seven."

"Yeah, and in a few hours it'll be dark as shit. No one cares as long as there's booze."

Caden looked at him while putting the milk in the fridge. As it rested on the edge of the shelf she could feel it begin to slip from her loose fingers. She looked down just in time to see it falling in slow motion. Caden scrambled to catch it, but it was too late. It exploded on the floor, spraying the kitchen with a translucent white sheen.

"You've got to be kidding me. Really, Caden?" The anger in his voice made her feel small. Her hands shook as she bent down to pick up the plastic jug that had burst open. Gabriel stormed over, grabbing it from her hands. "Be more careful, will ya?" He tossed it in the trash beside her. "Clean this up. Then go to the trunk of my car. The bags in there are for you. I'll be in my room." He raked his hands through his hair as he turned from her.

Caden stood frozen in shock. Her mother had always told her not to cry over spilled milk, but the tears came anyway.

By the time she was done cleaning the kitchen and putting

away the food, it was 7:45 p.m. People would be there soon. She felt sick to her stomach with anticipation, and Gabriel still hadn't come out of his room. Wiping her hands on her hips, she opened the front door and stepped into the brisk evening. It was nearly dark. The trunk of Gabriel's car was open, and she could see pastel blue bags in the side corner. Caden peeked inside to see soft fabrics and lace. She stared for a bit, remaining motionless as the information registered.

He'd bought her clothes?

A boy, no, a man had never brought her clothes before. Well, no one besides her father, and that had stopped years ago. What did it mean? She suddenly wished she had a friend to ask. Part of her felt taken care of and the other part of her felt a little creeped out. She inhaled a sharp breath as she grabbed the bags. What if he had bought her lingerie? If he did, she'd know what he wanted. Maybe he wasn't so different from Sean. After grabbing the bags, she closed the trunk behind her and headed back to the condo.

In the bathroom she went through the clothes, and they were beautiful but not *her*. The thought of wearing something besides black was a stab in the chest. Black was what she felt comfortable in; it had become part of who she was. *Caden can wear whatever colors she likes,* she rationalized. *At least he didn't buy me lingerie.*

She slipped on the light pink skirt and lace top that hung off her shoulders. They fit her perfectly. Her hands pulled at the skirt, wishing it was longer. She'd never shown so much leg before. She leaned toward the bathroom mirror, not recognizing the girl staring back. Pink was the worst color in the world, but maybe it didn't look so bad. In fact she felt kind of pretty, maybe even a little scandalous. She ran her fingers through her hair, exaggerating the part; it looked even blacker now, if that was possible. She tilted her head as she scrutinized her reflection.

Knock, knock, knock.

"Caden, get the door." It was Gabriel yelling from his bedroom.

"One sec," she called back.

Knock, knock, knock.

Not very patient, are they. She pushed the bags of clothes into the bathroom closet with the towels and opened the door in time to see Gabriel running down the stairs to the front door.

"I said I would get it," Caden huffed.

He looked her up and down. Anger still lined his face, but something else was there too. Shock? "You took too long," he said.

"Hey man, let us in," a voice yelled from outside the door. "It's freezing out here."

"Yeah, let us in," another hollered. Caden thought it sounded like a girl, and her heart stopped. She hated being around other girls.

Gabriel opened the door. "Hey guys."

The first guy came in and gave Gabriel an aggressive man

hug and hit to the shoulder. The girl followed, hugging Gabriel in such a way that every part of her seemed to seductively melt into him. Caden froze; now her heart wouldn't stop pounding and her brain felt fuzzy. It made her sick to see a girl touch him like that.

"Who is this? Lucky Charms?" the boy asked as he took Caden's hand and gave her an awkward swirl. Caden's feet fumbled around in a circle, her skirt flying with the movement. She quickly let go of his hand to grab her skirt. "Now I know why you took your time opening the door." He wiggled his eyebrows at Gabriel.

Caden looked toward Gabriel but he didn't give them a glance; he was too preoccupied talking to the girl as more people came in around them.

"I'm Caden." She put her hand out for the guy to take once more. He took it with both hands and shook her arm vigorously.

"Oh, Caden, I can't wait to get to know you better. Call me Face."

"Face?"

"Yeah, baby. Everyone loves the face. Where can Face get a drink around here?"

Caden pointed to the fridge. He did have a nice face: angular, with a full mouth and large blue eyes.

He winked, letting go of her hand. "You want one, Lucky Charms?"

"Ah, I guess," she said. Face was already on his way to the fridge. He came back again with two beers.

Face grabbed her hand and led her to the couch. "Sit down already. I'm getting tired just watching you."

Caden didn't know what to say. She had never gotten this response from a guy at a party. And where was Gabriel? She scanned the room. The heat doubled as more people flooded in.

"Where are the snacks?" someone yelled.

"Caden, get the snacks," Gabriel's voice bellowed. She still couldn't see him.

"I'm sorry, umm, Face but I've got to go help." She began to stand.

"No you don't, baby. Stay." He pulled her back down.

"You don't understand, I have an, ah, well, an agreement with Gabriel."

His face contorted. "What's that supposed to mean? You his property or something? That's F'ed up."

"No, no. Not like that." Caden stood back up, ducking through a group of people before he could grab her again.

When Caden got to the kitchen, she attempted to move around the bodies that were crowding her, crushing her almost. So far she didn't recognize any of them, and she doubted they would recognize her. Still, she kept her face down, her long dark hair covering one eye. Opening the cupboard she grabbed the chips and pretzels, filling the bowls on the counter and putting them aside. Hands grabbed for them, the bowls disappearing as they floated through the crowd. Next she opened the fridge to grab the cream cheese and butter. Eyes surrounded her and watched her work. She pulled out sugar, vanilla extract, and cinnamon. *Where did I put the toffee?* Caden spun around to see one of the party guests nibbling on the bag of toffee crumbs.

"Hey, that was mine!" he yelled as she grabbed the bag from his sticky fingers.

"Was not," she whispered.

Eyeballing the ingredients, she put them in the bowl and with a spoon used all her strength to beat them together. If ten people hadn't been blocking her way to the cabinet, she would have grabbed the electric beater, but the eyes watching her made her nervous. When she was done, she put the dip in separate bowls along with two separate plates of crackers. Caden looked up to see Face watching her. He smiled as she pushed one of the bowls of dip toward him. "Here. It's a snicker-doodle kind of dip."

His eyes went wide. "Hey, everyone. Lucky Charms here made us snicker-doodle dip." Hands full of beer lifted to the ceiling as the crowd moved in their direction. She ducked out of the way as the kitchen overflowed, hoping to escape Face and all the party people. She wanted to see Gabriel.

She went up the stairs, holding her skirt against her legs as she stepped around the people on the steps and opened the door to Gabriel's room. "Hey, get out of here!" someone yelled as something hit the door. She closed it quickly, letting out a breath.

Pushing back through the sea of bodies, she made it down the stairs to the couch, where she plopped down. Face was there.

"Here, baby, I knew you would make it back to me. Everyone comes to the couch." He looked pleased with himself as he bobbed his head up and down. "Have another beer."

Caden didn't even remember having a sip of the first one.

"The dip was a hit. Think it's gone."

Caden bit the inside of her lip and looked around once more for Gabriel. "I guess I should go make something else."

"No. Don't go."

"Yeah, don't go," a girl chimed in as she pushed herself over to the couch.

"Angelica. My girl. Come on over." Face opened his arms and she sat on the other side, nestling in.

Face was one of those guys? Caden suddenly felt less special.

"So, it's Caden right?" the girl asked. She was the girl who'd come in with Face, the one who molested Gabriel, basically groping him. Her bronze hair cupped under her chin, thick bangs concealing her eyebrows. Her blue eyes glistened against her pale skin.

Caden nodded as she pulled the neckline of her shirt to cover her shoulders; it slid back down.

Angelica was pretty, and Caden could tell she knew it. "What is up with you and Gabriel? You his go-to girl or something?"

"What?" Caden looked over at Angelica, whose face was a mix of bitter jealousy topped with a grin.

"You know, his ho?"

"Hoe? No, can't say I'm a fan of gardening," Caden replied with a fake smile. She felt bile rising in her throat. Competing with other girls, especially ones with more practice, was the last thing she wanted to do. Her confidence was fabricated, of course; her hands were shaking and she wanted nothing more than to hide behind her hair and disappear. *No, I'm not Rebecca anymore.* So Caden let the smile stay on her lips.

Face laughed, slapping his knee. "Fun, ain't she?"

"Yeah, real funny." Angelica got up to leave. "I'm going to go find Gabriel. Unlike you, I like to garden."

Caden's smile disappeared as she watched the girl get up to leave. Angelica's skirt was much shorter than Caden's, and it hugged her hips provocatively.

—Night—

It was nearly midnight and the crowd was still partying. Drunken kids ran in and out of the condo. Caden had expected the cops to come, but no one ever showed. She had seen Gabriel a few times earlier in the night. Here and there, he would glance over at her while talking to other girls. Face had kept her on the couch all night, making it impossible to look for Gabriel.

"Yo Ho?"

Caden looked up to see Angelica.

"Your boyfriend is upstairs puking in the toilet, calling for his mommy. Thought you were probably it."

She began to rise from the couch she had been glued to all night, but she got pulled back down. Face's hand held tightly onto hers as his body lay passed out, splayed in the opposite direction. She unwrapped his grip and headed for Gabriel's room.

"Gabriel?" Caden whispered as she opened his bedroom door just a crack.

In his bedroom's bathroom Gabriel's head leaned over the toilet, the rushing sound of vomit flowing from his mouth. Caden kneeled to the ground and placed her hand on his back. He coughed, spitting and breathing hard.

"You okay?" she asked, trying to sound gentle. Part of her wondered if he was still angry with her for spilling the gallon of milk.

He brought up his face from the toilet and lunged at her. Startled, she pulled back, but it was too late. He held her close, his face in her chest. It took her a moment to realize he was hugging her, crying.

"I—" *hiccup*, "—don't know what is—" *hiccup*, "—happening to me."

Caden shushed quietly in his ear, stroking his head. It was Tom; it had to be. "How are you feeling?"

"Like I'm going to die." *Hiccup.* "What is wrong with me? Who are all these people?" He held her tighter. She could feel the dribble of vomit on his lip pushing up against her skin. On any other occasion it would have made her sick, but the way Tom needed her was a good distraction.

"Shhh. Everything is going to be alright, they will leave soon. I promise."

"I want them to go now," he whined.

Caden continued to stroke his hair. He was twice her size; her body seemed to be concealed completely beneath him.

"Woho." Caden looked up to see Face towering above her. "What the hell is going on in here?" he asked, his expression sagging.

Tom looked up from her chest and hid his face again. "Who is that?" he whispered. "I don't like him."

"He's your friend, To—Gabe... Umm, he's your friend." Caden looked from Tom and turned to Face. "He just isn't feeling well."

"You're telling me?" He trailed his finger around the edge of a glass of water and looked down at the floor. "Heck, I think Angelica has some similar stories she could tell you." He gestured toward Tom, the water slushing in the cup. "You know, so you know what you're getting into."

"Angelica? Did they like—"

"Date? Yeah." He rubbed his face with his hand. "They ended it last summer. He only stays for the summer, you know?"

Face lowered himself carefully to the floor and lay back.

Caden didn't know. Her gut twisted.

"Yeah, some rich parents. They own this condo along with like a few dozen others around the States. Gabe made it real clear to the neighbors last year that if anyone called the cops on his parties he would evict them."

"Can he do that?"

Face shrugged. "That's what he says anyway. Plus we didn't get busted, did we?" Caden shook her head no. "Anyway," Face continued, dazed as he lay on the floor facing the ceiling. "You mind if I lie here a bit?"

"Yes," she heard Tom whisper.

"Go ahead," Caden said to Face, and Tom hugged her a little tighter.

"Anyway, like I was saying. Angelica and Gabe, they used to be pretty tight but he, you know." Face leaned closer, pointing at Tom with one hand, signing for crazy.

"You sure Angelica wasn't making it up?" Caden asked. She hated Angelica already.

"My Angelica, no, she's an angel. Can't tell a lie, that one."

Caden scoffed.

"Ah, don't be like that, Lucky Charms. I bet you two could be friends. She just needs to warm up to you. Like me." He winked and lay back down, closing his eyes. "We should get together and do this again." He spoke like he'd just had a brilliant revelation.

Tom pulled away and Caden reluctantly let him go. He gripped the toilet seat and retched again. Nothing was left to expel, but he coughed and more tears came. He let go and settled back into Caden.

"Yeah." Caden stroked Tom's head. "We should totally do this again." *There is no way I'm letting Gabriel do this to Tom, ever again.*

—Day—

When the heat against Caden's side vanished, she opened her eyes, her hand finding her neck. It hurt. They'd fallen asleep on the bathroom floor. Everything hurt.

"Tom?" she whispered groggily, rubbing the sleep from her eyes. Caden was alone in the small bathroom. She got to her feet, nearly falling over and catching herself on the wall. Where was he? Her eyes momentarily closed as she walked into his room, light shining from the windows and blinding her.

"All right, everyone out," Gabriel yelled. "Get out. Come on, off your ass."

Caden walked down the stairs to find him using his foot to roll someone over.

"I said *up*," his voice was becoming progressively louder.

Drunken kids slowly found their feet, their hangovers causing instant headaches as their eyes found the sun. Some of them grabbed their heads while others covered their eyes. A deep moaning hummed through the room. No one wanted to leave. They had probably only fallen asleep a few hours ago. An empty vodka bottle teetered on the floor, and red cups lined every surface. The bowls of dip were licked clean and one was broken in half. She knew she had a lot of work to do. Her eyes searched the crowd of faces; Angelica was gone and so was Face. They obviously knew better than to stick around until he woke up.

Caden looked down at her skirt to see that wrinkles scrunched it higher up her thigh. She could smell a distinct vomit aroma around the collar of her shirt. Her nose cringed. She would need a shower, but then again so would Gabriel. Her heartbeat quickened. She didn't know what he wanted from her. When Tom had fallen asleep, using her chest as a pillow, it had felt nice being needed. Like the times she had been there for her sister when she was sick. Tom made her feel strong and looked up to. She wanted to keep him and protect him. Men had hurt her, but Tom never would; he was too sweet and innocent. Waking up to Gabriel was a punch in the face.

Caden reluctantly felt a small amount of guilt creep into her. Gabriel did after all give her a roof over her head, her clothes, and a means to food. But that didn't change the fact that he was unpredictable and most of the time made her feel small and washed-up.

Where did Tom go during the day, and what was wrong with Gabriel? Pain bit into her palms as her hands formed into fists, her nails digging into the soft flesh. Couldn't anything be easy for once?

"Caden?" Gabriel looked up at her, the anger in his face softening. "Come help me with this."

Caden did a quick little walk, not wanting to move her skirt with a run and not wanting to see his reaction if she took her time.

"Grab this guy's ankle," he said.

She looked down at an unconscious boy. "Is he okay?"

"Do you know him?"

"No?" Caden looked up at him, perplexed.

"Neither do I. Who cares? Grab his leg."

Caden placed her knees together and slowly lowered herself to the ground, careful not to move her skirt. Her hands gripped around the edge of the unidentified kid's jeans.

"Okay, lift," Gabriel said. She did, though not far. "Follow me." It was hard not to when the kid's upper body pulled her forward. Gabriel had him lifted to his waist level while she stood hunched over with his feet only a foot off the ground. They walked out the condo's door and with a thud Gabriel dropped his half. The kid groaned. "Don't drink so much next time," Gabriel yelled behind him as he walked back through the door. Caden still held the pant legs, holding up the kid's feet. She set them down gently.

"Caden?" Gabriel peeked out from the door. "You coming?"

"Yeah." She wiped her hands on her skirt and stepped back into the condo. Gabriel shut the door behind her. *That was harsh.*

71

"Take a shower, you stink."

"I don't know, your vomit doesn't smell that bad," was her offhanded reply. It wasn't true though; it reeked. Still, she wanted him to talk about last night. He didn't look back at her as he went up the stairs.

"Don't take long. I want hot water for mine." He shut the door to his room behind him.

Caden stood naked in the bathroom, the humid air concealing the mirror. She braced herself on the countertop, looking into the fog as her mind streamed through the previous night. Part of her felt like she was imagining Tom, because nothing else made sense. *Sean always said I was crazy.* Caden ran a hand over the fogged mirror.

Knock, knock, knock.

"Caden, you done in there?"

"Yeah, one sec," she said, as she grabbed the towel off the shower pole and wrapped it around herself. She opened the door to step out. Her breath caught in her throat as her eyes took in the sight of his bare chest just inches from her face. The heat rose in her like a wave, and she feared her cheeks were red.

"Hi," Caden gulped, frustrated by the embarrassment of having almost run into him. Besides the towel around his waist, Gabriel was naked. It didn't seem to bother him that they were so close. Was it really necessary for him to be naked already?

72

Her eyes traveled down the length of his body, the smell of vomit wafting off of his skin.

"Hey. You done?"

"Ah, yeah." She pushed a wet strand of her hair behind her ear and moved around him. He entered the bathroom and closed the door. Her shoulders sank. She wasn't sure what she had expected. He seemed so unaffected.

Caden's eyes drifted over and around the condo. To say that it was a mess was a tragic understatement. She probably should have cleaned up before showering. The water turned on just as Caden remembered that her clothes were in the bathroom closet. *Damn. Why can't both bathrooms have showers?* If she waited for him to be done, they would both be clean, wet and nearly naked. She wondered if he would be angry that she hadn't started cleaning.

For now it was best to start with guaranteeing a place to live, which meant keeping him happy. She didn't want to be homeless again, and she couldn't leave Tom. She felt responsible for him, but there was something else, too. Some part of Gabriel, probably the broken part, appealed to her.

Turning toward the bathroom door to knock, she paused. Instead she let her hand grip the handle, turning it slowly. It wasn't locked. She pushed open the door, and warm mist hit her face as the rushing water got louder. Her stomach knotted. If he knew she was in there, would he yell at her to get out?

Being as quiet as possible, Caden tiptoed across the tile to the bathroom closet. Her fingers pulled on the small handle and a popping noise followed.

"Caden? Is that you?" He sounded unimpressed, and unsurprised.

She mouthed a few curse words. "Ah, yeah. Sorry, I forgot my clothes in here."

"I was wondering when you'd remember those."

He remembered but didn't tell me? A burning tingle filled her cheeks. She imagined they were bright pink. "Yeah, sorry."

Gabriel pulled back the shower curtain just enough for her to see his chest, wet and glistening. "You going to cook today?" he asked, oddly good-natured. Suspiciously so.

He likes my cooking. She felt like an unused balloon finally getting its first taste of helium. The new feeling felt right as it overcame her and expanded in her chest, like the anticipation of finally being able to fly after being left forgotten on the floor. Caden wanted the feeling to last but like all balloons, eventually she would deflate or pop; it was only a matter of time. She nodded, speechless, frozen to the ground.

"Good, I can clean and you cook. Maybe we can knock out the smell before tonight."

"Sure." She nodded again, grabbed her bag of clothes, and turned toward the door, wondering what was so special about tonight.

The condo was nearly spotless by the time Caden pulled the stuffed portobello mushrooms out of the oven. Gabriel hadn't said anything to her after he had gotten out of the shower. They had shared the quiet for over an hour, and it felt oddly peaceful. Caden thought being in a quiet room with someone was always awkward unless it was with family. She sure hadn't ever been able to share a silence with Sean, but now here with Gabriel it just felt right.

"Smells great. If it wasn't for the hint of vomit hanging around, I'd be in heaven."

Caden giggled. Her hair fell in front of her eyes as she lifted the first mushroom, soaked in butter, onto a nest of rice already on the plate. Her mom didn't like to eat butter. Caden didn't believe in cooking unless there was tons of butter. She poured the spiced gravy over the top of the mushrooms and placed the plate on the table.

"You're eating with me, right?" Gabriel asked as he put the window cleaner down on the counter before sitting.

"Ah, sure." She tucked a strand of hair behind her ear. *I thought you'd never ask.* Caden's stomach grumbled in agreement. She got another plate out from the cupboard and spooned a clump of rice onto the center. She quickly grabbed one of the mushrooms, her fingertips tingling from the heat. After dropping it on the plate, she spooned on the gravy and sat down next to Gabriel.

His mouth was already full of his first bite. "This is really great," he mumbled as he continued to chew, clearly impressed. "Where'd you learn to cook?"

She felt her old self resurface, the shy, timid Rebecca. She pushed it down. *I'm Caden, carefree and bold and whatever else I want to be.* "You know those trade schools you can start junior year?"

Gabriel nodded, shoving another forkful into his mouth.

"Well, I started at one for culinary arts."

"That's cool. Bet everyone really likes that, huh? I sure do."

Caden looked down at her plate. She wished everyone liked it. The mushroom broke apart as she poked it with her fork, the steam swirling delicately above it as the morsel vanished into her mouth. She shrugged, still not looking at him.

Before ten minutes had passed, Gabriel had eaten seconds and thirds. Appreciation felt good, better than good; it was the one thing no one had ever given her. If there was anything she knew about cooking, it was that it never lied; if someone liked what they ate, they would finish and ask for more. It wasn't like receiving a dress from your aunt at Christmas, one that you would only take out when she was around. That was why Caden had always liked food; it was honest, dependable, and delicious.

"So Gabriel," Caden hesitantly said as she washed off her dish. "Last night. You got pretty sick."

He set his dish by the sink, making her jump. She hadn't realized he had gotten up. "Yeah?"

"Do you remember anything?" *Like holding onto me? Crying? Choking on your tears?*

"Shit, Caden, I don't know. I just woke up. We didn't… you know, do anything?" His hand went to his forehead as he winced. "Is that what this is about? I don't remember something? Tell me I didn't make you some kind of promise."

On the outside Caden smirked, but on the inside Rebecca begged to turn and hide behind her hair, blushing furiously. Caden flipped her hair back and looked into his copper eyes. "You really don't remember?" She wanted to go farther, to list off all the pretend things that didn't happen just to make him nervous, but her Rebecca half stepped in and clamped her mouth shut.

Gabriel covered his face with his hand. "Shit, shit, shit. I should have told you about that. I tend to black out. Well, I don't know if black out is the right word, but I tend to forget things I've said." He let his hand drop from his face as he looked her in the eyes. "Or at least that's what I've heard.

77

I tried to steer clear of you last night, guess it didn't work." Gabriel grinned sheepishly, but somehow it looked devilish.

"Oh, is that why you ignored me all night?" She didn't actually believe that had been the reason why he ignored her, but she'd give it to him so they could move on. She used to pretend to accept Sean's excuses too, just to avoid walking into another hurtful night. Caden wiped her hands off on a towel, stepping closer to him. "Relax."

"What?" He sounded tired and a little bewildered. His eyebrows were still knitted together in apprehension.

She was so close to him now. She wanted to kiss him again, just once. Tom flashed in her thoughts, and she shrank away.

Gabriel grabbed at her arm and pulled her toward him again. He didn't seem to like her shying away from him. "What happened, Caden? What did I do to you?" Gone was the insecure Gabriel. He wanted answers.

Caden gulped. A pain formed in her arm where his hand tightened. He pulled her closer. Their bodies touched and molded together, not an inch between them. His thin running shorts didn't conceal even the slightest ridge. "I, umm…" Caden's hands gripped the dish towel trapped between their bodies. "Nothing happened."

"It didn't?"

"No, you just vomited a lot and, umm—"

"And what?" Gabriel held her tighter.

"Asked me not to leave…ever," Caden said. His heart beat

against her chest; it drowned out the beating of her own heart.

"Ever?" He smirked. Like a light, his aggressive demeanor suddenly shut off. "Well, as long as I was still Gabriel when I said it, guess it's as good as gold."

Still Gabriel? Does he know about Tom? Gabriel let go of her, the quick release making her unsteady. She watched him walk away with long, easy strides.

"So I thought we could go get coffee at Joe's Coffee Shop down the street. Sound good?" he asked over his shoulder.

"Sounds perfect."

—*Night*—

"Hey." Caden nudged Tom's shoulder with her own as she slipped onto the bed beside him. "I brought you something." She waited as Tom rubbed his eyes and sat up. Caden carefully unwrapped the delicate morsel of food. The chocolate muffin sat perfectly in the palm of her hand.

"What's that?"

"What do you mean? You said you liked chocolate muffins. I picked it up at Joe's Coffee Shop down the street."

His face lit up as he reached for it. "Yeah, but I've never tasted one before." He pinched the muffin with a little too much force and it broke in half.

"Never had one?" She watched as he looked at the muffin like it was a foreign object. He stroked the top of it and licked his finger. Unsatisfied, he picked up one of the half pieces and stuffed it in his mouth. His eyes widened as he chewed and swallowed, grabbing for the second piece. Caden pulled it away. "Wait a minute, slow down. You're taking too big of bites and you still haven't answered my question."

A pouting lip developed on his face, and his shoulders slumped. "Come on, give it to me."

"Fine, fine, but then will you answer my question?"

Tom nodded and stuffed the second half of the muffin in his mouth. Caden only sighed. She thought big bites wasted the taste.

"I've just never had—"

"Wait until you're done chewing," she insisted, giving him a mom's look of disapproval as crumbs fell from one corner of his lips.

Tom swallowed. "Sorry." He swallowed again. "I've just never had one."

"You said that already, but why would you tell me you loved them if you hadn't had one?"

"I just knew."

"Interesting. Well, I want you to tell me every other food that you just know you love too, all of the details, okay?"

Tom nodded, grabbing her hand as he did so. "Thank you." Their shoulders were still touching.

"How do you feel after last night?" Caden asked as she stroked his forehead.

"I feel okay. Can I have another muffin?"

"I don't have any more." Caden took her hand off his forehead. "Tom? Do you wake up sick often, you know, and throw up?"

"Sometimes." He shrugged. "Those people scare me."

"The people from the party?"

She watched as Tom turned his head to the side, trying to understand her words. "Party?"

"Yeah, you know, drinks, food, people."

Tom looked down at his hands. "I know what a party is. I've just never been to one."

"Yeah, you have. You were at one last night. I was here with you."

"That was horrible."

Caden sighed. "Yeah, I know, Tom."

Tom walked to the window, and she followed, standing behind him. Black asphalt covered the ground, and the lush forest hovered behind it.

"Tom." She found his hand and let her fingers fall in between his. "How many people know about you?"

He didn't say a thing as he dropped her hand and left the window, plopping back onto the bed. "I'd really like another muffin."

"I'll get you one tomorrow, Tom, but now tell me who you know. Do you know Angelica?"

He looked at her as if the name was another language.

Caden wondered if he would know her name at all. "You

know. Short brown hair, blue eyes, really white skin."

His eyes widened as he nodded. "She yelled at me. She called me some other name. The name you called me." His eyes narrowed.

Angelica must have called him Gabriel too, but of course she would have. Why wouldn't she? Tom didn't know Angelica like Gabriel did; Caden assumed it had been what broke them up. The darkness flowed through the room. Where did Tom belong in this world? "What about your parents?"

"My parents?" He looked down at his hands. "I don't have parents."

"But you know what they are?"

He nodded his head.

"Are you asleep right now, Tom?" she asked, and he looked at her like she was the one confused. Maybe she was.

"No, I'm awake. See, my eyes are open. Want to play a game?"

"Alright, let's play the memory game. I'll ask you for a memory and you have to tell me. Then we switch. Like, what's the first thing you remember?"

"Why?" Tom got up from the bed and crossed his arms over his chest as he paced around the room.

"Come on Tom, it's a game." She reached for his hand, but he pulled away.

He continued to glare at her. It seemed out of character and more like something Gabriel would do, but she ignored it.

"I don't have to tell you anything."

"Tom, you said you wanted to play a game." Her voice sounded like a whiny little girl's. "Come on, please." Caden got closer. "For me, Tom?" He was taller than she was, by a lot. She thought of Gabriel. They had to be the same person. Tom had to be sleepwalking or something. She felt uneasy because she liked Gabriel—maybe after today as much as she liked Tom. Still, no matter how much she wanted them to be, they weren't the same person, not really. She wanted to protect Tom like a brother but with Gabriel she wanted something completely different; she would just have to wait and find out if Gabriel wanted the same thing.

Good Morning, Beautiful."

Caden's heartbeat quickened as the mountains of hash browns wavered on the plate she held and the sunny-side-up egg yolks jiggled back and forth. Even the biscuits threatened to jump overboard as she corrected her footing.

"Morning," she said as she forced down Tom's name. "How did you sleep?"

"I feel great, best I've felt in a long time." Gabriel spun the chair away from the table and did a little skip before landing in it.

A giggle escaped her lips and he returned it with a laugh. She wasn't surprised that he felt well. Tom had wanted to go to bed early that morning, which meant Gabriel got a little more sleep. With that in mind, Caden placed the plate before him and turned to go back into the kitchen to clean up.

"Aren't you going to sit down?" He pulled out the chair beside him, patting it.

"I'm not really hungry. I ate while I was cooking, but at dinner we can eat together."

"Isn't that just dandy."

Caden cringed. He sounded put out. Would he throw another mug? She hoped not.

She was just about to make up some kind of apology when he said, "I'm just kidding, tonight works." He put a forkful of hash browns in his mouth, a bite so large she wondered how he could chew it all and still be able to swallow.

Dishes filled the sink to the farthest edge. If she was going to finish in time to make dinner, she needed to get started. She reluctantly made her way to the dirty dishes. Soapy water covered her hands as the plates and kitchenware went from one side to the other. "So, Face mentioned at the party that you only live here during the summer?"

It took a while for him to answer, she imagined, because his mouth was full.

"He said that, huh? Yeah, I saw him hanging on you all night."

He'd been watching her? Where had he been? Caden felt a little more confident knowing that she had had his attention that night. "So where do you stay normally?"

"With my parents, but probably not after this summer if I can help it. I finished up high school this year."

"Oh?" Caden's mind filled with questions. First and foremost, was he going to college?

"Yeah, I might try to stay here. Well, not *here*, here. Somewhere else. Maybe I'll move in with someone, Face or Angelica or something."

A sting of jealously rippled through her chest and made her skin feel tight, but he didn't elaborate. "You're kidding?"

"So Face told you about her too?" he calmly added a few moments later.

Caden looked at him from over her shoulder. How could he act so casual? Was he teasing her or was he just that cocky? His menacing smile didn't change as he met her gaze, as though meeting a challenge. She turned back toward the sink. As Caden continued to do the dishes, tears built up in her eyes; she felt completely mortified. Of course she had expected him to have been in another relationship before theirs. Theirs? What was she thinking? She wasn't in a relationship with him, and if she didn't get her head together she'd be out of his condo. The scraping of his fork slowed, but continued until he finished. Over the clanging of pots she heard him get up.

She felt his body heat and the soft current of his breath across her neck, and then the soft press of his lips touched her cheek. Caden let her eyes close as the tingle filled her body with anticipation.

"I've got to go. I promised Face we would hang out, but I'll see you around six for dinner?" His voice sounded quieter than usual, gentler.

Mustering all the neutrality she could, she nodded. "Yep."

At 5:45 p.m. Gabriel got home. He didn't say a word, just went straight to his room and closed the door behind him. Caden placed his nonmatching plates and glasses next to one another while humming her favorite death-metal song. Next came the food; she spooned out the fresh mashed potatoes, pushing a wedge of butter in the middle. The corn on the cob was too hot to hold in her hands, so she used two spoons as a makeshift pair of tongs to save them from the boiling water that threatened to overcook them. After setting them on the plate, she rubbed the butter on and salted them all the way around. Then came the main dish: orange pork. It had sat cooking on low for over an hour, smothered in orange juice, orange peel, garlic, brown sugar, and salt. She brought the pan over, placed a morsel on each plate, and spooned the sauce on top, feeling satisfied to see her hard work pay off.

As the clock struck 6:00 p.m., Gabriel opened the door to his room. Caden raised her eyebrows upon seeing him. He had washed up and changed into a button-down dress shirt that he left unbuttoned at the top and a pair of dress pants that she hadn't seen before. She didn't look half bad either; everything he had bought her fit, aside from the drawstring blue pants that were too long. They were all much more flattering than her usual clothes. The dark blue blouse made her black hair shine, and though her feet were bare, the skirt hit just above her knees and made her legs look long and dainty.

She watched as his eyes traveled down her body, eyeing

the new outfit. "What do you think?" she asked, and she did a small turn, but Gabriel just grunted. He pulled the chair out with force and sat down without a word. Caden's smile disappeared. Had she not been so excited to see him, it wouldn't have been such a letdown. "How was your day?"

He grunted again. His fork hit the pork with enough force to kill, making the plate squeal. The beauty of her work began to fade, his mouthfuls bordering on barbaric. It was enough to make her heart clench painfully.

"Excuse me," she said, placing her napkin on her chair. Her feet carried her to the door before she could think of a plan. She was so embarrassed. It was just too difficult to slave away in a kitchen all day without any consideration for her work. She deserved better than that. Not only that, but she had actually been excited to see him. She tried to keep her paces even and collected; she didn't want him to know how much he'd affected her. Her butter-slicked fingers slipping on the doorknob before opening it, and she walked out.

Caden tried to be quiet as she closed the dark gray door behind her and followed the sidewalk that weaved between the buildings. She hadn't even walked around the first corner when she heard him call after her.

"I'm sorry!"

She didn't turn around. It wasn't worth it, he was nearly as bad as Sean: unappreciative, negative, and angry. Then he'd try to make it up to her, only to treat her like dirt again later. She wasn't a yo-yo; they couldn't just toss her aside only to reel her back in.

He caught up with her, slipped his hand into hers, gave it a quick squeeze and let it drop. In an instant she wanted more of his touch, she wanted him to hold her and never let go, but she pushed the feeling away.

"I really am sorry, Caden. Let's go back inside."

A stinging in her chest pulled at her heartstrings. She still refused to look at him. He wasn't going to change; this was who he was. Yet Tom was different, and they were the same person. If he could be more like Tom, sweet and caring, things could work. Maybe he could change.

Without a word, she turned and headed back toward his condo. She wasn't going to starve on his account, and he had said sorry. Sean never said sorry.

She didn't make eye contact, just walked past him and sat back down. The rest of dinner was silent, aside from a few more apologies drifting through the air from Gabriel. He insisted on cleaning up. She sat on the couch waiting for him to finish, examining her nails and holding back the tears. The sooner she could see Tom, the better.

When the dishes stopped clattering, she lay down on the couch, waiting for him to leave her alone.

"Goodnight, Gabriel."

"Not so fast." Gabriel hurriedly wiped his hands on a dish towel and came toward her. She sat up as he came closer, landing beside her. "I'm sorry about earlier."

Caden didn't want to look at him; she wanted Tom's face.

"Come on." He placed his hand on her chin and lifted it, just as she had done to Tom, sweet Tom who would be awake now if she hadn't kept Gabriel up. She cursed herself for the slight change in his sleep schedule. "Practice makes perfect."

"Perfect what?" she deadpanned, looking up at him with a raised eyebrow.

"Eh—" he shrugged and looked to the side, "—practice makes perfect people, perfect me... Maybe perfect kissing?"

"Kissing?" Caden lightly pulled back. "Mine aren't good enough?"

"I don't mean that. It's just different, you know, kissing a new person. Plus there's always room for improvement." He looked at her from under his eyebrows.

She had only kissed one other person before, and who knew if Sean was a good teacher or not? What did Gabriel want from her? A chill ran down her spine as outrage and embarrassment settled in. *I bet Tom would think I was perfect*, she thought, but the thought was gone as soon as it came, leaving with the touch of Gabriel's lips.

The heat between them was powerful. The warmth of his lips seared the anger she felt until she melted in his arms. He carefully nudged open her mouth with his and let his tongue enter, inviting hers to do the same. It felt natural and smooth. Nothing like kissing Sean. She pushed harder against him, her hands on his chest, at the buttons…

Skin to skin. She stopped suddenly. Caden looked down where his hand sat on her thigh. Sean flashed in her thoughts, and she pulled away, fast and harsh. She didn't even have the protection of pants. *Skirts*, she panicked, *I hate skirts*. The pressure of his body suddenly felt heavy. His hand was under her shirt, not on her breasts but hovering at the clasp of her bra. How had she gotten here? She couldn't control herself. "This is too fast, Gabriel, I'm not ready." *After what Sean did to me, I might never be ready*.

Gabriel let go.

His eyes raged with the rejection.

He pushed a hand through his hair. "What is this, Caden? I swear you're sending me mixed signals. What are we doing?" His voice rose to new proportions as he stood up from the couch and began to re-button up his shirt, which she had nearly taken off. "You're homeless and I take you in, and you've been begging to stay. I thought—goddamn it, Caden—I thought you wanted to stay because of me. What do you want me to do? Cade, *you* kissed *me*, not the other fucking way around. Do you want me to just sit here with you and pretend it didn't happen, that I don't want to take it further? If you're here just to use the goddamn roof, then get the hell out." His hand pushed the glass cups off the kitchen counter and they shattered against the floor. His feet hit each stair with enough force to break them as he stormed off to his bedroom and slammed the door behind him.

Caden realized that those horrible choking sobs were coming from her, and as her body quaked and tears streamed from her eyes, she thought she wanted nothing more than to be left alone; deep down she knew even that was a lie. She cried until she fell asleep.

—Night—

"Why are you crying?" Tom crawled to the couch and looked over the armrest.

"I'm not crying," Caden said defiantly, glancing up from her crossed arms and wiping her eyes. He was close enough to kiss, and the thought made her stomach turn. She couldn't look at Gabriel's face, not after what he had said to her.

Tom reached for her hand, but Caden flinched, sitting up and moving to the far side of the couch. "What happened? Did you lose an earring?"

"What?"

"I know girls get upset when they lose earrings."

"Why would you think that, Tom?" She became mildly annoyed with his behavior, suddenly tired of his ignorance.

"I just know."

"Tom—" Caden rubbed her face with her hands, "—

you don't hang out with anyone besides me and I don't wear earrings."

"I know."

Caden wanted to scream. All she could think about was the possibility, or impossibility, that they were the same person, that she'd wake up one day and Tom would be Gabriel. "We need to talk, Tom."

"About what?" Tom jumped up on the couch like a five-year-old, a look of anticipation spreading into his features.

"Not a game." She pointed as if she was reprimanding him. She was sick of games. She didn't want to act this way, but she wanted to be clear that this was serious. He shook his head and reached for her hand again. She pulled back and pointed at him, giving him the eye. "Are you listening?"

He nodded.

"We are leaving, tonight." Caden could feel chaos erupting inside of her. She needed to get out of the condo, to clear her head, to keep Tom separate in her mind from Gabriel. The un-solved mystery of Tom was about to be tested. She wasn't sure what the plan was, but she thought if she could keep him awake for long enough, something might change.

"Where are we going?

"I don't know yet, but we need to find the keys to your car first." She could tell by the light in his eyes that this was as good a game as any. They got up and Caden flicked on the lights.

"Off, off," Tom whined.

She swatted at his hand as he lunged for the light. "No, Tom, they are staying on. Now help me."

Tom's eyes narrowed into slits as he turned toward the couch and tossed off the first cushion. She looked behind pictures and in drawers, but no keys. Caden thought back. Gabriel could only hide them in his room, because she was out here whenever he got home. However, Tom knew the room well and knew the keys weren't in it.

"They're outside, they must be. Tom, grab a coat, lock up, and meet me in the parking lot." Caden pulled on the coat that Gabriel had let her borrow earlier and zipped it up to her neck. She opened the door, ready to find the car keys.

It took less than five minutes to find the key. Storage cabinets hugged the top back wall above the Saab, and a single key sat hidden under the lower ledge.

Caden had the car running by the time Tom opened the door.

"What, I can't drive?" Tom asked.

"Pretty sure you don't know how to drive." She was also sure she didn't trust him enough to let him try. She looked him up and down; he wasn't in his pajamas anymore. He was wearing what Gabriel had had on earlier in the day.

"Not true."

Caden's smile widened. "Not a chance. Get in."

Tom got in the passenger side, his pouting lip disappearing

when he saw the inside of the car. She knew he probably hadn't ever been in a car before, not as Tom. She pushed the stick into drive and hit the pedal.

Darkness concealed the road, but the headlights cut through like a knife. A hint of moonlight illuminated the branches above them. Even in the car, she could feel the silence of the forest, and she could hear their breathing. She looked over at Tom. He sat with his face an inch from the window, quietly watching the darkness pass. After a few minutes he turned toward the glowing buttons. His fingers reached out in fascination as he turned on the AC and radio.

"Stop that." Caden turned off the AC, frustrated with his button pushing.

"This is my car?" he said perplexed.

Caden thought for a moment, and then settled with, "You could say that."

She didn't take her eyes off the road. Gabriel flooded her thoughts. *Gabriel, Gabriel, Gabriel.* It was Gabriel's car, Gabriel's hands that had been on the steering wheel, Gabriel's hands that were on her. Her body tingled at the thought of him touching her again, holding her...kissing her. Tom was just some other part of him. Caden almost wanted to be Rebecca again; she wanted to pretend that everything would be all right. She wanted to ignore the nagging feeling that things weren't going to work out, regardless of how much she wanted them to.

After a few minutes of the radio static filling the air between them, Tom asked, "Why don't I remember having a car?"

"I don't know, Tom." The Rebecca within her begged her to stop there, but Caden wanted to push a little more. If she said enough, maybe he would remember something. If Tom could make the connection to Gabriel, could things work out? "You haven't told me enough for me to figure all of this out. I could probably help, if you'd just talk to me." Caden tapped the wheel with her fingers, pushing Rebecca back down inside of her, telling her to be quiet. She didn't have time for weakness; she couldn't afford it right now. She noticed the clear sky above the road ahead of her and the flickering stars; it was a nice night. She turned on the heat, and adjusted the radio. Punk music traveled through the air as she rolled down her window. She let her elbow and hand drift out and catch the wind. It was perfect, just enough bite in the air to keep her awake for the long drive ahead. "Go ahead, start talking." She looked Tom in the eyes for the first time since they got into the car. "Tell me everything."

"About what?"

"I don't know. Your life. Okay, how about your first memory?"

Tom fidgeted with something in his hands and stayed quiet for a long time. "I guess," he finally said, swallowing hard, "I remember a hospital room. I mean, I think it was a hospital."

Caden looked at him. Was he trying to say he remembered being born? That was weird, and impossible. Rebecca begged her to stay quiet and let him speak. Rebecca always wanted to stay quiet, to let the man in her life rule over the conversation. Caden didn't like that, but she wasn't in the mood to argue. "Go on."

"I had a thick bandage on my head, my hands were bandaged too, and I was attached to all of these machines. The next time I woke up I was in my room."

"You're telling me you just remember being in the hospital? Why were you there? What happened?" She watched as Tom shifted in his seat.

"I just remember it being dark and cold. I was alone."

Caden watched Tom gulp as if he could swallow the memory and move on. Dark, cold, and alone. Were those feelings what made him Tom? Caden thought back to her high-school psychology class. Mostly she just remembered Rebecca scribbling Sean's name in the desk with hearts floating in every direction. There was something though, something they had learned regarding multiple personality disorder. MPD didn't seem likely because Tom only came out at night; maybe all he had was a severe case of sleepwalking. If he really had a disorder, surely he would be taking some kind of medication. "What about your parents, Tom? Were they with you? You know, at the hospital?"

"My parents?" He shifted again, the leather squealing in protest. "I—I don't know. I mean, there was a lady. I called her Mom, I knew she was my mom but I never saw her."

"You haven't met your mother?" Caden asked. What did it

mean? Of course he had met his mother, so what was he hiding? Caden wished she had been paying attention in her psychology class. "How can you say you called her Mom, but yet you never saw her? Never met her? That doesn't work."

Tom shrugged, turning toward the window, gazing into darkness. His hands continued to fidget with an object he held between his fingers, but she couldn't see what it was while it sat engulfed in the shadow of his hand. "I don't know. I remember parts about her. I don't know how to explain it. I knew her, I just never saw her before."

Caden's fingers gripped the steering wheel tighter. Her heart thumped against her ribs. What had she gotten herself into? Tom was crazy; he had to be. That, or Gabriel could really play out a joke. Part of her desperately wanted to know more. In the distance she could see the orange-and-yellow morning light seeping into the sky.

Caden pushed the gas pedal down farther and more wind filled the car, robbing it of its heat as they accelerated. Whatever Tom was, whatever was going on, it would be over when the sun came up. She needed him to last a little longer.

—Day—

As rosy daylight began to creep into the sky, Caden's mind continued to turn with possibilities. The questions she longed to ask were confusing. The answers she'd been receiving didn't even begin to put the puzzle together. Why had Tom ended up in the hospital? Had he been attacked? Beaten?

Tom believed he hadn't gone to school, hadn't learned to speak, or read, or write, and he had never eaten a thing aside from the chocolate muffin the night before. He said he just *knew*. And if he just *knew*, did that mean that if Tom learned on his own, Gabriel would acquire the knowledge as well? It seemed to be true the other way around.

Caden looked over at Tom, his soft black hair pushed to one side from the open window, his eyes slowly closing. She accelerated, pushing sixty on the curving forest road, each bend more hidden than the last. The orange and pink had seeped farther into the sky. It was her first morning with him—the turning point, she hoped. *Please Tom, stay awake.*

She wasn't sure what it was about him. Gabriel made her breath shorten, made her hope for more, but he also kept her guessing. Her heartbeat quickened at the thought of Gabriel's lips on hers. Caden shook away the feelings and looked over at Tom again. His eyes were almost closed.

"Don't you dare fall asleep, Tom."

"But I'm tired."

"Doesn't matter." Caden couldn't have him fall asleep, not now. It always happened like this; right before the sun came up, he'd pass out. "It's a game, probably the best ever. Whoever can stay awake the longest wins." Caden tried to sound enthusiastic, but really it sounded like a stupid game. She was tired and wanted to sleep too, but they had already made it this far.

Tom's eyes snapped open a little wider. "Okay," he said, sitting up in his seat. "What do I get if I win?"

"You name it, we're almost there."

Tom reminded her of a five-year-old, but some of his actions seemed older. Or maybe his body just played tricks on her, making him seem like the man he wasn't. He'd never had the experiences a kid needed to grow up, all of the trials with other kids, the messed-up relationships, and the fights with parents. She had taken those experiences for granted, had even wanted them to go away. She hadn't realized they were a part of growing up. It would take time, but he'd grow up eventually. She would help him. If she had been willing to wait for Sean to be a better man, she could wait for Tom to grow up. She had more faith in Tom than she had in Sean.

They parked the car and got out to sit on the hood. The colors in the sky seeped out from behind the earth, spreading into ribbons of light as pink and blue intertwined. They sat back as the colors drifted through the sky in delicate, wavy patterns. Tom remained silent as she stole a few glances to make sure his eyes were open. She could tell his eyelids were getting heavy, but she hoped he'd last a little longer. The gold light on his face made him more beautiful than she could have imagined; though his eyes stayed dark, the set of his mouth was calm and kind. His eyebrows relaxed, and his body peacefully molded to fit the shape of the car. *He's a genuinely good person.* Caden knew this, saw it reflected in every interaction they had, and she slid her hand into his. Their fingers slowly linked together, intertwining into a knot that she felt couldn't come undone. She hoped keeping him awake would be enough to change something.

"Come on, let's go."

Tom looked at her expectantly. "Where are we going?"

"We're getting food. Get in the car." Caden looked at him. His masculine jaw, his broad shoulders, his face lean and adult. She shook her head. He was something different.

———————————

It didn't take long to get to the breakfast joint, Alan's Café, on the other side of the mountain. It was a favorite of hers and Sean's because it was far enough away that it wasn't horribly crowded, but the food was delicious. She always wanted to work there and make it her own: *Cade's Café*.

The waitress, Victoria, liked to be called Vicky. She was the one who normally seated Caden when she was with Sean. Vicky had a turned-up nose and eyes that constantly searched her surroundings. Her apron had thick creases, while the rest of her clothes looked smooth and clean. She was probably only a few years older than Caden, but it seemed like more because she always had a lingering scent of cigarettes and coffee. Vicky wasn't her normal chatty self; instead she led them to a table without even acknowledging Caden.

Caden shifted uncomfortably; did she look that different? Instinctively she looked down at her black clothes, but they weren't black anymore. Her drawstring pants were baby blue and hung low on her hips, while her white shirt revealed most of her shoulders. She looked back up, catching Vicky eyeing Tom like a dog getting a meat delivery. Caden couldn't decide if it was good or bad though; it was better than how she looked at Sean.

Tom looked around as if he had entered a castle. "This place is amazing." He kept turning as if it was changing into something new and different. Vicky sat them at the table with the best view, per Caden's request; it overlooked the little town of Cloverdale. Tom sat wearily at the other side of the table. He looked out the window at the world. "Everything is so bright. All the green…"

Caden handed him a menu. He brought it close to his face and grew silent.

"What are you going to get, Tom?" She could hardly see his face hidden behind the menu. Part of her worried he would nod off while reading it.

After Vicky returned with two waters, she took their order. Tom ordered a large list of food and Caden laughed nervously before she asked for an extra plate so they could share. She hoped Gabriel's wallet was in Tom's pants and that there'd be enough money to pay for everything Tom ordered.

When Vicky arrived with the food, Tom's eyes went wide. Swirls of steam lifted from a plate of scrambled eggs. Two huge burritos were filled with mushrooms, olives, ham, eggs, and the restaurant's signature sauce. There was also a side of sausages and a bowl of fruit. Caden pulled the fruit toward her and began picking out the melon and putting it off to the side. She grabbed one of the burritos and eagerly took a bite, the heat and flavor overwhelming her senses. If felt good to eat; she always loved every part of it. It was as if every flavor hit her tongue at a different time before coming together to create something new. She wondered if Tom felt the same way. She watched as his eyes got larger with each bite he took.

They ate until they couldn't move. Not a word spoken between them, just smiles exchanged between bites. Caden watched Tom as he grabbed a slice of melon off the napkin she had moved them to.

"Why did you put these over here?"

She scrunched up her nose. "I don't like melon."

Tom brought the fruit up to the light. "Why is it green?"

"Try it."

"Nah." He put it down on his plate and stretched, his shirt pulling tightly across him, exposing the muscles on his chest and the biceps on his arms.

"Not yet, Tom. You can't fall asleep just yet." She pointed a playful finger in his direction, and he closed his mouth to hide an oncoming yawn. "I'm going to run to the restroom. I'll be right back. Don't fall asleep."

Tom nodded.

Three minutes tops, and she could tell he was already asleep before she reached the table. She sat down across from him and nudged his arm. "Tom? Wake up."

"Well, well, well, if it isn't my lost girlfriend."

A jolt of panic surged through Caden as she looked over her shoulder to Sean. He slid into the seat beside her, the plastic cushion wrinkling from his weight as he pushed her up against the window. His blonde hair was cut shorter than normal and his gray eyes hung piercingly on her blue clothes, looking her over.

"Hey, Rebecca. Miss me?" Sean grabbed her face in his hand.

"Let go of me."

"What's wrong? Scared your new boyfriend won't wake up to save you?" His eyes glanced at Tom, asleep against the table. A few of Sean's friends stood behind him, their deep laughs echoing in the small restaurant. Sean's wicked smirk enveloped his face as he turned toward Caden, his tongue extending to lick her cheek. Caden could feel Rebecca shrinking away, falling back into the void of helplessness. His saliva drifted over her clean skin, and she cursed Rebecca for being weak. "Think he can protect you?" Sean pointed toward Tom.

"Get away," she said, pushing at his chest.

Sean looked her up and down. "Since when do you fight back, Muffin?" His hand gripped her chin, his fingers pushing deep into her skin.

She winced. It always started this way, but she wouldn't let him get away with it, not like this. She wasn't Rebecca. She was Caden; she needed to be Caden.

"Get off of me," she growled. Sean got closer, grabbing her wrist. A scream broke from her lips. "Waitress, waitress. Vicky!" Her eyes searched the café. No one rose to help. Caden looked back toward Tom. "Tom!" She turned her attention to Sean. "Get off me." She attempted to kick him. He deserved to be kicked after what he had done to her, after leaving her on the side of the road after she had given him everything. She couldn't get her leg out from under the table, and she couldn't get his hands off her.

"I looked for you down at the bridge a few days back." His breath smelled of liquor. She stifled a gag.

"Have you been drinking?" She was disgusted; it was barely morning.

Sean gave her a little shake. "I figured you jumped off when I didn't come get you. Kinda sad you didn't."

"I don't need you, Sean. I'm not your Rebecca anymore. I have someone else." Caden turned to Tom. "Tom, wake up." Her voice sounded like a growl.

"Yeah." Sean looked over at Tom, fast asleep. "A real prince." He nodded in Tom's direction and his friends stepped over to grab Tom. She recognized them well enough. John went to the right of Tom; he was a stick of a kid who towered a foot above everyone in the town. Cliff followed, taking hold of Tom's left arm. Cliff had a man's mustache; it covered his upper lip and made him look older, especially because he insisted on wearing aviator sunglasses even indoors. They weren't the strongest of Sean's friends, but she feared anyone could hold Tom down. Caden bucked against the seat. They were going to keep him from getting up, from saving her. She knew it didn't matter; he was asleep. She'd failed to keep him awake. She continued to struggle, wondering why no one had come to her aid. Sean had probably paid off the waitress, Vicky. Or flirted with her.

"Tom, Tom, please wake up!" She kicked out, wishing she had taken him somewhere else, somewhere with more people, but then his eyes started to open. The light falling through the window exposed his soft skin and strong features, but the line of his mouth was hard and his eyes shone copper. "Gabriel, help me!" she screamed.

Gabriel's eyes shot open and took in the surroundings, his eyes flaming, his muscles tightening. He jerked his arm and found it caught by one of the boys. He pulled again, their bodies jostling from his strength. She could tell it wasn't the first time he'd been in a fight; he could protect himself, he could save her. He twisted his wrist, breaking free of the hold to deliver a clean punch between John's eyes, knocking him flat on his back. Cliff held on and Gabriel turned toward him, his free hand moving upward into Cliff's nose. The crunching sound made Caden jump, and she watched Cliff double over, holding his face. John began to get up, but Gabriel was faster. He stood over the boy with his fist ready to strike again. Caden screamed as Cliff jumped back up, grabbing Gabriel from behind in a chokehold. Caden could feel Sean's grip loosening in the anticipation of losing a fight and needing to flee. Blood flowed from Cliff's nose, and his mustache was matted down with red; it looked like an organ had fallen out and was resting on his upper lip. She watched as Sean recoiled at the sight; he couldn't handle blood. Gabriel broke free of the hold and hit Cliff again. He fell back and his body disappeared from Caden's view. It was Sean's turn. Caden turned to him with a smirk.

"Leave me alone, Sean." Then she did the youngest, pettiest thing she could think of; she stuck out her tongue just as Gabriel punched out his lights.

"Run!" Gabriel yelled. He reached for her hand and they ran, over the bodies and through the café all the way to the car. "How the hell did I get here?"

That was a good question, and Caden hoped she was a good enough liar to answer it. "You don't remember?" Caden asked. Playing dumb was a good tactic, at least a good thing to start with.

He opened the passenger door for her and she jumped in while tossing him the key. "No," he answered between breaths. She could tell his adrenaline was still pumping. She waited for him to get in the car, and the wheels squealed against the road as he hit reverse, pushing the gas pedal to the floor and creating a backward burnout. The nervousness in his eyes was nothing to play with; he was scared.

"What's the last thing you remember?"

"You telling me I was moving too fast." He gave her an eye and she gulped.

"Oh, wow, back there. That's weird. Well, then I suppose you don't remember how I woke you up this morning?" She gave him a devious smile and watched as his expression twisted into confusion. "Or how I explained that I panicked?" Caden tried to look at him as if she knew he was teasing her. "I mean, you're joking, right?" Her fingers crossed behind her back.

Please work. The red that lined his knuckles distracted her, until she remembered the blood was someone else's.

How would she explain any of it to Tom? Would he be in pain later? She imagined Reese waking up with a bloody hand and suddenly felt sick. No, Tom wouldn't take it well at all. She pointed to his hand.

"Does it hurt?" she asked him softly, and a little guiltily.

He shook his head no.

Good. She tapped the side panel of the car, not meeting his eyes as they sped down the curvy road. "Did you like breakfast?"

"I don't like olives."

Caden glanced at him, a little shocked. "Don't look at me, you ordered them." The silence continued.

He was angry. Caden obviously wanted to avoid the subject. Who the hell talked about breakfast when they were running from a bunch of guys who were looking to fight?

Gabriel shook out his hand. He had lied to her; his fist hurt like a bitch and he would regret the punch for days. He didn't regret what he did to those assholes, though. Caden made him act crazy, which bothered him. It seemed like ever since she had come to the condo to stay with him, he was split; it was a feeling he hadn't felt in a long time. Not only that, but she was going somewhere at night. He'd found wet clothes in his laundry basket after the second night she was there. He shifted uncomfortably in his seat, glancing over at her.

He felt an undeniable pull toward her; he wanted her, and he wished he didn't. He never let a girl get this close; he'd never really let a girl be there for him more than just at face value. Yet somehow Caden was already inside of him, picking away at something he had buried deep. Part of him felt like the days he'd spent with her were more like weeks.

He shook his head, trying to free himself of his thoughts. "Where the heck are we, Caden?" He didn't expect her to answer; from the looks of it they were on Crest Mountain, about an hour's drive through winding roads. Somehow she had gotten him inside a café, and they'd had breakfast without him remembering. Part of him did remember the flavors, the heat of each bite as he swallowed.

He gulped.

What was happening? He rubbed his tongue over his lips and gums, testing the flavor. He could definitely taste the olives.

He looked back and forth from her to the road and back again. The way her black hair traveled down the side of her body distracted him, and he wished he could lean over and tuck a few strands behind her ear so he could see her eyes.

"Who were those guys?" he finally asked.

She sat back into her seat and crossed her arms. The defensive, strong part of her was getting smaller, as if she continued to sink farther inside of herself.

"You going to answer me? Who were they? Who did I just punch?"

"Gosh, alright already." Caden uncrossed her arms but refused to look at him. She seemed different. "You know how I told you about my ex?"

"That was him?" He pointed over his shoulder. *What a jerk.* He wished he had punched him harder, broken the guy's puny neck. "Which one was he?"

"The one holding me down. The one you knocked out." A contagious grin spread across her face.

He looked back and forth again; she was laughing. That was the Caden he knew. He could feel the weight lifting off his shoulders and being replaced with pride. He would do anything to see that smile.

"Did you see his face?" She laughed harder.

"Yeah, you mean when you stuck out your tongue?" Gabriel stuck his tongue out toward her playfully and she mimicked it. It made him want to kiss her. He listened to her laughter die down as she took in deep breaths. "We can go back and I'll do it again," Gabriel boasted. He could feel the smile on his lips.

She looked over her shoulder, smiling too. He didn't remember the morning, but he did remember last night. His gut twisted in embarrassment. She didn't want him. If she did, she wouldn't have pushed him away. If she thought he was worth anything, she would have forgiven him for his behavior. Gabriel's smile contorted into a deep frown that he could feel take him over. Caden was just like all the other girls.

"What's wrong?" Her arms wrapped over her chest again.

"Why do you want to be anywhere near me, Caden? Sometimes, I don't know, I want to upset you." He ran a hand through his hair, feeling frustrated. *God, I sound like a complete idiot.* "I want to make you angry, make you hate me. I can't help it."

"Why would you say that?" She looked completely confused, and adorable. He wanted to feel her lips against his mouth and run his hands around her waist. Her sad, dark eyes were like some kind of drug he couldn't get enough of.

Why would he say he wanted to make her angry? He guessed because it was the truth, but he didn't understand why. Part of him wanted to push her away, while the other part wanted to hold her close. Sometimes the pull felt heavier toward one side. Which side, he never knew until it forced him to act. He wanted to give her everything while another part wanted to kick her out on the street, to get her as far away from him as possible. He went quiet. "Just forget it."

"What? No. I'm not going to forget that."

He looked over at her, her lips stuck in that stubborn way he'd seen the first day he met her. He took her in, the white tank top revealing her delicate shoulders and long neck. The serenity of being with her, the peace he felt, was dissipating; his anger crept back up inside of him. "I said forget it."

Her body jumped back a little at the sheer volume of his voice.

Gabriel tried to ignore it. He didn't want her to be afraid of him.

A flicker of movement caught his attention, and his eyes found the rearview mirror.

A black truck barreled over the dirt road, gaining on them quickly.

"Shit," Gabriel hissed. They were being followed. Two-lane roads didn't afford much movement and all the switchbacks were blind. Gabriel took the first corner fast. He pulled on the wheel, letting the car slide sideways on the dirt, his hands scrambling hastily to right the car.

The Saab whipped around, nearly completing a circle, and instead of letting it sit he hit the gas again, driving the car as fast as he could. Gabriel watched in his rearview mirror as the dust from his drift engulfed the truck.

The next corner was extra tricky. Trees lined the side. Gabriel took the turn wide, and Caden screeched when the branches hit her side of the car. Gabriel yanked the wheel hard, and the passenger-side mirror cracked against the edge of a tree trunk. The Saab corrected, their bodies tossing side to side as he accelerated again.

Caden held tight to the handle on her door.

"What are you doing? You're going to get us killed!" she yelled.

He wanted to shake her. This was her fault. He whipped his head back over his shoulder for a second. Caden looked back too.

"Oh, no," she breathed, the color and expression draining from her face.

"Yeah, your boyfriend."

"He isn't my boyfriend."

"Whatever, ex-boyfriend, same thing."

"It isn't the same thing, not even a little. We need to go to the police."

Gabriel took another corner, hard, the tree branches lining the road slashing his side of the car.

He went faster, glancing back. "That is a huge black truck."

"It isn't black, it's green."

Gabriel shot her a look. "You're kidding me. That is black."

"*Green could never be black*," she hissed; the same stubborn look lined her expression. She screamed as he took another corner and a tree branch hit the windshield. If he remembered correctly, there was still a good number of switchbacks up ahead.

The hum of the engine sounded sweet, a thick purr amidst the chaos, but it was interrupted by a sharp blow that sent them both forward. Behind them Caden's ex-boyfriend smirked, having just smashed his huge bumper into the trunk of the Saab. Gabriel watched in horror as Caden's head hit the dash. She pulled back in a daze, touching her forehead. Gabriel looked back at Caden's ex; the jerk let go of the wheel and lifted his arms, palms up with a shrug.

A deafening scream snapped Gabriel's head back. A car was coming toward them. His muscles tensed. He could miss it if he took the corner hard enough. Caden shut her eyes, waiting for impact. His heartbeat thumped against his chest, each beat ringing through his ears. He could handle anything thrown his way, he told himself. He swerved, a loud crash erupting a second later. He looked over at Caden, her hands covering her face like a young girl at a horror movie. The passenger mirror swayed back and forth, attached by only a few wires. They were okay.

"Hey, it's over." Gabriel shook her shoulder lightly. "You can look now."

Caden removed her hands from her face; she seemed shocked they had survived. Gabriel adjusted the rearview mirror to see the black truck crushed into a tree.

Caden whipped around in her seat to look behind them. "Oh my gosh. Sean hit the tree. It looks like the other car is okay though, they're getting out. We should go back and help."

Gabriel watched from his rearview mirror as they continued to drive. Caden's ex would have hit the car if he hadn't swerved toward the trees. His truck was headed for the junkyard. Gabriel wouldn't be able to pay for the damage to his car either, not without attracting his parents' attention, and it made him wonder if his car would be next in line for the dump.

"We aren't going back, he asked for it. Fucking dumbass if you ask me. And put your damn seat belt on."

She clicked the seat belt into place. "But he might be hurt."

He could see the glint in her eye, the longing for the asshole who had nearly gotten them killed. "Good riddance. Let the sucker he almost killed deal with that. I don't know how you stayed around that guy for as long as you did. And you know what?" He pointed ferociously at her face, not even an inch away. "He'd leave us for dead if he had the chance. I've known guys like him."

Caden's body shook from the shock of being in a car chase. She looked back once more at Sean in the distance. Gabriel was right; Sean would have killed them.

"I don't believe that I would come up here with you," Gabriel said as he shook his head and cupped his hand over his mouth.

"You wouldn't come to breakfast with me?"

"I wouldn't let you drive."

He seemed calm on the outside, but Caden knew it was all show; he'd blow up if she said the wrong thing. He moved his hand away, blood from the fight at the restaurant smearing around his mouth.

"There's something you aren't telling me. I can feel it." His voice was louder, higher. The car continued to snake back and forth with the bends of the road but with a new squeaking noise from whatever the car chase had jostled loose. His lips were hard as stone, a line that seemed unbreakable and straight, stained with a scarlet smear. "Tell me!" he screamed. *"Tell me something, anything!"*

Caden blinked, suddenly very aware of the earlier events. He had punched the boys at Alan's Café, effortlessly, looking like an animal with thick, strong muscles. But could he hurt her?

He yelled again, "Tell me, Caden!"

"Tom, stop," she cried. Her mouth quivered as she placed her hand on top of it, wishing she had thought first. Wishing she wasn't trapped in the car with him. She was so afraid, and just as she couldn't close out the world around her, she couldn't hold back the onslaught of tears that pressed through her closed eyes.

He didn't respond, or if he did she couldn't hear it through her own tears and broken hiccups, the same horrible wailing that only Rebecca permitted. What was happening to her?

Tom. She'd thought if she could keep him awake, she could have him for longer. She felt tired, but she knew she would never sleep again if it meant rescuing Tom. Tom would never hurt her; she could take care of him and be his family.

She hadn't meant to call out to him; it had been more of

a plea, but the wrong name for the right face. She had nearly done it before, a few times. How could she not? She was looking at Tom, his sweet face, hardened and smeared with blood.

Her body sat frozen, only allowing her lips to move. "I'm so sorry, Gabriel."

Silence.

He turned to look at her. "Where did you hear that name?"

Where did I hear that name? An answer could have been simple. "You have another half," or, "At night your name is Tom and he's your exact opposite." However, both played out in Caden's mind with the outcome of him being less than pleased.

"Gabriel—" She rested her hand on his thigh, only because she was afraid to touch his arm. "Have you ever been to a doctor?"

"Hasn't everyone?"

"No, not that kind, I mean a therapist?" He eyed her, and she continued. "Have you ever felt alone? Lost in the dark, it's cold and..."

"What are you talking about?" Gabriel asked.

"Well, sometimes, I guess people can, I don't know, behave differently as an adult because of childhood experiences."

"I had a great childhood."

"You did?" Caden watched the way Gabriel's face changed when he said the words. He looked as though he was pushing back a memory and locking it deep inside of himself, and she assumed it was because he was lying to her. "Maybe you don't remember it?"

"No, I do."

"Can you tell me about it then? You know, your child-hood?"

Gabriel looked down at her hand on his leg and tossed it off. "No. I don't have to tell you anything." He looked back at the road.

Caden sighed heavily, as if she carried the weight of the world; indeed she felt like she did, Gabriel's world at least.

"What is wrong with you?" Gabriel asked, and Caden laughed out loud at the question because something *was* wrong with her; she was trying to fix the unfixable.

She looked out the window, away from him—it was easier to lie that way—and said, "My crazy ex nearly got us killed. I'm just lucky he didn't know you're such a good driver, or fighter for that matter." Deflection didn't really count as lying, anyway. She looked back to him with a grin and bit her lip. She felt a pang in her chest when his eyes lit up at the sight of it, but he quickly tried to hide the excitement in his face. It vanished relatively quickly, but that strange feeling lingered for a bit longer.

"Look, Caden." He paused and Caden could tell he was searching for the right words, probably to toss her out. He took a deep breath and started again. "Look, I didn't bring a ton of money with me, enough for a bachelor lifestyle, not a lush life for two." He began to shake his head almost apologetically.

"Don't get me wrong. I like having you around but my money is disappearing faster than I thought. I could go home for a while, get some more cash. Credit cards might make my parents suspicious, so that's out the question. If I go, I want you to stay with someone. I can't stand the thought of you cold, hungry, and alone in that condo."

"Better than cold, hungry, and homeless."

"You seriously can't find a place for a week? Just while I'm gone?"

Caden's mind trailed off. He wanted her to stay. Her breath came up short and her chest felt tight. His behavior and moods changed quickly and without warning; could she trust him in a more permanent living situation? Could she live with a boy with two different personalities?

"Are you listening?"

"What? Oh yeah, sorry. I got distracted." Caden brushed the tendrils of her hair from her face and looked at him. *Gabriel*. Her eyes traced his jaw, his mouth, his nose, and then finally his eyes. *Her* Gabriel? Or was she simply getting attached to Tom, the equivalent of a puppy who needed her protection?

"Anyway, I was saying that maybe you could stay with one of my friends."

"Can I just stay at the condo when you're gone?"

Gabriel grimaced and ran a hand through his hair, his biceps flexing. "And eat what? I don't think it's such a good idea."

"Oh." Caden looked back out the window.

"We can hold off for as long as possible. Okay?"

Maybe this was how he was getting rid of her, like how Sean had told her he would pick her up at the bridge and never showed. If only she had realized Sean didn't want her for the right reasons, she would have never gotten into this mess in the first place. She would still be in her own bed at her mother's, listening to her mom complain about her dad, cursing marriage and love. Caden's stomach flipped at the thought. It was her mother's fault as much as her own; she'd told Caden that what she had with Sean wasn't real. Caden had just wanted to prove her wrong.

"You could always stay with Face. I'm sure he'd spoil you. He never left your side at the party."

"What? No way. And get called Lucky Charms until my ears bleed? I'll pass."

He laughed. "Alright, maybe Angelica?"

Caden pretended to gag. It wasn't that difficult. "The girl you dated? That would be really weird."

"Yeah, I didn't think that one through…"

Gabriel took a tight corner, making Caden grab the side handle as the force pulled her body in his direction. Whether she was meant to be with Gabriel or the Tom inside of him, she wished she knew. She gagged a little at the thought; it wasn't Tom she really wanted, the boy who had become like an annoying brother, but rather his sweetness. Gabriel needed the kind heart of his other half.

Maybe her mother was right. *Love is a deathtrap,* she would say, *it isn't meant to last. Some handsome man is going to pretend to be perfect, and then drop you eighteen years later for his pretty, young receptionist, leaving you with nothing but some stretch marks and the taste of regret.* That, of course, was what had happened to Laura, her mother, and was why she hated men. Her dad, to be exact. Caden hated her dad, too; he'd left them to start another family. He'd made her mom the *anti-love advocate* who'd driven Caden to try and prove her wrong. Gabriel's car rattled as it took another corner. She could see his face contort in frustration.

"So, Angelica. What was that all about? Doesn't really seem like your type." Caden looked down to pick at the corner of her fingernail in an attempt to look casual. It wasn't true—Angelica was definitely Gabriel's type, probably perfect for him. Just not for Tom.

"That bitch? Worst one yet." Caden watched as Gabriel's lips formed a hard line. She could feel the anger that lived deep inside him beginning to surface.

Caden crossed her arms and looked back out the window, dropping the topic as quickly as she had picked it up. She needed to keep him calm. What did throwing a coffee mug become when instead of a mug to throw, there was a gas pedal and a wheel? She feared what he was capable of and the potential accident that could follow from his rage.

"What?" Gabriel asked; the edge was clear in his voice.

"It's nothing."

"No, it isn't 'nothing.' I know when a girl says, 'It's nothing' it's always something. So what is it?" Gabriel took another sharp turn, and Caden's body leaned toward him again, their shoulders brushing. "Better uncross those arms and hold on or you're gonna get carsick."

She already was; her stomach twisted from the back-and-forth movement of the car. If only she had taken him to another café, maybe even the Wild Flower Diner down the hill. Caden grabbed the door handle once more.

"How many girlfriends have you had, exactly?" she asked, not looking at him.

Out of the corner of her eye she could see him glance at her before releasing a laugh. Her shoulders relaxed at his response.

"A lot." He laughed again. "Hey, don't look at me like that, I'm a respectable guy."

"Yeah? Well why did all nine end?" She said "nine" like a stage actor performing for the cheap seats, hand movements and all.

"Nine. You sure did pull that one out of your ass." He shook his head. "Nine," he repeated. "Try five, six if you want to count us but—" he looked her up and down, "—for me, I have special criteria for counting a girl as a girlfriend."

Caden winced; she hoped he wasn't implying what she thought he was, because if he was, then he was no better than

Sean. Sean, the brute; he'd told her everything she had wanted to hear and then transformed into a monster after he got what he wanted. She had been stupid, and she wasn't going to fall for that twice.

"Do you want to know what my criteria is for a boyfriend?"

Gabriel nodded as a long, sly smile carved into his features, features that were a mix of adolescent boy and man, like some mixed species.

Caden cleared her throat so he wouldn't mishear what she had to say. "Love."

Gabriel nearly swerved off the road. *Love.* He couldn't fathom what was so wrong with such a small word. Caden looked deeply satisfied with his reaction.

It was silent in the car for a few minutes. He took a left at the light. They were on the main road and only a few miles from home. Gabriel looked at her, his brain still blank and full of noise, like a dead channel on TV.

"Love, huh," he muttered quietly as he shook his head. He had never been in love before, and though he felt a deep connection with Caden, he doubted it was love; it reminded him more of safety.

He took the turn down Witter Gulch Road, and he could see the top of the condominium not far in the distance. It took a second for him to roll his weight to the left to fish the house key out of his pocket. His hand awkwardly searched the small jean lining to find only one thing, and it wasn't a key. Gabriel pulled it out, a thick crease forming in his brow. He turned it over to see the other side; a purple, blue, and green iridescence shone through the clear resin-coated Lepidoptera wing. How had it gotten there, and where was the house key? He rotated it through his fingers. Not only that, but why was it broken? When did it leave his nightstand? How could he not have noticed it was missing?

A heat was rising in Gabriel, a pulsing anger that sometimes took him by surprise. He would build it up around him like a wall that he tossed grenades over; it kept him safe and nearly always obliterated the enemy. Well, almost every enemy; all of them except for Caden. She hadn't run away, even though she had experienced his explosive tantrums firsthand. Anyone else would have called him out on his verbal abuse, and though he couldn't understand what made her stay, he hoped it had more to do with him than it had to do with her own problems.

"Where did you get that?" Caden asked. The way she said it made it clear she recognized the piece, not just as a butterfly wing but as something she had seen before, and that made him angrier. Had she gone into his room when he wasn't there?

"You tell me." The world around him went deathly silent as his mind shut down from fury, but she didn't seem to notice his current state of mind.

She shrugged. "I thought I threw it all away." She said it carefree—like it was dirt being swept under a rug. It meant nothing to her, and why should it?

"You threw this away?" Gabriel's voice rose in volume as he shook the iridescent, irregularly shaped object at her face. She flinched, as if she was afraid he would hit her.

Her hands shot up, palms open. "It was broken," she said quickly. "I was just cleaning it up." Her eyes frantically searched the ground to avoid his gaze. "Kind of like the coffee mug." She mumbled.

"You broke this?" He shook it again. Caden didn't know what it meant to him, and he didn't want to tell her. It was something he didn't want her to know, something he didn't want to share. He let his fist close around it, his hand now shaking from the outrage of what he had lost.

"I didn't break that coffee mug, did I? You know, you could take some blame once in a while because—" Caden cut herself off.

Gabriel could see the wheels turning in her mind and the chance she wanted to take. He felt guilty about the mug and the glasses he'd broken, but he hadn't touched the butterfly display.

Caden sat in the car beside Gabriel, perplexed. The way Gabriel drove, gripping hard on the wheel, pushing the speed limit, conveyed his anger. She was glad that for once she had kept herself quiet, like Rebecca, and it had saved her neck; she had almost told Gabriel that it was Tom who had broken the iridescent object in the glass case during the first night she stayed at the condo. Caden chewed at the inside of her mouth as she watched what looked like a broken, leaf-shaped piece of colored plastic slide between Gabriel's fingers. She still hadn't gotten a good look at what it was, but she remembered seeing Tom holding something as they drove. She just hadn't given it much thought. Why was it so important to both Gabriel and Tom?

The cowardly, meek Rebecca who still hid inside of Caden once again interrupted her train of thought, nagging at the frayed edges of her mind, begging her to sink down into its depths and apologize. Caden couldn't help but fight Rebecca's plea to say sorry; she hadn't done anything wrong.

She realized that if she didn't take the blame for breaking it, she would reveal Tom's existence. To sacrifice Tom just to win a fight would be to stoop to a whole new level. She looked back out the window, squeezing her eyes shut as she counted to three. "I'm sorry, I broke it."

Once the words were out of her mouth, she regretted them, because Rebecca was wrong. It wasn't fair; he had technically broken it and now she was lying to protect him from himself, at her own expense. She wiggled in her seat, wishing they were back to the condo. Her skin itched for a shower, or anything to get Sean's lingering touch off her body.

Gabriel's body looked hard and rigid. She wished Tom were beside her instead of Gabriel, or maybe Gabriel with a little bit of Tom's sweet side.

Caden looked back out the window, watching the trees pass. Little wires from the side mirror wiggled in the wind as dirt drifted up from the road. The best thing for her to do was to forget Tom. Obviously she had been wrong to think that if Tom stayed awake long enough, Gabriel wouldn't come back, or that they would switch places. If only she had been so lucky, she wouldn't have to try so hard to please Gabriel. It had been worth a try, but now she was out of ideas.

After a short silence, Gabriel spoke first. "So, what about the key?"

"The house key? You don't have it?" Caden asked, thinking about how she had told Tom to lock up; he'd been the last one out of the house. It had been stupid of her to expect something as small as locking the door and taking the key to be a task suited for Tom; Tom had only been out once before, and it had been with her. She rubbed her eyes, pressing her fingertips into their sockets. "We'll get a locksmith."

"What do you think I am, made of money?" His tone was uneven and harsh as his voice pushed through clenched teeth. "I'm out, Caden. Get it through your head. A few weeks at best, and we aren't going to have anything left. Hell, I won't have the money to even fix my car from today, and *that*—" he pointed at her, fear and pain lacing his eyes, "—is *your* fault."

Caden pushed herself farther into the seat and looked out the window again. They were almost at the condo. Once they got there, she knew Gabriel would flee to his room.

Gabriel floored the gas pedal to close the last twenty feet before his parking spot. In seconds he was in his marked carport and out of the car.

She ignored her shaking hand as she opened the passenger door. The car creaked with her movement, as if it might break beneath her. With her head down, Caden followed the sidewalk through the buildings to door twenty-five.

Smoke drifted through the room. She coughed as the fumes entered her lungs. A small fire licked the stovetop. Red and orange enveloped the hand towel she had overused since her arrival. Beside her Gabriel lifted a fire extinguisher and pulled a small pin.

"Don't freak. I got this." Gabriel shook the hose but nothing came out. "Come on. Come on, you stupid piece of crap. Work!"

Caden's eyes darted around the kitchen. She had dealt with small kitchen fires before; as long as it wasn't an oil fire, she'd be safe putting water on it. Noticing the faucet in the kitchen sink could be pulled out like a hose, Caden ran to it.

"Caden, get away from there."

The faucet turned on, releasing a stream of cool water. With one swift motion, she moved the hose out from its stationary position and directed it toward the fire. The orange light hissed and crackled as it began to shrink, quickly disappearing.

Black markings ran up the kitchen wall. The charred towel now looked more like a pile of ash that sat about an inch away from the stovetop. The burner closest to the towel was turned to low; it might have just taken a while for the flame to jump. Caden thought about her earlier episode with Tom and their hunt for the keys. Tom had looked in the kitchen—

Caden glanced up in time to see Gabriel disappearing up the stairs.

"Where are you going?" Caden ran after him. "Gabriel? What's wrong now?"

He slammed the door behind him.

"Gabriel, let me in. We should get out of here, let the smoke clear." It hadn't been a big fire, but the amount of smoke in the condo was suffocating. She pounded her fist against the door, worried for Tom. "Let me in, Gabriel." She kicked at the door. "Gabriel!"

"Go away."

"No." Caden crossed her arms over her chest defiantly, even though he couldn't see her through the closed door. "Gabriel, it's not safe in there with all the smoke, come on."

"Go, or I'll kick you out for good. I'll come get you at the coffee shop in an hour." It sounded like a nonnegotiable request.

"Fine." She coughed again, the smoke still hanging in the stairway. If he wanted to suffocate to death, fine. Like hell would she be dragged down with him. "I'll just let myself out," she said through gritted teeth; her daily threshold for being nice was running out. Her hand covered her mouth as more coughing wracked her body. Where were the smoke detectors?

Caden looked around and found one on the kitchen ceiling, entirely engulfed by smoke. She wondered if Gabriel had taken out the batteries or was too lazy to change them.

An hour at the café had quickly turned into several, and she couldn't help but feel uncomfortable as she waited. Without any money she was just some girl in a coffee shop, wasting the café's time and space. Joe's Coffee Shop had been made out of an old, gutted cabin and had a wooden deck in the front. She sat on the lumpy black sofa in the back of the little shop. She was glad it was only about a mile from Gabriel's condo.

It had started to rain again, but what else was new. This had been the rainiest summer she had ever witnessed. It was the topic of conversation in the little café. Business was booming, everyone wanting something warm to counter the chill in the air. It seemed impossible to believe she had watched the sunrise with Tom only that morning.

She continued to stare out the window, watching the rain as it fell from the roof in splashes which formed puddles. The raindrops rippled the water like pebbles tossed into a lake. Her mind drifted to thoughts of Tom. What had happened at the condo? Had Tom knocked the dial for the burner while he searched for the keys? They were lucky it hadn't burned the whole place down.

Where was Gabriel? Waiting for him reminded her of the bridge where she had waited for Sean. What if Gabriel never came to pick her up? She wished she had a car—at least then she would have a backup plan. Living out of a car seemed better than trying to survive the mess she was in.

Feet splashed in the puddle she'd been staring at, the puddle that had sucked away all concepts of time and space. Caden looked up to see an overzealous person waving through the window. *Darn it.* She had been worried someone would recognize her. Yet after the waitress at the diner hadn't noticed her, she had her hopes up that being Caden had changed things.

Caden returned her gaze to the puddle, which still rippled from the girl's splashing feet. She wasn't the least bit curious as to who it was. Only one person waved obnoxiously like that: Keira. The girl stood covered from head to toe in thick, pink, water-repelling plastic. Turquoise hearts sporadically covered the raincoat. The water poured off the sides of her hat and distorted the girl's smile. Caden waved back lazily through the glass. Hopefully she would take a hint and notice her complete lack of amusement. She knew it wasn't likely though; Keira wasn't just the obnoxious type, she was also blissfully unaware. *God forbid, if you sit with me... Ugh, just don't sit with me, please.* The back door rang with a soft jingle as Keira came in, shaking side to side as if she were a dog trying to dry its coat. She began to unbutton the long, bright pink plastic trench coat, which was still dripping on the rug below her feet.

133

"Rebecca." Keira turned, taking her hat off in a flourish to let her hair swoop out in lush long curls and drape over her dry body. The girl was probably a year or two younger than Caden but had skipped a grade and ended up in a few of Caden's classes the previous year. Luckily, Keira had also been in a couple honors classes, which spared Caden of her annoyance for at least part of the semester. "It has been too long."

"Has it?" Caden deadpanned.

"Oh yes, Ms. Rebecca Worden."

She watched as Keira sat down beside her and folded her hands in her lap. She looked like a plastic Barbie doll, and her lips were stretched tightly against her teeth, appearing as stiff and repelling as her raincoat. Her glasses were all foggy from the hot air in the café, and Keira quickly removed them and cleaned them before pushing them back onto the bridge of her tiny nose.

"Oh, will your mother be pleased with me today."

"My mother?" Caden sat up from her slouched position. *How the hell do you know Laura?*

Keira nodded happily and obliviously. She looked like a cat that was planning to eat the canary. Keira loved few things more than getting the scoop on someone and then telling the whole town about it. The second Keira left, Caden knew it would only be a matter of time before she heard from her mother. Caden reminded herself that she was safe as long as Keira didn't know where she was staying.

134

"She has been worried, sweet girl."

Caden hated the way Keira spoke, like she was some older sister or motherly figure that was too over the top, not to mention she wasn't a mother at all but someone her own age. It wouldn't surprise her if Keira leaned in to pinch her cheeks. Though if she did, she'd have another thing coming. Caden wasn't Rebecca any longer. She wouldn't sit back idly. She would return the favor and then some.

Keira continued to smile wide enough that her cheeks must have hurt at least as much as the headache Caden was developing. "You know, Rebecca, your poor mother hasn't slept in days, and now since Sean—"

"What about him?"

"Well, dear, he came to her around noon today all bloody from some car accident. He kept saying your name, pointing at your pictures."

Why were you in my house? "Is he alright?"

Keira didn't answer. "Do you want some tea? On me, of course."

"What about Sean?"

"Still or chamomile? Still is the chamomile with lavender, slightly different you know, but I think you'd like it."

"What are you even talking about?" Caden asked, her head up, her back straight, her eyes open and alert with her body now seated at the edge of the suede couch. *Sean.* He had gone to see her mother. That was bad.

"Tea, darling."

Caden swallowed a few choice words and relented. "Chamomile, I guess."

"Delightful," Keira chirped as she went to stand in line. She looked like a ten-year-old in her floral-pattern clothes, her toothpick legs in leggings and her skinny wrists decorated with dangling bracelets. Caden felt like Keira tried so hard to be an adult that she overshot it and landed in granny territory.

When the barista called for Rebecca, Caden didn't respond. Keira pushed at her shoulder and pointed to the man behind the counter.

"What?" Caden breathed, irritated by the motherly nudge.

"He is calling your name, silly."

Caden got up, mumbling under her breath, angry with Gabriel for taking so long.

Her palms burned as she gripped the cup, but she welcomed the slight pain and focused on it. She blankly stared into amber liquid. It beckoned her to drink it and burn her tongue. She watched as an assortment of dried-up fragments of flowers expanded in the water, floating delicately, clustered together in the bag that entrapped them.

Keira hadn't told her much—just that Sean had shown up at the house. She quoted Sean in a deep voice that shook Caden from her daydreaming: "Rebecca is wild and savage and is dating some abusive guy." She giggled when she finished.

Caden watched as Keira took a sip of her drink and let her

eyes drift around the coffee shop before she continued. According to Keira, Sean had led her mom to believe that the blood came from a fight; it was only after Mrs. Worden called the police that he mentioned how he ran his car into a tree. Caden wondered how much of his story her mom believed.

"Rebecca, Rebecca Worden. Are you listening to me?"

She hated that Keira used her full name. She didn't even know Keira's last name, or why she was so involved in a life that was none of her business.

"Why were you even at my mom's house?" she asked, refusing to look Keira in the eyes. Instead Caden poked at the bag of flowers in the tea, burning her finger as she pushed it under the hot water.

"Book club, every Thursday for like the last two years." She looked a little suspicious, as if her being forgotten was impossible.

The smell of drowning flowers filled Caden's nose. She took a swig and let the burn distract her from the twisting in her stomach. What had she been doing to not notice Keira coming over that often? Keira, whom she didn't even talk with at school, but shared homeroom and sixth-period math with.

"Oh yeah," Caden said, looking into the cup and contemplating another sip. "Book club, how could I forget?" Her tone felt like ice; it sounded like the tone Gabriel had used on her earlier. *Gabriel, where the hell are you?*

She looked back out the window, blindly watching the

rain. *I should go and find Gabriel. No, that would probably make him mad.* After waiting almost five hours for him to show up… *The hell with it.* Caden stood abruptly, ready to leave and resolute with her new decision. She looked out the window at the rain pounding the ground rhythmically.

Reluctantly she changed her mind, her feet frozen in place as her eyes traveled to Keira, who continued to blow on her tea and take tiny slurping sips.

Keira had a car. Caden could already feel the regret settling in. She wondered what this favor would cost her in the future, and if it was worth it.

"Keira?"

"Uh-huh?"

"Do you think you could drop me off at the library?"

Keira perked up. "An interest in the book club?"

"Absolutely." Caden smiled bitterly. "Ab-so-lutely."

—Night—

By the time Keira dropped Caden back off at the coffee shop, a few more hours had passed. Caden hadn't left with any books. She had read her fill, even ripped out a few pages to keep and read over later. At first she had been worried that Keira would never leave her side and would realize that she was only interested in the nonfiction section. Thankfully though, Keira had gone on a book hunt of her own the second they got there.

Caden turned back around and waved once more at Keira as she drove away in a purple Beetle; the blotchy paint job looked like it had come from a can. As much as Keira annoyed her, Caden was thankful for the company, the tea, and the free trip to the library.

At some point it had stopped raining. Caden darted around the labyrinth of rainwater pools as she walked through the dirt—now mud—parking lot toward the door of Joe's Coffee Shop.

When she looked up, her chest felt tight. Gabriel sat beneath the warm lights. He was turned away from the window, so she was unable to see his expression through the glass. His shoulders were hunched, and his head was turned downward. His fingers drummed anxiously on a maple table while his other hand loosely cupped a red mug of something hot. The coffee shop only let customers drink out of mugs if they weren't going anywhere for a while, and Caden wondered how long he had waited.

It wasn't horribly late. The library closed at nine, and when they left she had heard over the loudspeaker a closing-in-thirty-minutes warning. She guessed it was about 8:40 p.m., still pretty early. Seeing Gabriel sitting there waiting for her gave her some satisfaction. She considered it payback for the hours she'd wasted waiting for him.

As she opened the door to Joe's Coffee Shop, the thick

smell of oily coffee beans filled her nose and the warmth from inside surrounded her. Caden slid through the opening quietly, rubbing her hands over her arms to settle the goose bumps that appeared. Part of her wanted to rush up behind Gabriel and hug him, but a bigger part of her wanted to stay alive. She couldn't deny the feeling of desire; it grew whenever she was near him and lingered whenever she wasn't. With his deadly temper though, she'd never try to hug him. She would never get close without his okay.

"Hey," she said, walking up to the table, his back to her.

"Caden." The second he turned around, he wrapped his arms around her and lifted her body, carefree and light as a feather. He twirled around once, her foot awkwardly hitting a chair. Her cheeks were hot with embarrassment as he set her down, her body sliding against his. Caden took a quick look around the small shop. Everyone was staring. She looked up at him, noting the excitement on his lips; his voice was light and joyous, whimsical and kind. "I've missed you."

Was it that time already? Now that she thought about it, Gabriel did go to bed early; he must have fallen asleep. Which meant that he had forgotten to pick her up altogether. But that didn't explain how Tom was here. "What are you doing here?" she asked, resting her head on his chest as he held her in a thick, comforting hug, one that she felt she needed.

"I came to get you." He pulled her away from his chest, never letting go of her waist, and looked into her eyes.

It felt strange to have him touch her so effortlessly, though he didn't notice. He seemed to be ignorant to that kind of intimate touch. His hands wrapped around her waist like he thought it was natural to have her body against his. Was he growing up? "Tom, how did you find me?"

"What do you mean?"

"Tom, please." She pushed at his chest, and he released his hold. It was too strange having him hold her like he was Gabriel. "How did you know where to find me?" *Only Gabriel knew.*

"I don't know." He rubbed the back of his neck, frowning. "I just knew I needed to pick you up."

"Oh no, you didn't drive did you?"

"No." Tom crossed his arms. "I walked, but I could drive if I wanted to."

"You can't drive, Tom."

"You don't know that."

"Whatever." Caden's eyes moved around the room, and though the people were no longer looking at them, she knew they were listening. There wasn't anything better to do in a small town. "Let's go home." She grabbed his hand to pull him along.

"But I just got here and it's great. I don't want to go."

"No, I'm sure you don't." She suddenly felt like Keira and didn't like it; she didn't want to be his mother. With Gabriel she wanted to be something else, something special, but with Tom did she want friendship? What more could you ask for with a man who was practically a child? "How long is 'just,' Tom?"

He shrugged.

"He's been here a little under an hour, chugging coffee like a pro," the girl from behind the counter offered, her large, flirtatious eyes taking in Tom's body. Caden's stomach churned.

"Thanks," Caden murmured, uneasy that a pretty coffee girl had taken any notice of him.

Caden let out an exasperated breath; she had lost an hour with him and some barista had swooped down and enjoyed his company instead. She didn't want to lose any of it, not a moment, and especially not to someone else. She knew that if she could be with him every second, she'd be happy because something about him made her calm, collected; he made her feel like one whole piece instead of two separate ones. "What are you drinking, anyway?"

"Hot chocolate."

So it wasn't coffee after all. The barista didn't know a thing; she was probably trying to make Caden jealous. Caden's shoulders relaxed, and she took hold of his hand. "Let's go home, Tom." Her head was bent back to look at him, and she wished he would lift her into the air again like he had when he'd seen her.

"I want to stay."

"Tom, come on. We can play a game when we get home."

The barista behind the counter looked shocked, and Caden blushed. She didn't mean it to sound like that…not with Tom.

"Noooo." He was getting louder. "I want to stay and drink hot chocolate."

Like a real adult, Caden thought, her gears turning. If being an adult was his goal, she hoped it entailed more than just coffee. "Alright, finish your cup and we'll go."

They sat down. His dark eyes continued to look around with every sip. To Tom, everything was new and exciting. Caden tapped her fingers on the table, watching Tom linger on each sip, drawing them out. One by one. *Slowly*.

"Finished?"

His eyes smiled as he swallowed down the last gulp and showed her the empty mug. Caden pushed away her irritation and smiled back. His handsome face could make anyone happy, especially with his dark, messy hair and tight T-shirt. She could even see the darkness in his eyes glisten. Somehow the blackness felt enveloping, and she wanted to get lost in it. She shook the thoughts away, reminding herself it wasn't Gabriel, not really. Tom had a look of pureness about him. Caden wiggled her hand free of his. His smile vanished, melting into a kind of pout.

"I didn't finish fast enough?" He looked down like a lost puppy.

"Come on," she said. "I have a surprise."

———————————

Tom licked his lips; he could still taste the sweet chocolate liquid lingering there. Caden seemed upset. He reached for her hand again, but she evaded him. Tom looked back one last time at the lone red coffee mug. He wanted another hot chocolate, but Caden was nearly out the back door. Then he saw something bright. His eyes glanced over the mug to a girl outside of the front window, hidden in the shadows, her pink coat reflecting the warm light. Tom wondered why the girl wasn't coming inside.

"Tom, let's go." Caden pulled on his arm, and the pink coat with little hearts vanished with the girl. "Tom, now." When he didn't move, the warmth of her hand entered his. His smile reformed, and the girl outside was forgotten.

9

W hat's the surprise?" Tom asked for the millionth time, and for some reason Caden didn't feel annoyed. She was happy, happy to have him out of the coffee shop and to herself.

"If I tell you, will you shut up?" she teased.

"Nope."

"I didn't think so." Caden tried to glare, but it quickly dissolved into a laugh. Luckily Gabriel hadn't taken his wallet out of his jeans and had some cash. She and Tom had walked to the store and were carrying bags of groceries back to the condo. "Well," Caden said as they made it to the complex, "we are going to cook, and eat, for the whole night."

Tom didn't say a word for a few minutes. He looked a little disappointed. "Why?" he asked quietly.

Caden would probably have been let down had she not expected a similar response. They walked around the building to the condo door. Why would Tom want to eat—if not just for the taste—when he didn't need to? "You have the key?"

Tom reached into his pocket and pulled out a single silver key. Caden took it and unlocked the door.

She opened it, looking around the room. The kitchen wall that had been black from the fire was white again. A faint smell of paint and smoke lingered in the air. *No wonder he took so long.* The place even looked vacuumed, and new dish towels sat by the sink.

"Why would we eat throughout the night?" Tom asked, his tone soft and hesitant.

It made Caden's heart ache at the thought of what he had missed, of what he didn't know. "Because, Tom, contrary to popular belief, we don't eat in our sleep. We eat all day long, but you—" she pointed playfully at his chest, pushing him back a little with the force of her pointer finger, "—my dear Tom, are going to eat like it's day: breakfast, lunch, and dinner."

"But I ate this morning. I'm not hungry."

"Oh, Tom, do you know how much men eat?" She placed the bags on the counter. "I'll be right back. Okay?"

Caden went into the bathroom, closing the door behind her. Her hand went straight to her pocket, where she had stuffed the stolen pieces of paper from different books at the library. She pulled them out one by one, feeling her pocket flatten. The information she had found at the library seemed more real when she held the pages in her hand. She had been slightly worried that Tom would reach into her pocket and pull them out. It was a silly fear, but Tom wasn't a predictable boy.

Caden opened the bathroom cabinet and pulled out her old black jeans. After stuffing the paper inside their pockets, she folded the jeans back up and put them away.

Leaving the bathroom, Caden pulled her hair back with a small rubber band she had found. She grabbed an onion from the bags on the counter. Spinning around on her heel, she reached for the cutting board. In a second, the onion was sliced in half. She then placed the flat side down. She could tell Tom was watching, wondering. Her fingers stabilized the onion, and then she placed the flat side of the blade against her knuckles and pushed down and forward, creating the perfect slice. She did it again and again; Gabriel had great cooking knives and pretty good pans. Tonight she would unleash her mastery, starting with breakfast, all for Tom.

Tom took a step back as he watched Caden work. She was cutting onions and peppers while tossing butter squares over her shoulder. She threw olives into a pan with diced ham, listing off the ingredients with each movement. The food crackled and softened, mixing together in the butter like a whirlwind that Caden said would explode in his mouth with flavor.

"Here, Tom, take this."

Tom gripped the carton of eggs unsure of what to do. She showed him how to break an egg down the middle and leave its contents sloshing into a bowl. When he finally tried, the shell wouldn't break until his third crack. Little pieces of white shell clung onto the slimy insides and were dragged into the bowl, lingering at the bottom. Tom dipped his finger in the egg, attempting to retrieve the bits of shell, but he quickly pulled away once he felt their texture. He then tried to catch the pieces of shell with a fork, but they eluded him, again and again. *She won't notice*, he thought as he mixed them together like she had shown him and added the milk.

The bowl was gone in a blink, her hand grabbing it and tipping the creamy yellow mixture over the ingredients that had already settled in the heat. The eggs sizzled, filling the room with a glorious smell. It covered the smell that had been there before, one that made Tom think of fireplaces. His mouth watered, and he suddenly felt grumbles erupt from his stomach. He jumped. He had felt it before a few times, though he never understood why it happened.

"My stomach?" he inquired, asking Caden what was happening. He only used motions and fragments of words to convey his confusion, as if he couldn't speak. He could, he knew he could, but it was a strange experience and she always had an answer.

"Told you." Her face twitched upward, wrinkling her nose. He wanted to get closer to her, but he couldn't figure out why. His eyes trailed down the length of her body as she spun around the kitchen, her eyes bright with excitement. He could feel the happiness around her, a feeling he knew but never experienced except when he was with her. He'd never realized how fragmented he felt on the inside until she came and made him feel together, less broken.

He snapped back to attention when he saw things flying through the air. Food, he realized. Yellow pancaked things, which Caden insisted were omelets, were spinning, flipping and moving in ways that made it seem like the floor had a better chance to catch them than her pan. She finished the omelet with sprinkles of cheese and a fold, a cut down the middle, and a plate for each of them.

"I'd give you your own omelet," she said, "but I'm not sure how much you'll eat tonight." She paused, thinking, and looked at the refrigerator. "I don't want to waste it."

He went to get a fork, opening an empty drawer. Caden made a clicking sound with her tongue and pointed to another drawer with her foot, all while holding the plates. He could feel that tug again, the desire to be closer to her. The feeling made him uncomfortable. He hadn't meant to be so close to her at the coffee shop, but he liked it and a part of him that he didn't understand wanted it. Opening the drawer she had pointed to, he found forks; she was right again. Tom grabbed two forks and went to sit beside her at the table. Freshly poured orange juice already sat by the plates.

"Go ahead," she said eagerly, and Tom felt like she was waiting, watching.

He took a bite and instantly recognized a taste from the breakfast he'd had that morning. Caden took a bite too.

Then Tom heard a crunch.

"What the heck?" Caden opened her mouth, which was full of chewed food, and removed something white.

Tom tensed. The eggshell. He hadn't thought that would happen; he'd imagined they'd dissolve, or maybe get softer like the rest of the food. He looked away, not wanting to meet Caden's disappointed eyes. "Sorry," he whispered. He waited for an explosion of anger. Instead a musical, happy sound traveled through the air; she was laughing. Tom began to laugh along with her, unsure of what was funny but liking the sensation. He looked at her eyes, taking in the large creases from her upturned lips. They laughed and laughed, and he watched as Caden began to cry as she laughed harder. As they ate the omelet, the crunches continued, and with each one they laughed again and again.

"Oh, Tom, thank you."

Tom looked down at the plate, unsure of what he had done.

Caden couldn't wipe the smile off her face. She had been so worried that Tom wouldn't like the omelet. She hadn't thought about how he'd do with the eggs, what he would or wouldn't know. At the sound of the first crunch, she'd thought she had done something wrong. When it was just an eggshell she felt better, lighter. Part of her hadn't even understood the laughter that had exploded from her. It had felt good to laugh; it made her feel like her old self, the person she'd been before her parents had separated. Not only that, but she had been tense coming back to Gabriel's condo. She had expected ashes, and the burnt hand towel to be unmoved; all that had been left was the faint smell of burning, and even that was now covered by the smell of their first meal of the night.

Tom insisted on helping, so Caden directed him toward the dishes while she got started on lunch. It wouldn't take long to make, but because they'd gotten a late start, she wanted to get lunch over with to give their stomachs a rest before dinner.

Dinner was Caden's favorite, and she assumed that most people in the world would agree. So many things could be made. There was no rush, and it completed a hard day's work. Tom seemed to be doing a fine job with the dishes. Her thoughts trailed away to the coffee shop, to Tom lifting her and spinning her around. It had been so wonderful and natural and—

Knock, knock, knock.

Caden's heart leapt into her throat. Who would be here at midnight? Her mind flashed to Angelica, or maybe Face. Or maybe it was some other friend of Gabriel's looking for somewhere to stay.

"This is the police," a gruff, thundering voice said through the door. Tom dropped a plate, and Caden cursed under her breath.

"Caden, what do they want?" Tom's panicked eyes searched hers.

"Shhh." She came close to him, holding his shoulders;

he was already curling in on himself, sinking to the ground. "Tom, don't do that, get up. I need you right now." He slowly straightened. She could tell he was forcing himself to listen, but he couldn't stop shaking. "I need you to do something for me." She searched his eyes, the darkness pulling her in. "Tell them I'm not here."

"You're leaving?" His voice hit a high panic. "No, Caden, don't leave me." Tom's hand flew to her wrist, holding tight.

"Shhh, no, I'm not," she whispered. "I'll be in your room. Come and get me when they're gone."

Tom didn't nod an okay. He just stood, releasing his grip on her as she tiptoed over the broken plate and ran up the stairs to Gabriel's room. She closed the door behind her.

She didn't know for certain, but with what Keira had told her about Sean coming to her mom's house and making a fuss, it only made sense that her mother would try to find her. Caden just hadn't thought it would happen so soon. *Looks like asking Keira for a favor really was a bad idea.*

The lights were already on in Gabriel's room, and as much as she wanted to turn them off, she feared more police were outside and would notice the change in lighting. Caden could only faintly hear the police downstairs. Cold air filled the room, and Caden wrapped her arms across her chest, unsure why the air was lacking heat. She turned her head toward the open window, taking a step forward—*crunch*. She lifted her foot to reveal a small piece of broken luminescent material sitting on the carpet. It was the thing Gabriel had found in his pocket, the one he had been so distraught about seeing broken. Caden knelt on the floor, reaching for it. The fragmented piece felt as soft and clean as before, but now it was almost perfectly cleaved in two. She rubbed the pieces between her fingers before placing them in her pocket.

Not wanting her silhouette to be seen from down below, she began to crawl toward the window, determined to get a better look. The carpet scraped unforgivingly against the fabric of her pants; she hated the feeling. She grabbed the window's edge to look out into the night air. The moon cast a soft light on the bodies in front of Gabriel's front door. Caden squinted at the two figures—

"Rebecca? Rebecca!" The voice was shrill with panic and hope.

Damn it.

"That's her, that's my daughter, she's in there."

Caden pulled her head back in and quickly shut the window.

Her options flitted through her mind, coming and going just as quickly as they surfaced. She could talk rationally like an adult, or maybe she could claim it wasn't her mother. Caden shook her head in disbelief. How had her mother found her? Keira couldn't have told her—she hadn't given Keira any information, at least none that would bring anyone here.

Could they take Tom? No, on what grounds could they

take him? Kidnapping? Caden scoffed at the idea, but then her stomach turned; as long as she was under eighteen, her mother had full rein over her. Caden looked back to the door that kept her hidden in Gabriel's room, away from the kitchen, the front door, the police, and Tom. She ran to it, the seconds monumental; either she'd beat her mother or she wouldn't.

Caden flung open the door and screamed as she ran down the stairs, "Tom!"

Tom looked at her, his eyes wide. The policeman went to grab him, but he ducked down to the left. He spun on his heel and darted through the door. The wrong door. Tom headed out past the policeman. Caden screamed again, frustrated and confused. *Tom, you were supposed to run to me.*

Caden ran back into Gabriel's room. Her gut twisted as she watched Tom disappear into the forest from the window. This was her mother's fault. Why hadn't Laura just left her alone? Her body slouched against the wall. The anger faded into a fit of sobs and wails that only Rebecca could conjure. *I need to find him.*

Caden got to her hands and knees and crawled to the desk by the bed, hoping to find a pen and paper. From an almost empty drawer, she pulled out a crumpled sticky note and a dull pencil.

Joe's Coffee Shop, tonight -Caden

She moved toward the bed and placed the paper under the pillow.

"Rebecca?" Laura opened the door as Caden situated herself in front of the pillow on the bed.

"What are you doing here?" The bitter words cut through the air, making her mother take an uneasy step back. Caden figured it was probably because Rebecca wouldn't talk like that.

Rebecca—weak, pathetic, quiet Rebecca. Caden grimaced at the thought of her old self. Her tears had dried as she formed her plan and scrawled her note to Tom. She didn't need to cry anymore. She could take care of herself now.

Laura took a seat next to Caden and reached her arm out to tentatively touch her shoulder. Caden jerked away from her.

"*Don't touch me,*" she hissed. She caught the look of shock in her mother's eyes, their concern and sympathy turning into anger. The transformation scared Caden. It was probably the same gaze she would have been subject to when she ran away with Sean, had she confronted Laura instead of leaving a note on the fridge.

The heat under her skin burned from the inside out; she had been wrong, and her mother had been right about Sean.

Caden looked up toward her mother. She was wearing her ridiculous purple cat scrubs and her Crocs medical shoes. Laura was a nurse at a hospital about an hour south of Cloverdale. She worked late hours, and her friends called her Lala. It bothered Caden that her mother had such a playful nickname at work. Growing up she'd hardly seen Laura. Her night shifts caused her to sleep away most of each day, leaving Caden alone at all hours. And, in Caden's opinion, for most of her childhood.

"Honey." Caden watched as Laura cautiously placed a hand on her shoulder again.

"Shouldn't you be working?" Caden spat, violently turning her shoulder to escape her mother's hand.

"I got a call that they might have found you, so I left. Nancy took my shift." Her mouth moved as if she wanted to say more, but nothing came out. Her hand went back into her lap. She always liked to pretend she wasn't angry, but it never fooled Caden. In public, her mother glistened like an angel. Yet, like always, when they got home Laura would start screaming and probably restrict her from ever leaving the house. Public face was the most important thing in the world to her.

Her mother's long black hair draped over her shoulders with tiny white strands mingled sparsely between its darkness. *She must have cut it*, Caden thought, because she remembered it being much longer.

"Did he hurt you?"

"No, mom." Caden clenched and unclenched her fists, leaving little dents in her palms from the pressure of her fingernails. "He's good to me. I love him." She shouldn't have said that; she hadn't meant to say it. She wasn't sure it was even true. Yes, she was attracted to Gabriel, and she did care for Tom in a best-friend, little-brother kind of way, but *love* seemed like a drastic calculation of her mixed feelings.

"You may think that now, but honey we will get you help, we can get through this."

Caden shook her head. "Help for *what*? Get through *what*? You don't know what you're talking about, Mom, you just want everything to fail like your marriage. No one can be happy if you aren't happy. Why don't you just get a boyfriend and move away like Dad? Leave me alone."

"What have you done with my daughter Rebecca?" she asked, as if in disbelief that the little girl she remembered had turned into such a hard, unhappy beast. Laura crossed her arms over her chest. "No daughter of mine is allowed to talk to me in such a disrespectful way. You're only seventeen and until your birthday, like it or not, you're my responsibility."

"Your daughter is gone, *Laura*, my name is Caden. Rebecca is dead."

"Don't say that."

"You want the truth, don't you? Well, either way you can call me Caden. It's who I am, I like it and—"

"Did he give you that horrible name?" Laura pointed out the window in the direction of Tom. "That Tom?"

"Tom?" Oh, no. Caden didn't want her mother to know his name. Tom was her secret; if the police found out Gabriel wasn't exactly *normal* they could lock him away in some mental hospital. "No, Mom, his name is Gabriel. You don't know anything; you never know anything. You always jump to conclusions and won't listen to anything anyone has to say."

"Really?" Laura's face said it all; she hadn't ever been able to hide it. Caden knew the face too well, the "you're lying" expression that hung across her mother's lips, eyes, and in the slant of the eyebrows. She always pursed her lips and tilted her chin up; Caden figured it was to better look down on her. "Then why were you calling for a boy named Tom?"

"You must be hearing things," Caden said. "Old age can do that." Caden's eyes traveled across the room, searching for an escape. Gabriel's door was open, and a cop stood halfway up the stairs as if waiting for her to run. The cop had a smug look on his face, one that could have only meant he was listening to their conversation and that he'd heard it too. *Tom.* Caden tossed a glare at the cop, and he looked away with a smirk. She directed her eyes back to Laura, now pleading.

Laura looked over her shoulder at the cop, and he gave her a small nod of recognition. Or maybe it was a yes to her unspoken question. Caden wasn't sure. "We are going home now, Rebecca."

"Caden."

"Right, well, I have no home for a Caden, only a Rebecca."

"Good, because I want to stay here with…Gabriel." She'd nearly done it again; Tom's name had nearly slipped out of her lips. Her heart pounded painfully at the thought of him being alone and scared in the forest after dark.

"That boy has obviously caused enough damage. You're not staying here, young lady."

"Yes, I am. You said so yourself, there's no room for me at *your home*. I'm staying here."

"No, Ms. Caden, you aren't. You are under eighteen and as long as that is the case, you're coming with me. You don't get a choice. You can decide to never see me again and live with strange men when you're older, but tonight you're coming home." Caden hated that her mother always put on the act of the reasonable parent when they were in public; that always made her the reckless, rebellious, stupid young teenager people shook their heads at. No one ever stopped to think that her mother's act was just that: an act. Laura stood and outstretched her hand, which Caden ignored. She could barely stand looking at Laura, let alone touching her.

"Why now?"

"What?"

"You heard me, Laura, why now? I've been gone for weeks, and now you care?"

"Honey, not now."

"Yes, now. I don't care if they hear." Caden waved absently at the cop on the stairs.

"Well I do, this is family business and I would like it to stay that way. We can talk about it at home." Laura's hand reached out to guide Caden toward the door.

"No. Don't touch me. I want to talk about this now." Caden could see her mother's face pale.

"Alright, fine. What were you doing at this boy's house?"

Caden didn't want to answer; she didn't want to give her mother the satisfaction of being right about Sean or hear her make accusations about staying with Gabriel. She would make it seem worse than it really was. It wasn't bad, not really; Caden was nearly eighteen, and she hadn't slept in his bed.

"How the hell did you find me anyway?" Caden spat, crossing her arms over her chest.

"Keira called me."

"*Keira?*" Caden's stomach twisted at the betrayal, and she was suddenly worried that she might have accidentally told Keira something she shouldn't have.

"After she dropped you off at Joe's Coffee Shop, she gave me a call and I begged her to follow you."

"What? You had her follow me?" *And I didn't notice?* Caden couldn't stop herself from screaming, her clenched hands tingling with the desire to rip something apart. Laura took a step back from her. It was probably because Rebecca didn't yell; Rebecca never caused problems outwardly. Her rebellion was voiced with drawings and little things like dyeing the carpet or wearing nothing but black all the time.

"If you're going to be mad with someone, be mad at me. She called me fifteen times during your walk to the store and then to the condo. I had to bribe her with books." She let out a heavy sigh. "I had the late shift tonight, so I couldn't do much on my own; Keira lost track of you once you entered the complex. When I got there with the police, we knocked on nearly every door. You have to understand, sweetheart, that after Sean came to the house yesterday—"

"Sean? Sean's a liar!" Caden screeched, her voice breaking and tears rushing out from her eyes. She let herself fall onto

Gabriel's bed and pushed her face into the pillow. It smelled like him, like cinnamon. She missed him—not Tom, but him. Gabriel had saved her from Sean. "Sean lied, Mom, about everything, ever since the beginning." Caden spoke quietly, embarrassed by how broken she sounded. She could barely hear her voice through the thickness of the pillow, but she knew that her mother could hear.

Her hand drifted under the pillow to the note hidden there, and she squeezed it in her fist. Tonight she would see Tom, and tomorrow she would find a way to see Gabriel. The sooner she went with Laura the better. Slowly she rose from the pillow, careful not to move the note. Tearstains marked the fabric where her face had been.

"I'm ready," she said, but she didn't look at her mother or the policeman. Instead she took one last look out the window, hoping it wasn't goodbye for good.

———————

The car ride home was unbearable, but at least it was the better kind of unbearable: nearly dead silent. When the front door opened to Laura's house, Caden felt immediately out of place. She tossed her shoes off her feet and ran to her room, the room she hoped hadn't already been turned into an office. When the door flew open, baby pink walls lined with posters of death-metal bands welcomed her; a large dark red heart she had died into the carpet a few years back sat like a rug in the middle of the floor. Her shoulders released their tension. It made her feel a little better to see that her things looked un-touched. She flopped down on her bed, its sheets and comforter matching the pink walls. Looking up at the ceiling, she could see the drawings she had made. They weren't very good, but they weren't bad either. They had done their job—to make her mother mad. In fact, as she looked around all she could see were acts of her defiance, and it made her happy. Not that it mattered; she wouldn't be there for long. If everything went well, she'd escape and find Tom.

The thought of Tom out in the forest, alone and afraid after dark, scared her. What had made him run the other way? Caden reached into her pocket for the pieces of iridescent material she had found in Gabriel's room, remains of the piece that he had taken out of his pocket earlier that day. They were each about the size of a penny. She held them out in front of her, observing how the light shone through them delicately. She hadn't noticed that they were transparent, and she also hadn't noticed the delicate veins that traveled throughout the iridescence, shimmering. *A butterfly wing*, she thought, and the door abruptly opened.

"Can't you knock?"

"After what we went through tonight? I don't think so."

Caden quickly pushed the penny-sized butterfly wing fragments into her pocket and relaxed.

"What was that?" Laura asked as Caden's fingers came away from her pocket, empty.

"Nothing." Caden placed a scowl on her face to fend off any more questions about them.

Laura shook her head. "Rebecca—"

"Caden."

"Caden. I don't think this conversation is over, and I'm not happy about the way you behaved in front of the law enforcement. You know Margaret's husband works at the station, and now everyone will know about it."

"I can't believe you."

"Me? My daughter is running from boy to boy and you can't believe me? I'm just trying to keep this family together."

Caden lifted her head in the direction of her mother, and a few stray tears fell. Bitter, unwanted, weak tears. They trailed down her face unforgivably, and she wiped them away with the back of her sleeve.

"I know Sean must have hurt you. A broken heart can feel like the end of the world, I get that," Laura said. "Don't tell anyone, but I was kind of glad when he came here with a bloody nose—"

"What did you just say?" Who was this woman?

Laura had a faint smile. "A bloody nose. He had his hand on it, trying to stop the bleeding, and I was worried at first because I thought you were with him. But when I found out he'd been hurt following you, I was kind of glad. He had it coming. I know, I shouldn't say it, but he hurt my baby girl." Laura's hand came toward her, but Caden pulled away. Her mother sighed.

"Anyway, we had a long talk and he told me about this Tom Gabriel."

Caden took a step back.

"Yes," Laura said, "Tom Gabriel. Sean told me you called him both names at different times."

"His name is Gabriel, Mom. Sean doesn't know anything."

"See—" she pointed a finger in the air, and it rocked up and down in a nonthreatening way, "—that's what I thought, but then when we were at that condominium, you called for Tom but insisted his name was Gabriel."

"Yeah, well—"

"Don't lie to me, Reb—Caden."

It was true; Laura had extra keen lie-detector senses. She could always see through Caden's false faces, voices, words. It was annoying. "His legal name is Gabriel, but—" Caden shrugged, "—he likes to be called Tom sometimes, like I like to be called Caden."

"I see."

"But Mom, don't tell the cops that."

Laura didn't seem to like the comment, but she nodded and got up. "Sleep well, and don't make me regret coming to get you." Laura walked away, closing the door behind her.

She knew her mother was pleased to see her daughter so broken. It meant that she had been right, and that Caden was the unruly teenager that Laura insisted she was. It meant that loving someone could only bring misery, and that Laura was better for knowing it. She liked seeing the proof of her belief reflected in Caden's misery.

Caden wasn't going to make any promises to her mother. Most likely, Laura would regret coming to get her. There was nothing she could do to make her happy anyway. Plus, Caden had a plan. She just hoped that Tom had found her note and could read her scribbled words.

Patience wasn't one of Caden's virtues, though she did try. She took a shower and put a bag together. She grabbed a black sweater, two pairs of black jeans, and even a black dress. Her hair, though well brushed, sat wet on her back.

A chill shot down her spine as she opened the window. Moisture drifted through the air and filled her nose with the promise of rain.

"Hasn't it rained enough?" Caden grumbled as she swung a leg out the window. She had been sneaking out for years. Her room's window led to the roof, and if she followed it around the side of the house, it sloped closer to the ground. And just as she had so many times before, she disappeared into the night.

When Caden got to the coffee shop, her breath was ragged from running. There were no sounding crickets in the distance, and she hadn't passed a single car. Only the wind whispered through the moist night air. The windows of the coffee shop were as dark and opaque as a black hole. Even though she knew the place would be packed in the morning, it looked as though it had been deserted for years. A few streetlights illuminated the empty parking lot, but she couldn't see Tom.

The deck in front of the coffee shop was only one step up from the dirt parking lot surrounding it and was mostly enclosed by a railing. She stumbled onto it and collapsed against the outside resting bench, releasing a deep sigh as she removed her backpack and placed it beside her. Caden reached out to rub her cramping leg. It was entirely possible that Tom had already been there and left. She hoped not.

Caden turned around and looked back into the dark window. Joe's Coffee: the small-town hangout that was always booming.

"Hey."

Caden turned. "Tom." She practically jumped up off the bench and threw her arms around him.

"What the heck? Get off." He pulled at her arms, and she released him, confusion and hurt stinging in her chest.

Caden took a step back, realization dawning; it wasn't Tom. "I'm sorry, I don't know what got into me."

"Who's Tom, Caden?"

"I don't know, I didn't mean to say it, I just—" She looked at Gabriel in shock. It had to be three or four in the morning. It was Tom's time, not Gabriel's.

"Answer me, Caden. Who's Tom? This has happened twice. I deserve an explanation." Half his face lay masked in shadow, his shoulders rolled in, his head down. She took another step back. His voice was deadly quiet, dangerously low yet somehow vulnerable. "You better start explaining." He shook his head as if in disgust and took a step closer, slow, measured, and calculated. The boards creaked under his weight.

Caden didn't move. He stood so close their bodies nearly touched. She let out a breath, tilting her head up to look in his eyes. Even in the dark the vibrancy of his copper irises was breathtaking. When the night air stirred, it carried his cinnamon scent.

"I'm so sorry, Gabriel, don't be mad." Her shaky hand rested gently on his chest, but he pushed it away.

Caden's heart began to race. She took a step back from him as if from an angry dog, or in this case, a stalking wolf.

A deadly grin stretched across his lips. "Mad? Mad, Caden? I woke up in the woods. It took me an hour to get to my *unlocked* condo. I found your note." Gabriel crumpled the note in one fist and tossed it to the ground between them. It teetered back and forth before resting motionless. "What is this? Some kind of game?"

"It isn't a game, Gabriel."

"I won't ask again." His voice rose to a yell as he enunciated, "Tell me who Tom is."

Caden shrank backward until the backs of her knees hit the bench, making her fall onto it. "He's you."

Silence.

Gabriel ran his hands through his hair, the boards creaking as he turned to face the other direction. Silence, then: *SMACK*. Caden whimpered in fear as he hit the wall with his fist, anger soaring through his eyes.

He pointed at her, blood dripping down his knuckles. "Don't you lie to me." The timbre of his voice was low with warning and more terrifying than any of his angry outbursts.

"I'm not." Caden shook her head incessantly, her eyes wide and desperate.

"Damn it." Gabriel hit both fists against the wall and leaned into it, his head dangling between his arms. "How often?"

"What?"

"I said, HOW OFTEN!"

Her body was shaking. "Every night," she whispered.

"Every night? EVERY *NIGHT*." He turned around and began to pace. "No. NO." She watched him pull at his hair. "I should have known—the memories, all the memories."

Caden didn't say a word; she didn't know what words there were to say. She brought her knees to her chest, wrapping her arms around them. What would she do now? How would she protect Tom?

"So. You like him better than me?" Gabriel said, pointing to his chest, his voice beginning to rise once again. "Is that it, Caden? Is Tom better?"

"I—I don't know." Tears ran down her cheeks. She wanted to lie and tell him there wasn't a difference, but there was. Tom needed her like Reese had, but she couldn't be there for her sister—she only had Tom and Gabriel… She didn't know how she felt. Tom made her whole, while Gabriel tore her in two.

"TELL ME, DAMN IT," he bellowed, taking quick strides to loom over her. He lowered his voice to a whisper as he brought his face down to her eye level. "What has *Tom* told you?"

"Nothing." Caden shook her head back and forth; she didn't remember ever feeling or sounding so miserable. "Nothing," she repeated, the tears coming faster. She sniffed loudly and wetly. She knew she looked like a splotchy, disgusting mess, but she didn't care. She wanted to go home. She wished she hadn't come.

"God forbid, Caden, if you don't tell me." He came at her with what looked like a punch. She closed her eyes and squealed before she realized she'd never felt an impact. Instead she heard a loud thump as Gabriel hit the side of the cabin again with his fist.

"He's innocent. We just hang out. Play games."

Gabriel scoffed, "What kind of games?"

"Just innocent games, kids' games."

"I knew something wasn't right." Gabriel ran his hands over his face. "Damn it, Caden, I haven't heard a peep about him for nine months. You did this."

"Wait. You know about him?" Her anger flared in

response. She pushed herself up off the bench, her legs trembling with the effort.

A low laugh escaped from Gabriel. "I thought he'd left. Stupid. I was fine until you came along. You brought him out." He nodded, as if convincing himself as much as her.

"I didn't," Caden yelled through her tears. "He was there that first night."

"So you stayed for *him* the whole time."

"I stayed for *you*, Gabriel." It was true, whether she liked it or not, she was falling in love with him. Being with him would never be easy, but it still felt right.

He stepped closer until their bodies almost touched. His lips were dangerously close to hers. She thought about what Face had said at the party, how Tom coming out was common. Caden didn't mention it. She let out a long sigh and touched his chin, lifting it so he'd look in her eyes.

"I want to be with *you*, Gabriel, not Tom."

Gabriel grabbed her, gathering her to him with all his force, crushing his lips against hers. She gasped, shocked by the sudden desperation in his touch, the heat of his mouth. Hunger ran through his long fingers as he gripped the edges of her shirt. She opened her mouth further, letting the kiss deepen. He slammed her body against the unrelenting wall, and a moan escaped her from the pain and pleasure overwhelming her senses. He pushed harder, their bodies melding, their tongues knotting together. Gabriel's hands encircled her waist, hoisting her up so she'd wrap her legs around him. His hands slid down her back and around her hips, up under her butt. She gasped as his hands trailed up her back and down again, his fingers catching at the back of her pants, sliding under the fabric.

Her breath caught in her throat as she tried to pull away from his lips. "Gabriel, we're in public."

He bit into her neck, making her moan again. "I want to know you really want me." His voice rumbled like rolling thunder, but there was a desperate edge to it that she'd never heard before. The warm whisper of his breath against her ear, sent bumps surfacing across her skin.

Caden pushed him back and looked down at him. Her height surpassed his because of the way he held her against him, her legs still clinging to his waist. "And I want to know that you really want me. I'm not just some girl you can use and leave behind."

His hands let go of her body as her legs awkwardly found the ground. He pulled at her arms around his neck, refusing to look at her until she let go.

"So that's it. That's what you think of me." He nodded, as though convincing himself, before turning to walk away.

"Gabriel. What the heck? What do you mean? Gabriel!" He continued to walk away, and she screamed into the night for him to come back.

What had he meant? That she was obviously someone he would eventually leave behind or someone he cared about?

Her fingers brushed against her throbbing lips as the anger surfaced.

"Tom would never treat me like this." She spat at the ground, wiping at her mouth with the back of her sleeve.

"Doesn't matter." He shrugged, suddenly very calm, not bothering to turn around as he walked toward the car he had parked in the darkness. The resignation in his voice frightened her. "You'll never see him again."

11

It had taken Caden nearly an hour to get back home. The rain started not long after Gabriel left her, and it didn't appear to be letting up soon. The roof of her house had been slick and hard to grasp, making it difficult and dangerous to get back to her room. She wished she had closed the window when she left; her room was just as cold as it was outside, reminding her of that first night at Gabriel's. A knot formed in the pit of her stomach; she'd hurt him. Not telling him about Tom was as good as lying to him, and even though she'd stayed for Gabriel, she'd also stayed for Tom. How could she explain any of it? Part of her wished she hadn't gone to meet Tom tonight, but the other part of her swam in the depths of Gabriel's kiss. The heat of his body pressed against hers had been all she'd wanted for days.

Caden glanced around her cold room, noticing that the heart-stained carpet had gotten wet from the open window, causing the dye to smear. Caden knew her mother would notice. It was a stupid heart anyway, a lopsided heart. She changed out of her wet clothes and got out an old towel. Frustrated with how she always seemed to be crying, she took to cleaning up her mess. Her hands and arms became red with dye from scrubbing the stained carpet with all her might.

—Day—

"I see you were up late last night? I'm assuming that's why you slept in until two in the afternoon?"

Caden shot out of bed, ready to defend herself, and she saw Laura eyeing the carpet. She hadn't been able to get the dye out. However, it no longer resembled a heart, and the once-deep-red color now looked pink. Caden had ended up rubbing it around, trying to blend the color in with the rest of the carpet.

"Maybe we should just get you new carpet, honey. Or a rug?"

Caden rubbed her eyes, lying back down. "Maybe."

"Get dressed and come downstairs. The police need to talk to you."

"What? They're here?" Caden pulled the sheets up to her neck.

"Yep. Up, up." Laura patted the side of the bed and walked out, closing the door behind her.

When Caden got downstairs, two men were sitting on the living-room couch drinking tea out of the fancy china that Laura only got out when company was over.

"Want any tea, Rebecca?"

Caden glared at her mother.

"Oh, right. Officers, this is my daughter Rebecca, but she is going by Caden right now."

Caden grunted in embarrassment as her mother tossed a wink in their direction. Adults winking: it was like patting a six-year-old on the head and saying, "Yeah, kid, you'll be president someday."

"Thanks for joining us, Caden." The man nodded at her. They weren't the same men from the night before. They seemed younger.

"Yeah. Whatever." As Caden landed on the couch with a thump, her mother attempted to save her tea from splashing over the edge.

"Careful, darling." Laura eyed the guests, as if they couldn't see for themselves what a troublesome child Caden was. "We have company."

"Yeah. I know." She rolled her eyes.

"Caden, we just wanted to ask you a few questions, and if you give us your cooperation, we will be on our way shortly." She nodded and the man continued. "Alright. This Tom Gabriel, does he have a last name?"

What a stupid name, Caden thought, *Tom Gabriel.* Why were they doing that? "It's just Gabriel."

"We were under the impression it was Tom Gabriel."

Caden looked up, shaking her head. "Just Gabriel, and I don't know his last name either." She watched the other man scribble on a piece of paper. He didn't say a word.

"Has Gabriel shown any signs of aggression, anything you can think of, anger problems maybe? Yelling?"

Caden thought about the shattered coffee mug, the way he had punched the wall and left his knuckles bleeding, the way he yelled at her, how he'd fought off Sean and his friends at the restaurant without a second thought. How he needed someone willing to defend him just as he defended her. "Nope." She shook her head slowly from side to side. "Can't say I have noticed anything like that."

"Honey, are you sure?"

"YES, MOM." *Oh, no, not the famous lie meter.* "Why can't you just believe me for once?" *That's right, turn it around, make her feel bad in front of guests. Laura hates that.*

"I do, honey, and keep your voice down."

Success, Caden thought, and she turned to the cops, their navy blue uniforms tight on their bodies. "Anything else, officers?"

"Yes, do you know a Sean Ryan?"

Oh, yes, Sean Ryan, what an ass. She couldn't believe she'd ever wanted to marry him. Rebecca Ryan, she used to say, and think, and scribble on all of her school papers. She shuddered in disgust. "Yeah, what about him?"

"He is pressing charges against Gabriel. He states you were there during the fight?"

"That little ass," Caden hissed.

"Rebecca. Watch your language. The company."

"They're cops, Mom, I'm sure they've heard worse."

The cop nodded at her mom as if to say, "Not to worry, ma'am."

Caden sighed. "It wasn't a fight. It was self-defense. He held me down and wouldn't let me go." Laura gasped. "Yeah, Mom, like I said, he's an ass. Then he had his asshole friends hold down T—Gabriel."

The cops looked at one another, and the quiet one wrote something down again.

"They would have killed us or something. I swear." Caden moved anxiously on the couch. She'd nearly used Tom's name.

"They?" The officer looked confused. It figured that Sean hadn't mentioned his friends.

"Yeah, he wasn't alone. He had Man-Mustache Cliff and Tall John with him."

"Cliff Harrison and John Johnson?"

"Yeah, them." She smiled smugly at the cops knowing their names; it was typical of small-town Cloverdale police to know the rambunctious teens.

When the cops were gone, Laura made a point to remind Caden that Margaret's husband was a cop, and just how much of a gossip Margaret was. She would tell the town everything, soil the family name, *blah, blah, blah*. Caden stopped listening after her mother's famous *our family's reputation* line.

"Okay, Mom, but I'm going out."

"I hope you're not going to go see that boy."

"Nope." She grabbed her bag, tossing it over her shoulder. *I probably won't be able to find him.*

At the condominium Gabriel's parking spot was empty, and no one answered the door.

"Damn it, Gabriel, where are you?"

A middle-aged lady in a patterned dress came out of door twenty-six, eyeing Caden nervously in her black outfit like she was a little devil. Caden waved hello as the lady dashed around the corner. She wished she had kept some of the clothes Gabriel had gotten her, but she'd left them all in the condo, and the ones from the night before were still soaked.

Caden looked up. A tree stood not far from door twenty-six. If she climbed the tree, she might be able to make it around the edge of the roof to Gabriel's bedroom. The Rebecca inside her remembered the story her mother would read to her as a child, of Pollyanna, the girl who fell out of a tree and was paralyzed from the waist down. Her mother had practically raised her off the book. Caden pushed Rebecca's thoughts aside. Her mother was overly paranoid; everyone knew it.

Caden put her hand in her pocket, rubbing the slick, cracked butterfly wings she had gotten from Gabriel's room. She had looked at them that morning and decided they were covered in something slightly thick to preserve them, like resin.

Whatever coated the wings didn't take away from their delicate nature. She wondered what they meant to Gabriel, and to Tom.

The afternoon sun loomed high above her, filling her surroundings with light. The low hum of an approaching car grabbed her attention. Caden moved around the side of the building near door twenty-six. Ducking low, she went to the back of the condominium, which gave her a view of the road. The sheen of a glossy black car reflected the sun as the car sped toward the carports. Her heartbeat accelerated upon realizing it was Gabriel. He took a quick turn into parking spot twenty-five. That was all it took for her to register that she wasn't ready to see him yet.

Even from a distance, his car looked horrible with its scratched paint and dangling side mirror. He looked from left to right before lifting a small panel of wood hidden under the carport shelves. When he was done, his car key was gone. *His new hiding place*, Caden thought. *He would be paranoid enough to change it.* Though she supposed with everything that had happened, it made sense. He disappeared from her view as he walked toward the path that led to his front door. Caden ducked down farther, hoping the side of the building and the bushes concealed her.

Gabriel's dark hair moved from side to side with the light breeze. His navy blue shirt clung to the muscles of his upper body as he reached into his jeans for a single key. Caden bit her lip, trying not to remember the kiss and the heat of his body against her. He opened the door and shut it behind him.

Her shoulders relaxed. He hadn't seen her. Still, what would she do if she couldn't get to his window? Beg to come in? Why not just use the front door, or better yet, leave? She rubbed her hands over her eyes in frustration. If she got on the roof, would the window still be open from the other night? The sound of a door slamming shut startled her as she ducked down behind the bush.

"Yeah, we can hang out." Gabriel locked his door before rushing down the path on his phone. She hadn't known he had a phone. "You know, if you would have said something a few weeks ago, I could have avoided a lot of this."

Caden leaned closer. His voice grew fainter with the increasing distance between them.

"I'll come get you. No, no, stay there." Caden watched as he took his car key from the hidden spot in the carport. "See you in ten." Gabriel ended the call, shoving his phone in his back pocket as he got in the car.

Caden let her body slouch against the wall. She needed to make sure Tom was okay, or at least that was what she told herself. The plan was simple: climb the tree and camp out until Tom woke up. She could smell the moisture in the air. The sky above her was blue and free of clouds. The tree looked semi-climbable. *Ugh, please don't fall,* she told herself. Her hand reached for the nearest branch and pulled. Her arms ached in protest as she placed her foot in a small knothole and pushed. *How do people do this? It always looks easy in movies.* Grunting and whining, Caden heaved herself over the first thick branch, the bark scratching every part of her exposed arms. After hoisting herself up, she stood on the branch. The pent roof wasn't very high, probably about twelve feet. After a few more minutes, and more branches beneath her, she managed to cling to the edge of the roof to pull herself up.

"I'm never doing that again." She could feel the heat of each shingle as she lay quietly against them, panting. *This is pathetic. It's supposed to be easy.*

Caden got to her feet and carefully walked across the pent roof. She passed the window for twenty-six and stopped beside Gabriel's bedroom window, the one that had been open the night before. She pressed her sweaty palms against the glass, pushing upward. Her hands slid and squeaked, and the window didn't move.

"Great, great, great." She moved her hands farther up and again placed her palms against the glass like large suction cups. "Come on, come on," Caden pleaded, unsure of what she would do if she couldn't get in, not entirely sure what she would do if she *could* get in. Using her foot as leverage behind her, she pushed against the window, and up. Her hair fell in her eyes, and she pushed the strands away hastily. The roof tiles held, though she feared she would slip off them, just like Pollyanna. She pushed harder and felt the slightest movement. "Yes, a little farther." Caden put all of her body weight forward, angling it upward against the window until a small gap formed. She slipped her fingers in the gap and pulled up.

The musty, cinnamon air streamed out into her face. The room, illuminated only by the light streaming in through the windows, was fairly dark. She could make out the unmade bed and a few clothes scattered on the ground. Caden took off her shoes and placed them on the desk before opening the first drawer. Empty. The second, empty. Caden ran her hand through her hair, twisting it nervously around her finger. She needed to figure out what was wrong with him so she could help him through it. Any kind of clue would be better than nothing—medication, medical bills, a home address, anything to help her understand his situation.

Caden opened the door to Gabriel's private bathroom and looked on the shelves, finding nothing interesting. Then she opened the closet and pushed back the clothes. She couldn't see anything out of the ordinary. The smell of Gabriel filled her nose, making her think of the night before and his arms around her. A tingle trailed down her spine when she touched her bottom lip and felt where his teeth had been.

What was wrong with him? She thought back to the library. She had looked up books on personality disorders. At the time she hadn't been sure what to make of it, but a mental illness did make the most sense. Though the possibility of Gabriel being Tom, and Tom being Gabriel, confused her. She didn't really want them to be the same person; it was too weird. So far it was the only thing that made sense. Tom wasn't real; he wasn't a young kid but a young man with traumatic experiences. Which meant when Gabriel kissed her, Tom was technically kissing her.

It was late afternoon by the time Caden decided to search Gabriel's living room. The second she reached the bottom of the stairs, she was overcome by goose bumps. Ripped paper lined the floor like torn confetti. The dining room table and couch had been turned over. All of the kitchen cabinets were emptied onto the floor. Coffee mugs lay broken across the carpet, shattered against the wall by the front door.

Caden bent down to grab a small piece of ripped paper, taking another look around as she stood. It looked like someone had ransacked the entire flat, or maybe Gabriel had gotten to it during one of his fits. Her eyes darted toward the paper once more. The very top line made the breath catch in her throat: *their other personality is in control.*

He'd found the pages she'd stolen from the books at the library.

Caden ran to the main bathroom, where she had folded her clothes and placed them neatly in the bathroom closet. More pieces of paper were scattered, ripped to shreds. The pants pocket that had once protected them was turned inside out. Caden's knees collapsed and her hands reached out to grab the pieces. Her fingers trembled as she glanced over the words, desperate to put something back together. She wondered when he had found them, and if it had been before or after they had seen each other last night.

Caden's fingers brushed the bathroom's cool tile floor as she pieced the papers back together. The edges of the paper were wrinkled, and in places they lifted, making the page imperfect but readable. "'The identity of two or more separate and'—" Caden pushed down the paper's edge with the tip of her finger, "—'distinct states of personality'—" she moved the pieces around to find the next line, "—'control the individual's behavior at different times. When under the control of one identity'—" the papers shifted and she matched up the last two, "—'the person is usually unable to remember the events that occurred while their other personality is in control.'" Caden looked over her shoulder. A mess of other pieces was scattered over the floor. She reached up to push her hair away from her face to find that her cheeks were wet. Her heart ached for Gabriel; she couldn't imagine what she would do if their roles were reversed. And what about Tom? He didn't even have a life of his own.

The soft click of a key fitting into the front door broke her serenity; her foot pushed the pieces of paper out of order before she ran up the stairs to Gabriel's room. Praying he hadn't seen her, she grabbed her shoes off the desk and held them tightly to her chest as she moved aside the clothes that were in her way and nestled into the back of the closet.

"Ugh, what a freakin' mess," a girl's voice squeaked as the door closed. "I can't believe you would bring me to your dumpy condo without at least cleaning it first." Caden strained to hear through the wall. Angelica?

"You'll get over it, the bedroom is fine." Gabriel mumbled.

The voices were getting closer and becoming more recognizable as they came up the stairs.

"Oh, and you think you can get me in there so easily?" Caden's heart lurched in her chest. It had to be Angelica. What was she doing here? She felt a lump form in the pit of her stomach and thought she might be sick; there was only one thing Angelica would be here for.

Caden heard the bedroom door close, and she pushed her body against the closet wall, hoping to conceal herself. She felt the overwhelming realization that she never should have come.

"Do what you want, you're the one who's been all over me since last summer."

"Yeah, and you didn't return any of my calls." Caden peeked out from the clothes to see Angelica motioning at Gabriel with exaggerated hand movements. "Then you invited me over for a party when you already have some ho-bag girl living with you."

"Don't talk about Caden," Gabriel said.

"What, you can't handle it?"

"Shut up, Angelica."

"Why?" Angelica tapped her foot impatiently; it slowed as she thought about the situation. "Oh... I see. You did that to your living room because she left you, and you invite me over to soothe the pain? You thought I'd come over and take off my clothes without saying a word about it? You can't use me anymore, Gabriel." Caden could hear the sharp smack as Angelica's hand hit Gabriel across the face. "I'm no fucking rebound." Angelica already had tears streaming down her face.

Gabriel's hand cradled his cheek, and for a moment he looked broken and small like Tom. Then his back began to straighten and his mouth formed into a tight, hard line. Caden winced at the sound of his knuckles cracking as they hit against the adjacent wall. Angelica's hand covered her mouth. He stood with his back turned away from her, as if he couldn't stand to look at her any longer. Caden looked away, feeling as if she was invading some kind of secret space, letting the clothes drape back over her vision.

"You know," Angelica said in a tear-choked voice. "I used to fall asleep next to you and wake up with you sleeping on the floor. But I never told you how many times I woke up to you cowering in a corner telling me you didn't know me. I loved you, but you broke my heart. Every night," she cried, "you broke my heart."

"You think I wanted that?" Gabriel whispered.

Angelica didn't seem to hear him. Her broken sobs became a shrill, hatred-filled shriek. "Something is wrong with you, Gabriel, and you might act tough now but you aren't. No, you sure as hell aren't. I'll walk home."

"Don't you dare leave me, Angelica, not after this," Gabriel yelled as their footsteps left the room; they grew quieter until the front door close behind them.

Caden's shoulders relaxed, but she still felt like she couldn't breathe. Her gut twisted. She wanted Gabriel to want her; they had a connection she couldn't deny, but Tom made a relationship impossible. Tom was so innocent and sweet; he just wanted a friend. She didn't want to be the next Angelica in Gabriel's life. There had to be a way to bring the two boys together, to somehow connect Tom to Gabriel.

Time passed slowly as Caden waited in the closet, afraid to even check if it was safe to come out. The only sounds she could hear came from her breath hitting the fabric around her. Caden felt like she was waiting for a bomb to go off, the panic keeping her muscles taut. She let her eyes close for what felt like only seconds.

—Night—

Bang.

Caden's body went rigid at the sound of the front door slamming shut. The footsteps got louder until she was sure Gabriel was back in his room. The wood creaked as he shut the bedroom door. A clanging, metal-on-metal sound filled the air. *Dead bolts,* Caden realized. *He installed dead bolts.*

Gabriel hissed under his breath, his whispers hardly reaching her ears, "Just try to get out." He wasn't talking to her, she realized, but himself. He was going to lock himself in, and unfortunately lock her in with him. Caden prayed he wouldn't check the window lock.

The clothes moved above her, tickling her face as the chime of keys stopped and began again. *He's hiding the keys in the closet?* Caden's heart began to beat in her ears. She felt nauseated with the anticipation of being caught. The keys chimed once more as the shirts moved again. Her heart seemed to stop beating as she waited. If he was hiding the keys in the closet, she would find them.

The floor creaked as Gabriel walked away, and the bed springs squeaked. He'd left the closet door open. Again Caden felt vulnerable. Did he know? Was he watching her?

Caden held her breath as the room became quiet once more. She waited for what felt like an hour, taking care not to fall asleep this time. When she was sure the coast was clear, she peeked out from behind the clothes. Darkness filled the room as thin streams of light drifted in through the window from the street lamps outside. How long had she been there? A pang of fear hit Caden as she wondered if her mom would show up again.

There was movement coming from the bed. She watched as he removed the covers, panic lining his face. Everything told her it was Tom, but she needed to be sure. She watched as he grabbed the door handle and pulled without success.

"Come on," Tom said, pulling harder. His anger sounded foreign.

"Tom. Psst. Tom," she whispered. Realizing the room only held the two of them, she cleared her throat and pushed down her fear. "Tom."

Tom looked around the room. "Caden? Caden, where are you?"

"Down here." Her back felt stiff from sitting for too long. A painful tingle invaded her legs as she tried to move around.

"What—what are you doing here?" Tom came to her side and grabbed her arm to help pull her up. "How did you get in?"

"I came in through the window."

"Oh, the window? When?"

"I have no idea, probably like eight hours ago. My mom is going to kill me." Caden grabbed onto his shoulder and stood the rest of the way up, ducking as the hangers hit her head. She let her arms wrap around Tom's neck. "I missed you," she whispered, though she could feel his body stiffen at her touch.

"It's been...a day."

Caden let go of Tom, wishing she had waited to say anything. She wanted him to tell her he missed her too, like he had before. "You didn't miss me?" She felt small as she reached out and took his hand, the skin rough with scars. If the skin had truly belonged to Tom, it wouldn't have had a scratch. "We should get out of here."

Tom's face was flushed, even though the darkness in the room hid most of it. "It's locked."

Caden couldn't help but stare at Tom. His lips looked soft and kissable. She reminded herself they were Gabriel's lips, and they were soft... Caden pushed away the thought.

"We could find the keys. Or we could go out the window? It could be an adventure. Get something to eat? Are you hungry?"

"Not really." Tom looked away.

"Why am I not surprised? Well, let's get out of here and see if I can cook us something that will change your mind."

"I told you the doors are locked." A hint of anger shot through Tom's voice. "The. Doors. Are. Locked. Don't you listen to anything I say?"

Caden took a step back. "Why are you acting like this?" She looked at the door. They could find the key; it probably wouldn't take long. That wasn't what bothered her though; she wanted to know why Tom sounded so much like Gabriel on a bad day.

"You just never listen, Caden." Tom put a hand through his hair and walked back toward the bed. He didn't seem young, he seemed like Gabriel. Wasn't that what she wanted? Her hand twirled the ends of her hair nervously. Did Tom even know about Gabriel?

He sat on the far end of the bed facing the window, facing away from her.

"Tom," she whispered. He didn't respond. "Tom, sometimes, you act very...young." She gulped. "Other times, you act older, but you can be mean. Do you know what I'm talking about?" She watched his unmoving silhouette in the frame of the window. "Tom?"

"You don't like me."

Caden froze. What? "Of course I like you, Tom, we're friends..." She took another step forward. "I just wish you understood..." *that I need you to grow up. I want Tom Gabriel to be one person with one name. I want you to hold me and tell me you'll never leave my side.* "Tom, the summer is going to end. I'll go back to school and, well, I think you'll go back home, wherever that is."

"Caden?"

"Yes?" Caden's heart hammered in her chest; she was close to him now.

"I lost something, a kinda... Ah, good-luck charm." He still didn't move, looking out the window from the side of the bed. "Have you seen it?"

"I don't know, Tom. What does it look like?"

"It looks like butterfly wings."

Caden stopped the hand that was about to rest on his shoulder. "The thing you broke the first night I met you?"

He nodded.

"Why would you want that, Tom?"

"I think I need it."

Caden pushed her hand into her pocket. The two pieces were nestled next to one another. Her fingers grazed their soft surface. "Are they really butterfly wings?"

"Yes. Have you seen them?"

"No." Caden let the pieces fall back into her pocket. "No, I haven't." She slid her arms across his shoulders. There was no way she was giving them back now. So far they were the only thing she'd found that they both cared for, though she couldn't fathom why.

Tom is Gabriel. Gabriel likes me. Tom needs to grow up. Tom is really Gabriel. Caden repeated these things in her head as the awkward seconds passed on. Tom still hadn't looked at her. He still hadn't said anything besides that he wanted his good-luck charm.

"Tom? Have you ever kissed anyone before?" It was a long shot, hoping her kiss with Gabriel had been memorable enough for Tom to remember. She figured she was the first girl they both knew and interacted with, and Tom was technically Gabriel. Maybe he felt the same way. A tingle traveled through her body from the thought of Gabriel's lips against hers. She pushed away the memory, trying to focus on Tom. But the silent Tom was hard to tell apart from his daytime counterpart.

Tom shot up from the bed, pushing her hands off his shoulders in frustration. "What are you talking about?"

"You know, a kiss?" Her throat tightened. What would happen if Tom kissed her? Part of her didn't want to know—it was too strange. Caden let out a deep sigh as her mind tried to figure out what to do, what she should do. "Look, Tom, this is going to sound weird, but if you want to kiss me… I'm okay with it, I guess. I mean, your first kiss should be with someone you trust." *Though I'm sure your other half has kissed dozens of girls.* The thought of Gabriel kissing someone else made Caden's stomach turn.

Tom's face wrinkled, and his eyes narrowed. "I don't know why I'd want to kiss you."

"And I don't know why you wouldn't," Caden snapped back. Something had changed. Tom wasn't the scared little boy he had been nights before. He was stronger, angrier, but then again, so was Gabriel. "I bet you don't even know what a kiss is." It sounded petty even to her.

Tom crossed his arms defensively over his chest. "Yeah, I know what a kiss is."

"Prove it."

"No."

"Fine, be that way." She didn't really want to kiss him anyway.

The stress in the room felt like a physical substance keeping her from breathing. All her emotional energy was spent. Her therapist years before had said that everyone reacted differently to stress. For her it was a combination of fatigue and muscle pains. She let herself plop down on Gabriel's bed. The sweet scent of him filled her lungs. He was everywhere. Caden felt a pang of guilt; what did Tom smell like? The same? Did he even have his own identity?

"What are you doing?" Tom asked.

Caden had already closed her eyes. "What does it look like?"

"But you just got here."

She didn't respond. Her mind drifted in and out, wondering what it would feel like to kiss Tom, wondering if she could figure everything out with Gabriel before school started.

"Maybe you should have kissed me," she said with a yawn. Her head sank farther into the pillow, the weight from her worries drifting off. She felt whole when she slept. The faintest touch skimmed her lips, and part of her wondered if it was Tom, but the thought vanished as sleep took over.

12

—Day—

A calming thump of a heartbeat pulsed through her ears and traveled through her body. The rhythmic pattern was soothing and constant, as was the warmth she clung on to. Her eyes began to open, irritated by the orange that teased her eyelids. A body lay next to her—Tom's or Gabriel's, she couldn't tell; they smelled the same. He looked peaceful lying beside her in his jeans and wrinkled T-shirt. She moved into him once more, wanting to enjoy his warmth, his touch, while it lasted.

Caden gripped Tom Gabriel more tightly. "Who are you?" she whispered. The idea of Tom lying beside her in the night was thrilling, and it made her body feel light with hope that Tom wasn't as far from Gabriel as he sometimes seemed. Though how Gabriel would react when he opened his eyes to find her beside him, she didn't want to find out. Most likely, he would add a few hundred dead bolts to the window. Caden let her hand drift over his chest, committing to memory his peacefulness beside her. *If only Tom and Gabriel were the same, things would be easier.* She looked down at his face, the sun illuminating his features, and she knew, like her, they were only *one* when they were fast asleep.

I wish I could stay, she thought as she leaned over to kiss his cheek. He groaned softly before turning over and going still once more. Caden's heart pounded a little faster knowing she needed to escape before Gabriel woke up. She gingerly rose from the bed. Leaning into the closet, she grabbed her shoes, and then she opened the window and placed them on the roof. Her body still felt heavy with sleep, and each movement was like a drunken attempt to be sober. She wasn't a morning person. The dawn light blinded her as the wind twisted its icy fingers into her knotted hair. By the looks of it, it had rained during the night. Caden crawled out of the window and onto the roof, put on her shoes, and closed the window behind her, leaving just the smallest crack at the bottom.

"I'll come back tonight," she whispered, and she carefully began her descent off the roof.

By the time Caden made it home, it was obvious her mom knew she had been gone overnight. For one, the window to her bedroom was locked. A little note taped on the outside of it, wrinkled from the rain, read: *You should know better. Don't make Pollyanna's mistake.*

Caden got back off the roof and went around to the front door. Another note was taped on the door: *Be back later, went shopping. Mom.*

Laura *would* do this. It was punishment.

Caden grunted with frustration as she got on her hands and knees to try and find the hidden key. There wasn't one under the mat or behind the garden's turtle statue. Did her mother think she had gone to see Gabriel? Or could she maybe pretend she had gone somewhere else?

An hour passed before Laura pulled up in the driveway.

"Help me with these?" she called out. As Caden walked toward her mother's car, the trunk popped open to reveal a dozen plastic bags.

A few other cars came up seconds later. There was Keira's blotchy purple Beetle gurgling and puffing smoke like a decrepit fat dragon, then a flashy BMW that belonged to Mrs. Dering, and pulling in last was Ms. Burby, a local schoolteacher. Her car looked even worse than Keira's; it was completely unrecognizable aside from being some kind of truck.

"Is it book-club day or something?" Caden asked as Laura passed her a bag of groceries.

"Yes," Laura whispered. "Unless you would rather it be an intervention?"

"Intervention for what?"

"For you. God only knows what you do when you sneak out at night."

"I don't do anything bad, Mom, plus I'm pretty sure interventions work better if you use the person's friends."

"Well, if you had any friends, I wouldn't have to use my own."

Caden huffed. It was definitely a book-club meeting. No one bought cheese dip for an intervention. Plus Laura didn't like other people thinking that her family wasn't perfect, and an intervention would let the cat out of the bag. Even after Caden's dad left with another woman, Laura insisted on telling everyone she had kicked him out. No one knew they had been left behind, and Caden didn't mind that. She did mind the front, though. Everything was always *just dandy* in the Worden household to the eyes of the public. It wasn't. Caden hadn't been doing well in school since the divorce, and Laura had gotten depressed and lost a lot of weight. It wasn't until the month before Caden left to live with Sean that Laura got back on track.

"Hey Rebecca!" Keira chirped. "I'm so glad to see you again."

Caden looked away, rolling her eyes.

"Be nice," Laura whispered, her tone sharp and demanding.

"Whatever you say, Mother." Caden turned back to Keira with a look that could turn people to stone. "So, Keira," Caden gritted the words through her teeth, "what have you been up to these past—I don't know—two days?" *Besides spying and playing kiss ass for my mom?* They began to walk toward the front door; Keira, not seeming to notice Caden carrying all the bags, clung to a single book.

199

"Well, you know we are meeting twice as often this summer. We've been reading two books a week. Your mom thinks it is a good idea to read as much as possible."

"Two books a week?" Caden asked while Keira nodded vigorously.

"That's why I was so excited you wanted to go to the library with me." Keira turned to Laura. "Mrs. Worden, I have some new suggestions for next week's reading."

"It's Miss Worden now, you know that, and I thought I told you to just call me Laura." Her mom walked into the house with a weary smile. "Caden, I'll expect you to stay with us for the book discussion."

"Who is Caden?" Keira wrinkled her nose in disgust.

"Oh, that would be Rebecca, she is changing her name."

"Really?" Keira looked at Caden with wide eyes then back at Laura. "You're letting her do that?"

Caden looked at her mother's back as they walked into the house. Laura shrugged. "Doesn't seem like I have much choice these days."

Keira took off in a little jog, leaving Caden's side to walk with Laura. They lowered their voices so Caden could only hear bits and pieces of them talking about her. Caden stayed to hold the door open for Mrs. Dering and Miss Burby. The ladies nodded their thanks, continuing their conversation and following Laura and Keira into the living room.

"Caden? Set everything up for us, will you? And meet us in

the living room," Laura instructed.

Caden let out a sigh, closed the front door, and hobbled into the kitchen with the overflowing bags of groceries in tow. Her hair was still in knots and her clothes were a mess from being slept in. All she could think of was seeing Tom again, and hopefully finding a way to get Gabriel to forgive her. She missed him.

Emptying the grocery bags, Caden grabbed the salami, cream cheese, and pepperoncinis. She pulled out the large serving dish and set it aside as she spread the softened cream cheese over a slice of salami and rolled it around a pepperoncini, pinning it with a toothpick. It didn't take long to stack them neatly on the dish until it was full. She placed the remaining cream cheese in a bowl, adding some sour cream and garlic. A can of artichoke hearts sat open in the fridge. She drained them, chopped them up, and added them to the creamy mixture. Last she grabbed a glass dish and filled it with crackers.

"Artichoke dip, crackers, and salami rolls. Does anyone need a drink?" Caden asked as she entered the living room with the tray held high.

"Oh, how delightful." Mrs. Dering clapped her hands together. "Oh, Laura, we should have your daughter cook for us all the time."

Laura nodded in agreement with Mrs. Dering. She looked equally surprised.

"Thanks," Caden said. What could she say? Keira had

probably already told everyone that she had found her with a strange boy. Everyone also probably knew that she had been missing before that to go live with Sean. Should she deny it or tell the truth? "My mother has just been so forgiving of my adventures, I thought I should do a little something for her." Caden attempted to keep her voice even and kind. If her mother decided she was antagonizing her, it would make her situation worse.

Laura shot Caden a glare as Mrs. Dering and Miss Burby exchanged a glance. *Made it worse, guess I should have lied.*

Caden continued in an attempt to make her mother happy. "I've been pretty irresponsible lately." Caden handed Mrs. Dering the dip and placed the platter of salami rolls on the table. "Growing up is harder than I thought it would be, and I've made some mistakes… But I'm trying to be a better daughter."

Miss Burby made an exaggerated pouty lip. "Oh, sweetie. You know I always tell my kids how hard it is to grow up, you just don't know until you have to go through it. You're lucky to have your mom." Miss Burby didn't have kids of her own, but she liked to refer to her students as her children. "Do you want to talk about it with us? I'm sure we can postpone the book club for a little heart-to-heart. I always think talking about problems is the best way to solve them."

No, no, no. "Really, my mom has already helped so much." Caden plastered on a sweet, uber-fake smile. An honest heart-to-heart would be a death sentence. Laura would kill her just to divert the gossip.

After an awkward silence Laura cleared her throat. "She's fine. Why don't you go start some tea, Miss Caden, and grab some waters?"

"Yes, Mother."

Once in the kitchen, Caden turned on the kettle and opened the fridge. The cool air hit her face as her eyes searched for something to eat. Her mom would snap again if she took too long, but she was starving. It seemed like her cooking had been put on hold since her mother found her. She needed to cook; it kept her calm, sane. Part of her wanted to find Gabriel, even if he yelled at her and locked her out again. He was better company than her mother. She grabbed a jar of pickles, olives, and some sliced ham. Closing the fridge, she glanced over her shoulder to see her mother walking toward her.

"What are you trying to do out there? Make me look bad?" her mother said in a low voice.

"What? Honestly, for once, no. What did you want me to do, Mom? Lie?"

"Yes. For all the years you have filled this house and my life with your lies, you couldn't do it for me now, in front of my friends? You may have lost your quiet streak, but you still know how to manipulate, just like your father."

"What? Like Dad? I don't do that." *I survive, I dig myself out of the holes your divorce has caused. You've ruined my life.*

"Yes, you do, and do you know how hard these last few weeks have been? Do you have any idea how difficult it is to keep it out of the gossip channel of Cloverdale? First you left to live with Sean, then Sean came over here all bloody. I'm sure Keira has already had a field day telling everyone about you and that boy, Tom Gabriel."

"Rrrrr. Mom, stop calling him that. It's just Gabriel. Plus, you should expect as much, making Keira your little lackey."

Laura shook her head. "I know, I swear I can't breathe—she's always calling and texting me. I almost wish I hadn't asked her to follow you, but you put me in a horrible predicament. Probably everyone in this small town already knows," Laura finished, crossing her arms.

"Knows what? I told you, *nothing happened*, Mom." *Didn't you care about the fact that I was gone? Homeless? Hitchhiking?*

"Really? Because when she called me it sounded pretty bad, Caden. He changed you, parading you in slutty outfits, hanging onto him in public, and who knows what you were doing in his room. I hope you're at least using protection."

"Shut up. Just shut up. You don't know what you're talking about. That little brat, Keira," Caden kicked at the trash can, which clanged. "Ugh. She's just a deceiving little bitch. She's spoon feeding you her bullshit, and you're eating it all up."

"Rebecca, keep your voice down. How the hell do I know you're telling the truth? You'll say whatever you need to say if it means staying out of trouble." Laura put a hand through her hair and let out a frustrated breath. "You're really making this hard, I have to work tonight and I'm afraid—I'm afraid that if I leave you, you'll do *who knows what* and show up on the news. Do you know how hard it was for me after your father left? I don't need this again. I won't let you take the rug out from under me when I've worked hard to make this life for us."

Caden closed her eyes, counting to three. *Stay calm.* "Why the heck do you care about what everyone else thinks? Even when it's not the truth? Especially when it's not the truth?" Her voice rang out as a sharp whisper in the quiet of the kitchen. Though they both had been keeping their voices down, Caden knew the women in the other room were probably straining to listen.

"I don't need to answer that, it's beside the point."

"Why? You haven't even noticed me since Dad left. You've been in your own little bubble and I've been alone." Caden could hear her voice rising out of the whisper. "Why do you think Dad left? It was *your fault* because you only care about what everyone else thinks."

"Take that back, young lady, or I'll make sure you never see that boy again." Laura's eyes bulged out of her face, red lines streaming through them, ready to pop. "Do you think I wanted to be left?" Laura gripped the countertop with both hands, lowering her head. "Go to your room."

"But Mom—"

"Don't. Go to your room and stay there. I'll be up when the company leaves."

"That's real mature, I make a point that you can't argue

205

against, so you send me away? You know why you can't stand the town knowing about anything that goes on in this house? It's because you can't bear to see the truth everywhere you go. Your *life* is a lie."

"REBECCA, GO."

Caden let out an exasperated sigh.

"I'm going," Caden grumbled as she got out a plate before heading back up the stairs to eat in her room.

In minutes the jar of olives was finished, and she had wrapped the pickle slices in the ham. She scribbled at a piece of loose-leaf paper as she bit into the rolled ham. Her hand glided across the page again and again. Caden cursed silently as she crushed the piece of paper in her fists and tossed it into the trash can on the far side of her room. She couldn't draw people. None of the attempts looked anything close to Tom or Gabriel.

Gabriel was leaving at the end of the summer. She would finish at the trade school and finally be done with high school. After all that, hopefully she would go to a culinary school to finish her training, but her thoughts kept going back to Gabriel.

After about an hour of drawing, Caden got up and glanced across the hallway. Reese's door was shut; a boy-band poster was haphazardly taped halfway up. Caden's mom loved "R" names, and when she became pregnant with Reese, she had a mad craving for Reese's Peanut Butter Cups. Her dad had used to say that the first time he held Reese, he'd joked about the name, and it stuck.

Caden walked across the hall and opened the door to Reese's room. Reese was spending her first summer with their dad, and she missed her. The princess-themed room was clean and organized for her return. Caden's eyes darted to a large spot on the floor. A stained heart lay in the middle.

"She wants to be just like you, you know?"

Caden turned to her mother walking up the stairs, the company having left for the evening.

"I cried so hard the day she dyed that heart into her carpet. I was thinking, 'Gosh, my little princess is going to go Goth and fall head over heels for horrible boys just because she wants to be like her big sister.'"

A lump formed in Caden's throat. So her mother's biggest fear was that Reese would turn into her. Was she really such a horrible person to be? It wasn't fair. She couldn't be held responsible for what Reese was doing. Caden closed the door to the room.

"Rebecca." Her mom's voice was hard and distant. "Maybe it would do you some good to move in with your dad when the summer is over."

"What? No, I'm not moving in with him and that...that tramp." Caden's voice echoed through the house.

"I don't like it any more than you do, but I need to think of what's best for Reese, and you're not a good role model."

"So you think you can just get rid of me?" Caden's hands formed into fists. "Why did you even come get me? I was happy. I was doing just fine."

Laura shook her head from side to side. "I'm sorry to mess that up for you, but you can't go living with—"

"Sorry? You aren't sorry. You only think about yourself. You're only 'sorry' that by me not living under your roof, the town has more to talk about. You're only 'sorry' that the only way you can avoid gossip after all the crap that has happened is to lock me away where no one will remember to talk about me."

"Look who's talking. Maybe if you thought about someone besides yourself, we wouldn't be in this mess. I mean, really, Rebecca, what is all of this?" Laura pushed past her to motion at the walls and ceiling of Caden's room. "What happened to my princess?" Her eyes trailed around once more before landing on the drawing of Tom. "You'll never learn, will you?" Laura shook her head. "I want you to stay up here, and don't you dare come out. Think about all the pain you have caused others."

"I don't want to stay up here." Caden's voice cracked as tears streamed down her face.

"You will. And while you're up here, think about how you would feel if Reese turned out like you. Disappearing and sleeping with boys who don't actually love her."

Caden's heart stung. She had only been with Sean, once, and he'd said he loved her. He had to have loved her, at least a little. At least at first. She took a step back, falling onto the bed as her mother slammed the bedroom door shut behind her.

"Really, Rebecca. Have I taught you nothing?" Laura yelled

through the door. Caden shut her eyes. "You have a lot to learn, young lady. These boys don't love you. They will use you up and leave you, all of them!" she yelled again.

Caden pushed her fingers in her ears, and sobs escaped her lips. How could her mother possibly know if Sean had ever loved her? She curled up on her bed and cried herself to sleep.

She dreamt she was Rebecca again. She could see herself curled in a ball in the middle of the forest, the moon shining down on her bare skin. The fear Rebecca felt lived in the air as she lay motionless amidst the wet grass. She could feel Tom's presence before she could see him approach from the trees. He knelt down beside Rebecca, oblivious to Caden watching from above.

"Why are you crying?" he whispered, but Rebecca didn't respond. Tom lay beside her, never touching her.

The fog rolled in, and when it cleared Rebecca hadn't moved but Tom was gone. Gabriel came in through the forest and stopped at Rebecca's body.

"I found you," he said, and he bent down to scoop her up in his hands. Caden watched from above as Rebecca's limp body bobbed back and forth in his arms. Then Gabriel looked up.

Caden's eyes snapped open, and she took in a breath of air as the dream dissipated. Gabriel's copper eyes grounded her; he had looked at her as if he'd known she was always there. Caden lifted her head off the tear-stained pillow and looked around. It was dark. "Tom," she breathed.

13

—Night—

Caden grabbed a coat before slipping out the window and running through the night air to Gabriel's condo. *With some luck*, she thought, *Tom will already be awake.* By the time she reached the condo, she was out of breath. She reached into her pocket to touch the pieces of butterfly wings. Their smooth surfaces slid together effortlessly.

She hadn't meant to lie to Tom about having his so-called good-luck charm, yet she couldn't bear to part with the butterfly wings, not when they were the only thing that both boys seemed to care about and want. The commonality had to be some sort of link that could lead to figuring it all out. Or at least that was her hope.

If Tom was awake, he would be locked away in his room again, and she didn't want to climb onto the pent roof every night she came to visit. Caden shook out her hands and grabbed on to a branch. The sting of the cold air in her lungs and the damp mist hovering over her skin propelled her up the tree.

"I hope I don't fall," Caden muttered as she pulled herself up and over each branch, heading toward the roof's ledge.

Once on the roof, Caden crawled on all fours, afraid of the slick surface. The full moon reflected a cool gleam across the wet pavement down below. Light shone brightly from the neighbor's window, and Caden moved down onto her stomach, using an army crawl to maneuver underneath. Peering into Tom's window at last, she could see him. His head rested in his hands as he sat at the edge of the bed.

Tap, tap, tap.

Tom looked up. She wondered how well he could see her in the dark with only the moon and the neighbor's window illuminating her silhouette. She imagined most visitors used the door, not that anyone would be visiting Tom.

"Caden!" Tom called out excitedly. He ran to the window. His voice sounded muffled through the glass, and the light that streamed in was enough to reveal his smile. She was surprised but pleased that he seemed happy to see her.

Open the window, she mouthed while motioning the action. Tom nodded, his hands gripping the window and pulling up. She watched the gap form as he repositioned his fingers and lifted. "Thanks," Caden said before turning around to take off her shoes, leaving them on the roof, and jumping through the window.

"You came back." Tom's hand found hers. She looked up at him, his broad shoulders, his thick neck, the line of his jaw. Gabriel's extremely kissable lips… *He isn't Gabriel*, she reminded herself.

"Of course I came back," Caden whispered before turning back around to close the window.

"So you wanna play a game?"

Caden's shoulders dropped. *A child within a man.* She pushed away the thought.

"What kind of game?" she asked, still unable to look directly at him. She could smell Gabriel again, the sweet comfort that drifted throughout the room. Her eyes glanced over his body, knowing Tom sat trapped inside. She sighed, "Or we could, I don't know, cuddle?"

Tom wrinkled up his face. "Cuddle? What kind of game is that?"

If Tom had been part Gabriel last night, Caden could tell that was gone today. "It isn't a game, Tom." The exasperation threaded through her voice and made it raw. "You just hold each other. It would be nice." She missed Gabriel, there was no denying it.

"But why?" Tom backed away from her.

"Come on, Tom, I know you cuddled me last night. I was in your arms—"

Tom shook his head, and Caden whirled around to face the other wall. She shouldn't be mad. It was Tom. She knew he was childish, but she wished he would grow up a little, or at least start to.

"Fine. We'll play a game." Her mind spun with possibilities. *Tom is Gabriel.* "If I win, we cuddle."

"What? That's stupid, what do I get if I win?"

Caden brought her finger to her lips and kept it there, thinking. "If I don't win, we keep playing till I do. That way you get to play more games."

"That's not fair." Tom tilted his head to the side as if he didn't quite understand. "But I do like playing games."

A numbing pain traveled through Caden as she looked at Tom. He would never understand.

By the fourth game, Caden was tired of losing, or at least tired of trying to figure out who won. Plus her legs were going numb from sitting cross-legged for so long.

She could feel herself sinking into a dark hole without air. Her mother's words circled her. *These boys don't love you. They will use you up and leave you, all of them.*

Tom wouldn't, Caden thought. *Tom won't leave me, but he'll also never love me the way Gabriel could.*

"Hey, you awake?" Tom flicked her in the knee.

"Ah, yeah." Caden shook the thoughts from her head. "New game." She twisted the ends of her hair, her teeth clamped painfully shut. Her stomach felt like a million cotton balls were stuffed inside of her.

Caden stood up and began to pace the room. *Tom can grow up; he just needs some incentive.* "Truth or dare." The words were out of her mouth before she could think twice about it.

"What's that?" Tom stood up too and put his hands in his pockets. His red shirt hugged his body in a way that revealed his toned chest.

Caden bit her lip to repress her want for him. Every part of her ached to run her hands down his chest and wrap her arms around him. *This is Tom, not Gabriel.*

"Never mind, Tom. We'll play something else."

"No, I wanna play that game."

"You won't like it."

"I wanna play Truth or Dare." His voice was on the edge of whining; she couldn't handle that.

"Okay, okay. I ask you truth or dare. You pick one, and I either ask you a question or tell you to do something." Tom nodded, his eyes wide. He loved new games. "But Tom? You have to do it. You pick it, and you have to either answer the truth or you have to do the dare. That's the game." She pointed at him and let her finger poke his toned chest as he nodded vigorously. "Now. Truth or dare?"

"Truth."

Caden relaxed a little. Giving Tom a push in the Gabriel direction was what she wanted, but it didn't mean it would be easy. "Do you like me, Tom, like really like me?" Her fingers knotted together in her lap, waiting.

"Yeah." Tom shrugged.

Caden raised an eyebrow. "Is that it?" Her stomach knotted. How could he just say *yeah*?

"I don't know. I have to say more for the game? Umm, yeah you're really nice."

"Nice? But, Tom, do you like me? Like, *like me* like me?" She knew it sounded stupid the moment it left her lips, but was there another word for it other than love? Love was down the road, not for tonight. It would take Tom time to understand the meaning of love, and it would probably take Gabriel years to admit anything close to it.

"I said, 'yeah.' Okay, truth or dare?"

Caden pulled at the ends of her hair, grunting with frustration. He didn't get it. He would never get it. "Dare."

"Okay. I dare you to run around the room howling like a monkey."

"Tom, that is so stupid." Caden pulled at her hair tighter. She really didn't want to play little-kid Truth or Dare; she wanted the PG-13 version.

"You have to do it, Caden. That's the game." He crossed his arms over his chest with a pouting lip.

"Fine." Caden let out a semi-monkey sound but didn't run around the room. Tom laughed, seemingly pleased with himself. "Okay, Tom. Truth or Dare."

"Dare."

Really? Caden bit her lip as her eyes trailed around the

room. She knew what she wanted to say, but she wasn't sure if it was ethical to ask him, with him being so childish in a super-hot teen body. *Technically he is almost nineteen...* "Okay. I dare you to kiss me." She'd said it, and the wide eyes and raised eyebrows on Tom were enough to make her bright red. In fact, the heat traveling up her face was proof of her flushing cheeks.

A few moments of silence passed in the room, but it felt like an hour to Caden. Tom just kept staring at her. His eyes darted from her eyes to her lips. He took a step forward. Caden ran a hand over her arm and looked away. She couldn't do it.

Tom got closer.

"Tom. Don't, it's okay, we don't... You don't have to..."

In that moment his warm lips were against hers. Caden's body tensed, but when he didn't pull away she got closer, her arms a little shaky and unsure as they wrapped around him. His hands were cupping her cheeks, holding her face against his. Every inch of her that touched him sent a chill down her spine.

When he pulled away, his dark eyes peered into hers, and for a moment she thought she could see a glint of copper. She wanted them both.

Her whole body tingled from the simple kiss. Their faces were still close, too close. His mouth hovered near hers, his breath stirring her hair.

"Again?" she whispered, and she waited a moment before

rising on tiptoe to let their lips brush. Tom's eyes swirled with copper as he pulled her against him.

Her heart leapt. She parted her lips lightly, and he followed. Each passing moment became more powerful as the kiss deepened. Tom's hands wrapped around her waist, a hunger in his touch as his tongue brushed hers. She gasped a little at the contact, at Tom's kiss, his kiss that was so similar to Gabriel's.

His hands loosened, and she took a step back to sit on the edge of the bed. Tom had kissed her.

He joined her on the bed, and their shoulders brushed as their heavy breathing filled the quiet room. An awkward tension hung between them as his eyes, eyes that should have been much darker, continued to search hers. When he turned toward her, he put his hand on her leg; it sent a heated tingle though her body. His eyes were almost like Gabriel's…

Sucking in a breath, Tom slid his hand up her thigh toward her hips. But then he stopped.

"Tom?"

His hand rested on the pocket, his fingers sliding back and forth. "What's in your pocket?"

Caden suddenly felt cold. Tom's eyes were dark again.

"Nothing's in my pocket."

"You're lying, Caden. It's in your pocket, isn't it? Let me see." He held out his hand, refusing to look her in the eyes. "Let me see it."

Her hands began to shake as she reached into her pocket, the smooth surface gliding between her fingers. "I'm sorry, Tom—"

"Give it to me!" he yelled. His face was red, his lips forming a hard line.

Her hand opened, and in her palm lay the piece of butterfly wing, broken in two. She looked down at it as the light from the moon streamed through the window, illuminating the veins that came to life like a dance.

Tom's fingers were shaking when he took them from the palm of her hand.

"Tom? What is it? What does it do?"

He let them rest in his palm for only a second before closing his fist around them. "You should go," Tom whispered.

"I—I don't want to go."

"I don't think you should come back." His eyes were focused on his closed palm.

Her mother's words ran through her mind. *Think about all the pain you have caused others.* "I need you, Tom." Caden wiped her cheek with the back of her hand, feeling the tears she hadn't realized were falling from her eyes. No matter how many times she wiped them away, more would appear. She felt like she was a child again. "I'm not leaving." Her hands were shaking. "What is that thing?"

"I don't have to tell you anything," Tom said, as the darkness of his eyes blazed with copper.

What is happening to him? "Please, tell me something. Maybe it will help me understand."

"Get out, Caden. Get out and don't come back."

Caden cupped her face in her hands and turned to climb out the window, her trails of tears turning icy in the night air.

14

Caden crawled back into her bedroom window as the rain began to fall. She'd just barely missed it. *At least one thing went my way*, she thought wryly. The warmth from her bedroom gave her goose bumps as she bent down to remove her shoes. Dirty footsteps marked her entrance. She cursed quietly, wishing she had thought to take her shoes off on the roof like she'd done at Gabriel's.

"Not much for learning, are you?" Laura stood in the threshold in neon blue scrubs and purple medical shoes. Caden wondered if she'd skipped work after realizing she wasn't in her room. "I hope it was worth it."

Caden glanced away. She could still feel Tom's kiss. She'd lost the butterfly wings. He'd found out she had lied to him. *No, it wasn't worth it,* Caden thought; she would have been better off staying home. Thunder cracked outside the window. "I'm sorry, Mom," Rebecca blurted. She collapsed to the floor in tears. Rebecca was back—weak, apologetic Rebecca.

The pounding of rain began to hit the roof in a rhythmic song, playing along with the patter of Caden's tears hitting the carpet, taunting the storm inside of her. "Mom, I'm so sorry." The tears continued as Caden felt herself disappear, losing her grasp on reality, losing herself in the storm. She wasn't sorry, not at all; she just wanted Laura to leave.

"Oh, honey." Laura came to her, nearly crumbling on the floor beside her, stroking her dark, knotted hair while making soothing noises beside her ear. "Tell me what happened?"

For a moment, Caden felt the air in her lungs vanish as Rebecca took over. "He doesn't understand, Mom; he doesn't understand me. He doesn't want me."

That isn't true, Caden whispered, though the words didn't break past her lips. *Well, maybe it's a little true*, she amended. She fought the deep, dreamy fog around her. Rebecca's weakness was smothering her, and so was Laura. "Let go!" she screamed. The room went silent, the tears vanishing.

"What has happened to you?" Laura's eyes were large and glossy.

Caden thought back to a time before the divorce, when her family was whole. Back then, Rebecca had been quiet and polite. Though as the divorce developed, she slowly slipped away. Life became void of color, and she began spending her free time drawing dark pictures as an escape. Then Sean had found her. He'd made everything worse.

Maybe if her dad hadn't left, her mother would have noticed the small changes in Rebecca. Maybe she could have stopped them. Caden had come around when no one else was there to help. After all, Caden was just the side of Rebecca that wasn't afraid to be strong, flawed, and self-serving.

"What happened to *me*?" Caden could feel the fog drift away as she pushed Rebecca back down inside of her. "You never noticed *me*. You never heard Rebecca crying, you never noticed the bruises Sean gave her. He was the only one who would give her the time of day, the only person who saw her. But that ass, he didn't *see* her, he was breaking her. He was finding me. He was finding Caden." Caden looked across the room; the window was open. She thought she had closed it. "He made me this way. He left Rebecca empty, and I took her place."

Her feet lifted her off the floor and carried her away from Laura. She broke into a run for the open window. Caden's hand grabbed the windowsill and pushed her body up and over the ledge. The rain fell quick and relentless, weighing her down. Her feet could feel the sandpaper texture of the roof as she ran across it and jumped.

Moist dirt encircled her fingers as her hands sunk into the soil. *Now what?* No Tom, no Gabriel, no mother, no father, no friends. Sean's face flashed in her thoughts. She pushed it away. "No Rebecca, no more Sean!" she yelled into the rain.

Water seeped into Caden's mouth as she ran through the storm, the pale moonlight venturing behind the clouds and back out again. It couldn't rain any harder; in the morning, the news would call it the worst rainstorm all season. Thunder shook the sky as lightning split through the darkness ahead. Caden didn't know where she was going. The water ricocheted against the road as her bare feet scraped against pebbles. The small town ahead wouldn't provide much shelter, but she knew the bookstore had an awning that could cover a small group of people. There was that, or the café across from it that had an outdoor seating arrangement, though she would need to jump the small fence in front of it. Caden kicked at a puddle, the splash disappearing in the mess of rain. She wished she had shoes.

Honking filled the air as headlights blinded her. It wasn't her mother. No, her mother would have been coming up behind her; this car was coming toward her. It slowed as it approached. The black car shone in the light of the moon, rain hammering off its roof.

"Caden? Hey, Caden. My Lucky Charms, it's me. Face." Caden squinted into the black shadows of the car. His chiseled chin was hardly noticeable through the dark, and a figure sat next to him, unmoving. A shiver of cold passed through her as he turned on the overhead light in the car. Angelica was glaring at her from the driver's seat while Face leaned over her breasts, seemingly oblivious, to get closer to the window. "What are you doing out here?"

"Does it matter?" The slap of her words mirrored the crack of lightning. The warm light in their car called to her. "I mean, I'm out in the rain. Whatever way you look at it, the reason can't be any good."

"Fair enough." He nodded. "You need a ride?"

Caden shook her head no. She had been through this once before. "Not if you intend to drop me off." The moon disappeared back behind the clouds, thunder shaking the ground beneath her bare feet. "I have nowhere to go."

Angelica looked away from her toward Face. The air carried the bite in her tone as she whispered to him. The path of the road curved down before coming to a hill that Caden didn't want to climb. Then again, she thought she would climb it if it meant not dealing with Angelica.

"Well?" Caden yelled through the rain. As much as she wanted to sit around waiting for an answer, the sooner she started up the hill, the better. Angelica looked straight ahead, her face blank and unmoving.

"You can stay with me. Get in!" Face yelled. He got out of the car, his coat pulled up over his head.

"What are you doing?" Caden asked him.

"He's opening your door, you idiot," Angelica snapped. "Get in."

Face opened the back door and motioned with a hand to Caden. "Anything for you, Lucky Charms." The grin on his face caught the rain, and he readjusted his coat.

Caden smiled, rolling her eyes. "Thanks," she breathed as she got in.

Angelica whirled around in her seat. "If you ruin my heated seats, I'm so going to make sure you pay for it."

Yes, this situation was all too familiar. Caden shrugged. "I don't have any money, you'll just have to kill me and use my skin to reupholster them."

A demonic grin spread across Angelica's lips.

Face came around the car and climbed into it. "Whooeee, that shit is *cold.*" He began to vigorously rub his hands together in order to get the heat flowing back through his fingers. "What the heck are you smiling about, Angel?"

She shrugged. "Caden said I could use her skin to reupholster my seats. I think I'm going to take her up on it."

"Way to take one for the team, Lucky Charms." He winked at Caden before turning back to Angelica. "Take us away, El Capitan."

—Day—

"Wake up." Caden nudged Angelica with her arm.

Caden had slept on the floor that night, in Face's T-shirt and a pair of pajama pants from Angelica. They had gotten in around four in the morning. She had slept restlessly for a few hours before her growling stomach woke her up. Face and Angelica lived in an old brick house in town, one of the few that was down by the shops and not up on a hill.

That morning, she had wandered into the kitchen to find an older woman with a newspaper and cup of coffee. Caden had to admit the woman was rather calm about seeing a stranger in her home. The woman, Cassandra, was Nikolai and Angelica's mother, and she stated that she did not know a "Face."

When Caden offered to make Cassandra and her kids breakfast, the woman eyed her suspiciously as she sipped her coffee, but she consented to the offer. It resulted in a slightly awkward hour of Caden asking Cassandra what she could and couldn't use in the kitchen as she performed her prep work. The contents of the little kitchen only allowed for one kind of breakfast. She had taken the eggs, butter, and a lemon off the table, adding a pinch of cayenne and a sprinkle of salt.

Cassandra watched her over the edge of her newspaper as Caden created a homemade double boiler. She whisked the egg yolks together while making crepes with the milk, eggs, and flour. Eventually Cassandra offered to help. She minced the ham and cooked it with garlic as instructed. Then Cassandra broke the ends off the asparagus and tossed them in a pan with oil for Caden to take over. A thick, heavenly scent filled the air as Caden whisked and flipped and stirred.

It was all ready now. Cassandra told Caden she would wake up Nikolai if Caden just wanted to wake up Angelica. Caden wanted to switch places, but she felt a sort of respect toward the woman for having never asked her where she'd come from or who she was. It felt right being in their home.

"Wake up." Caden nudged Angelica again. "Breakfast."

"Breakfast?" Angelica wiped at her face, her hair a mess. "What time is it?"

"Early, but Nikolai is going to eat it all if you don't get up."

"Nikolai? Who told you... Mom? She's home?" Angelica pushed the covers off, bounding past Caden into the kitchen. When Caden walked in, Angelica had her arms around Cassandra's neck, holding her tight. Face was already sitting in his seat, half of the breakfast on his plate gone.

Caden sighed; she would never understand large-bite takers. "Hey, Nikolai." She grinned, punching his shoulder.

"Morning, Lucky Charms." Food peeked out from the corner of his mouth as he smiled.

"Lucky Charms?" Cassandra lifted a brow. "The chef is named after the cereal with marshmallows? Come now, Nikolai, surely you can give a pretty young girl a better nickname, something with 'chef' in it."

"Thanks, Cassandra. It's fine really, names don't really matter to me." Caden took a seat between Nikolai and Angelica. *As long as it isn't Rebecca,* she thought.

"This is delicious. Who would have thought ham-and-asparagus crepes could taste so good? And the homemade hollandaise sauce is wonderful. Do you have a job as a chef yet?" Cassandra asked, taking another mouthful and covering her mouth so she could continue eating. "I think there is a job

227

opening down the street for anyone who can make something this good in a kitchen that has nothing." She looked happy and maybe even a little proud, like Caden was one of her own. "What is your name anyway, hon?"

"Caden. It's Caden."

"What a lovely name."

"Thanks."

"Yeah." Nikolai smiled. "Real lovely." He wiggled his eyebrows as Angelica tossed a napkin at his face.

"Give it a break," Angelica's firm voice ordered. Caden looked at Angelica, expecting to see the acidic tone matched with a horrible glare, but Angelica looked happy. They were all grinning. "Mom?" Angelica turned back to Cassandra. "What time did your flight get in? I thought you weren't coming home 'til late tonight."

"I got a redeye flight because I wanted to see you, sweetie." She rubbed the side of her daughter's cheek with her thumb. "Plus, I'm glad I did or I would have missed this fantastic breakfast Caden made. However, I do remember telling you kids not to bring strangers over. After what happened last year..." Cassandra shook her head as she dabbed at her lips with the corner of her napkin. "We will talk about it later, and you're lucky Caden is so charming or you would be in even more trouble." Cassandra turned toward Caden. "I hope you'll be staying with us for dinner. I'll get you anything you want from the store."

"I'd love to." *Food is a magical thing*, Caden thought. "Anyone want seconds?" Hands flew up.

When they finished eating and cleaning, Cassandra sat down with a fresh cup of coffee and patted the seat beside her, gesturing to Caden. Dark wood floors and warm cream walls surrounded Cassandra, who sat on the edge of an old teal couch nestled into a corner. Sunlight poured in through the window as steam from Cassandra's coffee danced in the air. Specks of dust hovered like dull glitter as Caden made her way over from the kitchen.

"Thank you for taking me in, Cassandra."

Cassandra nodded as she took another sip. "You're too kind. Really it was my children who took you in, I just didn't kick you out." She chuckled to herself.

Caden leaned back, sinking into the throw pillows that looked like they had been made from old floral curtains. Cassandra's arms moved forward to help cradle the rocking liquid in her cup.

"Sorry." Caden's cheeks reddened, wondering how the mood would have changed if she had spilled Cassandra's coffee on the teal couch.

"Honestly you'd probably be doing me a favor, I need a new couch. Just can't seem to part with the old thing." She smiled as her wrinkles broadened across her face. She wasn't horribly old, just old enough for the first signs of aging: the crows' feet and the laugh lines. "What brings you here, Caden?" She tilted her head ever so slightly to the side, as if she could see it written across Caden's face.

Caden shifted uncomfortably on the couch but didn't reply.

"I see," Cassandra said, looking back at her coffee. "Family trouble and boy trouble?"

Caden looked up at Cassandra, her throat dry. Was it really written that clearly on her face? Caden opened her mouth to speak, but the words wouldn't come.

Cassandra looked up from her coffee mug. "Oh, don't look at me like that. I've been there, I can tell. It hasn't always been sunshine and rainbows in this house, and I have a teenage girl; I know the look of boy trouble."

Caden opened and closed her mouth, unsure of what to say. She hadn't thought she was alone in her problems. Well, maybe she did *feel* alone. It didn't seem like others had as much to worry about—they didn't have a crush on a guy with two personalities. They didn't have a mother who could only love the safe, easily managed, quiet girl. She needed a mother who could love her even through change.

"How did you—"

Cassandra waved a hand in the air. "Oh, sweetie, I'm a mother. I can't say I've been a perfect one but I've been there, we all have." She tapped her finger against the ceramic mug. "Would you like some coffee?"

Caden nodded. "Yes, please." She didn't like coffee, but the burn of hot liquid in her throat sounded soothing.

"Angelica, sweetie, will you get Caden some coffee and

bring over the cream and sugar?"

"Yes, Mom," Caden heard Angelica reply from her bedroom.

"Well, would you like to hear our story? Maybe then you won't feel so bad."

Caden nodded. Angelica was walking toward her with a mug adorned with colorful little cats dancing up the side. A delicate ring filled the air as Angelica placed the dish of sugar on the table and followed it with the cup of coffee and a small carton of milk.

"Thank you, Angelica," Cassandra said.

Angelica kissed her mom on the cheek. "You're welcome, Mom; we missed you."

"I missed you too, honey."

Caden grimaced. *What is it with Angelica? How the hell can she be such a slutty bitch but still be a mama's girl? God, I hate her.*

Cassandra turned back to Caden. "Where were we? Ah, yes, about five years ago, I was married. I'm not anymore, see?" Cassandra wiggled her ring finger, then held it out in front of her as if admiring a beautiful, invisible wedding ring. "Anyway, it didn't work out. Sometimes they don't, sometimes they do. Mitch and I, we wanted different things." She paused and motioned toward Caden's mug. "Drink your coffee, it will get cold."

Caden nodded, taking the cat mug and pressing the hot ceramic to her lips. The dark liquid sloshed back and forth as she brought it to her mouth, slurping it through her teeth. The

231

bitter taste stuck to her tongue unforgivably. "I need sugar," she coughed. Cassandra leaned over and passed her the sugar bowl.

"So Mitch and I split up, but the divorce was terrible. I couldn't eat, couldn't sleep. A few friends around town... some friends—" Cassandra scoffed, "—told me he had another woman in his life. I was mad, jealous, and still in love with him." She shook her head and took another sip of her coffee as she looked out into the distance. "But while I was fighting my own battle for self-worth and trying to figure out how I would support the children, my children were having a difficult time." She paused. "They never liked each other, you know? They've only recently become inseparable."

Caden looked to the open bedroom doors, expecting to see the siblings. "Really?"

She nodded. "Yes, but they didn't support one another during the divorce. Everyone took sides. No one could smile. I slept the days away in depression, might have drank a little too much, too."

"What changed?" Caden took another sip of her coffee. The cream and sugar helped with the bitterness.

"Well, things take time. I just realized that I should live for what I have and not what I lost. I went back to college and got a marketing degree, and now I work with an advertising firm. Aside from the business trips, it's fun and it gave my family this home. In fact now that I think of it, the only thing really left from our old life is this couch." Cassandra looked at it as if the teal cushioning was an admired companion. She stroked the armrest. "I need a new couch," Cassandra murmured to herself. Finally she seemed to realize her wandering thoughts and looked back up at Caden. "I just had to accept the change and learn to adapt. We can all adapt."

"Maybe." Caden looked down into the swirling coffee.

"You can; trust me, honey. All your problems, they will get better. Wounds will heal. There might be scars, but they will heal." She leaned over to pat Caden's shoulder. "Until they do, you are welcome to stay as long as you like. It will get better. Just learn to accept change and be open to possibilities. Oh, and as for boy problems, Angelica has had her share. I'm sure the two of you will have lots to talk about." Cassandra got up off the couch. "I need to get ready for work."

"Cassandra?"

"Yes, sweetie?"

Caden twisted the ends of her hair; she didn't know what to say to Cassandra. The only thing that came to mind was, "You don't happen to have a computer I could use, do you?"

15

Angelica pulled up a chair, placing Caden's clothes from the night before on the side of the desk. The clothes had just come out of the dryer, and Caden could feel the heat radiate from them and drift into the air. As much as she wanted to grab them and put them back on, she continued to scroll down the images on the Web page. She had searched *iridescent butterflies* hoping to find a match to the butterfly wings Tom had, but so far nothing was an exact match.

"You have a thing for butterflies? I thought you said you kicked me off the computer for an emergency?"

"Angelica—" Caden stopped scrolling through the images and turned to face her. Her short bronze hair was pulled back in a ponytail, and her bangs were pinned to the side of her face. Her dark eyelashes looked long and soft, and her skin glistened with perfection. Caden wondered what *she* looked like; she hadn't looked into a mirror for a while. She shook the thoughts away before starting again. "Angelica," she repeated, clearing her throat. "What do you know about Gabriel?"

"Besides that he is a total dick?"

"Watch your mouth, you dirty, dirty girl." Nikolai passed with a grin as he carried a large basket of clean laundry to another room.

Caden turned to watch him go. "And why didn't you tell me your name was Nikolai? Why Face?"

"Everyone loves the face," he yelled back.

Angelica shook her head, smiling. "He has trust issues. Likes to keep people at a distance until he knows them better. Plus we go to a lot of parties. It's easier if people don't know us." Angelica looked down at her hands.

"But you used your real name?"

"Yeah, because Gabriel already knew it. I trust him, or…I used to."

Caden nodded and put her hand in her pocket. She could feel the uncertainty creeping back into her; she could feel Rebecca on the edge of breaking free. "What happened?" Caden's fingers stopped searching when she remembered the broken butterfly wing was no longer in her pocket.

"Well, like I said—" she glanced at the door Nikolai had disappeared through, then she turned and whispered. "He's an ass. I don't know. He was one way one minute, and like another person the next. I'm sorry I was mean to you at the party, by the way." She sighed, leaning back into the chair.

"That's okay." Caden shrugged. It wasn't okay; she still felt uneasy around Angelica, and she probably always would. *I hate her, I hate her, I hate her.* Rebecca's words echoed through Caden's mind, distracting her.

"My mom had just been gone for a week, which is the longest yet, and I hate when my brother hits on girls. No offense, but he always picks losers. Plus you were staying with Gabriel. Kind of a double negative."

I'm not a loser, Rebecca argued. Caden squirmed in her seat. "You aren't over him?"

"Over him? How could I be? Talk about an amazing body. And have you ever seen copper eyes like that? They aren't brown; they are like seriously copper or maybe even gold. Gosh, I could look into his eyes all day." Angelica looked up at the ceiling and bit back the smile covering her face.

Ugh. She's probably daydreaming about him. A deep growl hummed through her head. She ignored it, pulling at the ends of her long black hair nervously. She could feel the bite of jealousy emanating from all parts of herself; it was as if her skin was stretching feverishly tight across her face. "What happened?"

"Long story short? I don't know. He had, like, these insane meltdowns, like all the time. No, I'm not even kidding. All the freakin' time. He would cry at night and act like I was some kind of disease. I mean, I'm practically naked in his bed and he shies away from me like I'm a monster. What is up with that? Who does that?"

Caden grimaced. *Practically naked?* Her gut twisted. The

fog inside of her thickened, and Rebecca clawed at her to get out, not wanting to hear any more. Rebecca would never let the things that traveled through her thoughts out in the open. Rebecca would take over just to hide behind fake apologies and pretend it was okay. "What did you do?"

"Nothing, at first, but it happened again. I woke up with him hiding in the corner. I tried to talk to him but—" she paused, "—he lied and said he didn't know me. We broke up a week later and he moved back home. I didn't see him again until the party and you were there."

"I'm sorry," Rebecca chimed. *That he likes me better,* Caden retorted. She squeezed her eyes shut, concentrating on the rising current inside of her.

"It's okay. I'm over it. Well, almost." Angelica grinned. "So what's up with the life-or-death butterfly?"

"Nothing," Rebecca answered. Caden pushed her aside and took over once again. "Have you seen it before? At Gabriel's?" she asked, feeling Rebecca dissipate along with her unease.

"A butterfly?" Angelica tapped her chin as she looked at the butterflies on the screen. "I don't think so. Why?"

"No reason," Caden and Rebecca responded simultaneously. The echo bounced in Caden's ears as she kept a straight face. If one thing hadn't changed, it was that Caden didn't want company when it came to solving problems.

"Well, I'll leave you to it." Angelica eyed her warily and got up to leave. "Let me know if you need anything. Actually...feel free to bother my brother."

Nodding, Caden turned back toward the screen of the computer. Her mind was already elsewhere. Hours passed before she found a drawing; the image looked to be scanned from a book, with a bit of text peeking out from the side. She leaned closer to the screen. The curve of the wings delicately brought the eye toward the body of the butterfly. The artist hadn't been able to render the iridescence, improvising with a chunky scribble of blues and purples, mixed with gaps to portray the transparent quality. Though she could see similarities, she knew it couldn't be a match. Tom's butterfly had thin orange veins. Caden scrolled down to the bottom of the page, frustrated.

She leaned back in the chair. It bothered her that she hadn't found anything in all the time she'd spent searching, but it didn't stop her from wanting to find out more. She wasn't ready to give up just yet. Part of her thought that if she could get the wings from Tom, she would have an easier time finding information on the butterfly.

"Hey, Face?" Caden yelled, still looking at the computer screen. "I mean Nikolai."

Nikolai came out of the doorway, dripping wet, a towel around his waist. "You called?"

He really is handsome, Caden thought. *He could call himself Body instead of Face and get away with it.* She quickly looked back to the computer. "Can you drop me off at the library and pick me up sometime around five o'clock?"

Caden lifted one hand to shield her face from the glare of the sun. Her other hand waved overenthusiastically at Nikolai as he pulled away from the library entrance. The library was just a cover for her real goal, finding Gabriel. It was a few miles away from his condo.

Her feet moved forward into the woods behind the library. The fight to stay Caden took more energy as Gabriel flashed in her thoughts. Rebecca had it all wrong; they weren't going to make friends, they were going to find the butterfly wings. It made her stomach twist. A huge part of her wanted to see Gabriel, though whether it was Rebecca or Caden who was driving the desire, she couldn't tell.

Nearly an hour had passed before Caden reached the condominium. The walk was a blur of green and a fight to be in control once again. By the time Caden could see clearly, the desperate, pathetic Rebecca part of her had already weaved through the paths of the condos and knocked on door twenty-five. The pain of digging her nails into the palm of her hand kept her focused as she waited.

Caden wanted to get inside. Her body felt magnetically drawn to Gabriel; it was almost painful. *No, only Rebecca needs a man in her life, not me. I'm not here for Gabriel, I'm not.* Something had changed when the butterfly wings had sat in her pocket; they were her one power over the boy she was falling hard for, but they were also hope. She craved the feeling of holding on to something tangible, something she felt could maybe change their outcome and make them one person instead of two. Unease squirmed inside of her. The Rebecca part of her needed to see Gabriel like a child wanted a toy. The feeling crushed her, as if without him her bones would bend inward, creating a cage to trap her. It had been one of the reasons Caden came around in the first place; Rebecca couldn't handle men. Sean had done the same thing to her. He had been the cause of her desperation, of her need to be needed. It clawed at her insides and made her want to pull out her hair. Caden shook away the yearning inside her. It was Rebecca's problem, not hers.

The door opened. Gabriel crossed his arms as his body relaxed against the now-open door. "What do you want?" His voice was quieter than she would have expected. His hair was a mess, sticking up strangely in all directions. His pajama pants hung loosely around his hips. His chest was bare. Caden gulped. Was it shirtless-guy day?

"I wanted to see you," Rebecca whispered. Gabriel took a step back, ready to close the door, but Caden took control, putting out her arm to stop it. "I want to see *you*, Gabriel. Let me in." *I need to find that butterfly wing; I need to understand what it does to you.*

"Sure you aren't here to see Tom? Because he only comes

out at night." The sarcasm in his voice thickened the air, making it hard to breathe.

Rebecca receded inside of her, and it made Caden feel stronger, no longer having to fight her. "It isn't night, I'm here to see you. Kick me out the second it gets dark."

Gabriel scoffed before leaving the door. Caden stepped inside.

"So, now what?" Gabriel asked as he flopped down on the couch.

Her eyes drifted around the condo. Everything seemed to be in place. The papers that were once on the floor were gone, the table and chairs sat upright. The kitchen sparkled. Had she imagined the whole thing? Her eyes traveled over the couch to look at Gabriel, his face set into a deep frown. Where would Tom hide the butterfly wings? Probably in his room since Gabriel locked him in every night. She'd have to sneak in again and hope he wasn't home; she would need to get out of there before he went to sleep and Tom woke up again. Or maybe he would let her in, if he trusted her.

"It isn't raining."

"So." Gabriel shrugged.

"So, want to go to the park?"

Gabriel stared at her calculatingly. Silent seconds passed as their eyes stayed locked on one another.

"I'm bored anyway." He slapped the side of the couch. "Make yourself at home, we'll leave in five." Caden watched as he got up and headed to his bedroom, closing the door behind him. Her shoulders relaxed until she heard Gabriel's door open once more. His voice carried well through the small condo. "Change into some of your other clothes, would you? You're killing me in all that black. They're in the bathroom where you left them." The door closed again.

After a few minutes he knocked on the bathroom door. "Ready to go?"

Caden ran her fingers through her hair, giving herself one last glance in the mirror before she opened the door. "I'm ready." A thin teal T-shirt clung to her body tightly, stopping an inch before her pale blue skirt started, and her toes felt cold as she wiggled them in the air, free aside from the sandal straps. The sun was out, but it wasn't a warm day. She wrapped her arms around herself as they headed for the door.

Gabriel placed his hands in his pockets and glanced at Caden as they walked toward the park. He hadn't wanted to let her into the condo so easily, but it was better than him coming after her. Plus she had a point; Tom, whoever he was, didn't come out in the day. That could only mean she was telling the truth. She wanted to see him.

They walked a good distance before the park came into view. The swing set swayed in the light breeze, not a child in sight. They hadn't spoken since leaving the condo, and Gabriel's mouth felt dry from the anticipation of who would talk first.

Still, it wasn't an uncomfortable silence; it was pleasant.

There was so much that had been left unsaid, unmentioned, like the kiss at Joe's Coffee Shop. *God, I want to kiss you again. I want to hold you against me.* His hands turned into fists as he thought of that night; part of him hated her for it, for calling him Tom. He hated how she made him feel, and he hated how easy it was for her to hurt him.

Gabriel stopped as Caden walked on toward the swings and sat down. Her feet held her in place as she rocked back and forth. The edge of her skirt crinkled against the swing's chain, revealing more of her legs. Gabriel rocked back on his heels before following and taking a seat beside her.

"I missed you," Caden said, wincing a second later. She squeezed her eyes shut and let out a long breath.

"Where did that come from?" It completely threw him off when she did it, acted small and needy. Those actions didn't fit the girl he knew.

Caden giggled nervously. "Sorry, what I mean is—it's nice just being here with you." Her long, silky black hair fell in front of her face, and she pushed it back.

His fingers ached to touch her.

"Yeah, well…" He trailed off, looking straight ahead. He hadn't seen her for nearly two days. It was driving him crazy wondering where she was staying, who she was staying with. A knot in his stomach twisted when her ex came to mind. "Where have you been, anyway?"

"You know, just around." Her eyes wandered away from him, as if she felt guilty.

"I thought you said you didn't have anywhere to go?"

"I don't."

"What changed?"

"Nothing, really." She looked away from him again.

Part of him felt like she was hinting that he should already know. For the millionth time he wondered what had happened that night when he woke up in the forest. He still couldn't remember how he got there. "Tell me you didn't go back to that jerk." Gabriel kicked at the sand before turning to her, his swing rocking him gently. She didn't say anything. "Caden?"

"I didn't. I haven't even seen him since he hit that tree."

Gabriel let out a small laugh, surprising himself. He could still picture the car swerving at the last moment and freeing them from his grasp.

"So where are you staying?"

"Some friends."

"Oh? I thought you didn't have any?"

"I made some," she snapped back. "I *am* a likable person." Her face reddened as if she didn't actually believe it. "What about you? What have you been doing?"

He could tell by Caden's expression that she too felt as if it had been a lifetime since they last saw each other. The kiss they shared that night seemed to have left some kind of energy between them. He remembered playing with magnets as a child and how holding the two correct ends together would make them stick; they were drawn together. Holding the two wrong ends together would only make the pieces repel each other. That was how he felt about Caden; their attraction depended on who they were at the time, but it seemed like it was impossible to really know who she—or he for that matter—was at any given time.

What have I been doing? Thinking about why I'm such an ass when you're around. "I don't know." He licked his dry lips and reached for her hand. In his peripheral vision he could see her glance over, surprised. Their bodies lightly swayed in their separate swings, their hands dangling between them. He gave her hand a quick squeeze before remembering his dream the night before and letting it drop. "I dreamt about you."

Caden swallowed hard. "I hope that isn't a bad thing." Her voice was even and steady, but there was a soft hum that sounded foreign; the lack of sarcasm made her seem like a different person.

He shook his head, smiling. "We were in my bedroom. Kissing." *I wanted you. Damn it, I wanted all of you. I was so close. It felt real.* He attempted to smirk carelessly but didn't continue. Part of him felt empty inside, as if that dream had robbed him of the one thing he truly wanted: Caden.

Caden opened her mouth and closed it again. She seemed shocked. Embarrassed? Her hands cupped her cheeks as they grew rosy. Gabriel put a hand on her back, afraid she might stop breathing and have some kind of panic attack. "What the hell is wrong? Don't worry." When she still didn't say anything, he continued. "I liked it." Gabriel added the last part in case she thought of the dream as something he couldn't like, which would make him question her overall sanity. How could he not?

Caden closed her eyes, and he could see little pools of tears spilling from the sides.

Shit, what did I do wrong now? He turned forward again in an attempt to pretend that he didn't see her crying and then cleared his throat. "Will you come by tomorrow?"

She opened her eyes and quickly turned to face him, but the look on her face was strange, as if she didn't really believe what she was seeing. Gabriel looked away, regretting his words, but then she sniffled loudly. When he looked up at her, her lips were tightly pulled into a smile-grimace, and her eyebrows knitted together in an expression that he couldn't read.

She opened her mouth and paused long enough that Gabriel thought she wouldn't say anything, but then she spoke. "Okay."

16

Bye," Caden said as she parted ways with Gabriel. He had been kind, more than kind.

Who was he? She couldn't deny that his two sides had messed with her head and her heart. Guilt for kissing Tom thrummed through her body; it felt sour and toxic inside of her. He'd remembered. Did that mean she'd really kissed Gabriel?

At the line of trees, Caden collapsed into the grass and twigs. She felt weakness settle into her, as well as the desire to succumb to it. She could feel herself reaching for Rebecca, the timid girl who could pretend none of it mattered.

Gabriel had spoken with such sweetness, and he had held her hand the way Tom had… But when she had looked into his eyes they'd been copper, not brown.

Caden curled into a ball on the ground and cried. She had gotten used to blaming Rebecca, and now she wanted to blame her again but she couldn't feel her.

"Everything is so messed up," Caden groaned. The heat on

her face dissipated into the cold ground as she closed her eyes and counted to three. Nothing changed. There was still no Rebecca. Caden let the realization set in. She hadn't really thought Rebecca was a different person from Caden, but she also hadn't wanted to taint her new image with the insecurities Rebecca lived with. When she opened an eye, the vastness of her surroundings settled in. *It's just me; I have to deal with this alone without blaming Rebecca. Rebecca isn't real.* Hot tears trailed down her face. Caden felt like the realization of this was going to make everything else that much harder to bear.

—Night—

Cassandra didn't mind a late dinner, so when Caden finished cooking at 8:00 p.m., they all sat down for a meal. Cassandra had insisted on helping, all the while begging Caden to teach her some of her cooking tricks. While the chicken roasted, Caden had taught her how to properly cut vegetables. She told her how in school they told them overseasoning is always better than underseasoning. When they were all sitting, Caden placed the prepared dishes in front of each of them: honey-glazed carrots, garlic-stuffed chicken, hummus mashed potatoes, and Caden's homemade gravy full of spices. She felt a little calmer now, though part of her kept searching for Rebecca.

After they ate, Nikolai insisted on doing the dishes and Caden stayed behind to help as Cassandra and Angelica went into the other room to catch up on the week they'd missed together.

"Must be nice," Caden said, handing a plate over to Nikolai.

"What's that, Lucky Charms?"

"You know, to have such a nice mom. To be…wanted, I guess." Caden could feel the uncertainty of Rebecca in her voice, but she didn't fight it; it felt right, like it was the right level of sincerity she wanted to convey. She reminded herself it wasn't Rebecca, and that Caden didn't need to be right, or perfect, or strong all the time.

"Eh, it wasn't always so easy."

"I know, she told me about the divorce and stuff."

Nikolai grabbed the plates and turned on the water. "Talking about it and experiencing it are different. She wasn't always the perfect mother she seems to be. Still isn't if you ask me, but we all make mistakes. It's how we forgive them that defines us."

Caden scoffed. "Deep. Real deep, Nikolai."

"What?" He grinned, looking up at her. "I'm not kidding, it was hell. She turned into some other kind of person during the divorce, and the person she is now isn't who she was when I was growing up. I'm not complaining or anything. It's just—" he shrugged, "—people change."

"People don't change." She could feel the hard edge in her voice again. *People become new people, but they aren't changing. They're dying and being replaced.* She suddenly questioned the thought; hadn't she just realized hours before that Rebecca was part of her? That she herself had changed? The only difference was that she'd also changed her name.

Nikolai's hair fell into his face as he leaned forward to scrub the dishes in the sink. "I like you, you know?"

"What?"

He turned, giving a faint little smile. "Not like that." His cheeks turned red, and Caden looked away. *Why can't I like Nikolai? He isn't complicated like Gabriel and Tom.* The thought of Tom made her heart hammer painfully in her chest. When would she see him again?

They finished up the dishes in silence. Caden stood around, unsure of what to do next. As comfortable as she felt with the family, it still wasn't her home; she couldn't just go do her own thing—it felt too weird. She leaned up against the counter as Nikolai dried off his hands on a dish towel.

"I want to show you something." His hand found hers and pulled. She could feel the dampness of his skin and the wrinkles that had formed from having his hands in the water for too long.

He looked around the corner, to make sure his mom and sister didn't see as he pulled her into his room and closed the door. Caden felt instantly self-conscious. He wasn't the same cocky guy she'd met at the party; instead he seemed gentle and sincere.

Her eyes trailed around the length of this room. Posters of constellations hung on every wall, and little planets dangled from strings attached to the ceiling.

"Close your eyes." He held her hand a little tighter.

"Why?"

"Just do it." She could hear the smile in his voice.

Caden shut her eyes. He pulled lightly on her hand, and she followed.

"Now, there is a bed right in front of you. Just lay down, okay?"

"What? No. Why?"

"Come on, it isn't a big deal. I promise you're the first girl on my bed."

Caden became uneasy. "Just sit back, I promise the bed is under you." Caden let her knees give out. The awkward *close your eyes* game felt a little weird, a little like playing with Tom. "Lay back."

Caden opened her eyes, ready to protest, to protect herself from this game. Her heart stopped. All around her were twinkling constellations in the night sky, an endless black world full of stars. She leaned back on the bed, silently searching the glowing lights. "This is amazing."

"You weren't supposed to open your eyes yet." Nikolai lay down beside her, and her heart quickened. "LEDs. I installed them myself to match the sky. Some are dimmer to gauge their distance, but in general it's inaccurate. Really they're all too bright, but I like it that way."

They sat there for a long time in silence. The serenity of lying next to him no longer felt foreign or strange. "Stars, they move, you know? Just a little; you'll never be alive long enough to see them move a noticeable amount. Now people, they change slowly too; and sometimes, like the stars, it might be too slow to see. Other times a star might fall, granting someone a wish and killing itself in the process."

"What do people have to do with shooting stars?" Caden asked.

"Nothing, really. I saw a shooting star the night I met you."

Caden blinked as a star shot across the sky. She didn't say a word. The ceiling couldn't have shooting stars. She was going crazy; she'd known it the day she had met Tom. The warmth of tears entered her eyes again, and she blinked them away until she fell asleep.

—Day—

Birds chirped and fluttered their wings as Caden rubbed her eyes and turned over, her head sinking into the soft pillow. Bright light streamed into the room, and she turned again, pulling up the sheets to cover her eyes. Only after the sheets were over her head did she realize she wasn't on the floor, or in Angelica's room.

She pushed back the sheets, panicked.

Where was Nikolai? What would Cassandra say? Would they kick her out? She jumped to her feet and opened the door.

"Morning, Lucky Charms," Nikolai said, smiling as he stretched his hands out over his head. "I would have loved to wake up with you in my arms, but Mother noticed just a little while after you fell asleep and kicked me to the couch." He grinned.

Caden's shoulders relaxed and dropped a little. "Where is your mom?"

"Mom? Oh, she left for work a few hours ago."

"What time is it?"

"Beats me." Nikolai shrugged. "Probably…"

"Eleven," Angelica snapped, and Caden turned to look at her crunching away violently on cereal. "Did you sleep well in my brother's bed?" Caden cringed at Angelica's tone. It didn't matter that nothing had happened; she wouldn't live this down. Caden leaned in a little closer, examining her cereal: Lucky Charms. "Mom isn't happy about it. Says she should have told you about purple."

"Purple?" Caden asked, looking at Nikolai for help.

"You know. Boys are blue—"

"Girls are red," Nikolai joined in.

"They make purple. Purple isn't allowed in the house unless you're married to the person. So it better not happen again unless you intend to marry my brother." Angelica's voice was laced with ice.

"I'm sorry," Rebecca chimed in as she wrapped her arms around herself. Caden didn't fight it. *It isn't really Rebecca, it's me*, she reminded herself. *I'm Rebecca too.*

"Back off, Angel, I told you guys nothing happened. I was

253

just showing her the world."

Angelica rolled her eyes as she took another vicious bite of cereal.

Nikolai walked past Caden, lightly squeezing her arm before disappearing into his room.

"Can you take me to the library?" she asked before he closed the door. "Like, soon?"

"Anything for you," Nikolai said.

Angelica looked up at the closing door, glaring through slits. "First you steal Gabriel, and now you're taking my brother from me?"

"If it helps any, Gabriel said I wasn't his girlfriend. He said he had special criteria for that position." She smiled weakly, hoping Angelica realized it had never gotten far between them. As for Nikolai, there was nothing to say.

Angelica pinched a piece of marshmallow from the bowl of Lucky Charms cereal and made a show of crushing it.

It was noon by the time Nikolai dropped Caden off at the library. She turned and waved before running into the forest toward Gabriel's.

Knock, knock.

Gabriel opened the door, stepping out beside her. "Come on," he said, and she followed him to his car, the side mirror still only dangling by a small wire.

"Where are we going?"

Gabriel shrugged, getting into the car. Upon opening her door, Caden noticed the mud stain still rubbed into the beige carpet from the day he picked her up in the rain.

"Where did you get that shirt, anyway?"

Caden looked down at the shirt Angelica had given her. She had called it trash. Yet the blouse looked near perfect and fit her nicely. She shrugged, wanting to avoid a conversation about his ex-girlfriend.

Trees began to blur as Gabriel drove faster down the roads. He turned on the heat, and they rolled down their windows. It wasn't a cold day, but it wasn't hot either. She let her hand hover in the wind and watched the trees thin. Nearly an hour passed before they turned off the main road. A sign hung loosely, dangling on its side. "14 Miles" was hardly readable, but she recognized it from a trip she'd taken with her parents before the divorce.

"Brandon Beach," she whispered. "You know about this place?" She turned to look at Gabriel, whose eyes were trained straight ahead.

"Came here once with a babysitter."

"Did your parents ever take you?" Caden asked, looking out the window. The moist, salty smell lingered faintly in the air. She could feel her old quiet self as she sat there comfortably, enjoying the wind on her face.

"No, my parents never took me anywhere." He cleared his throat. "I was raised by a bunch of nannies and babysitters. I might as well not have had parents."

Caden looked over at him and felt guilty. She at least had had some kind of family life before the divorce. "Are you an only child?"

He laughed. "Yeah, and I'm pretty sure I was a mistake." He tapped his fingers aggressively on the wheel. "I figure the only reason my mom didn't get an abortion was because of my grandparents. Yet they never bothered with me after I was born."

The wind whipped in the car, sending her hair flying back with the sea breeze. She wanted to take his hand, to feel the roughness of his skin. She moved uncomfortably in her seat, wondering when she could get into his room to look for the butterfly wings. The allure of the wings made her uneasy; they had a secret, one that she thought would bring her closer to Tom and Gabriel. Maybe one that could bring them together. Caden just wished she knew how it would all work out.

Gabriel moved his hand to rest on the center console, and she leaned over to lace her fingers between his. She thought he would pull away, but his grip tightened.

Gabriel's eyebrows drew together as he opened his mouth to speak, but he hesitated. Licking his lips, he started again. "I've been thinking about what happened at the coffee house.

I was mad and I thought you were lying to me." He gritted his teeth. "I just..."

"I'm sorry too, I should have told you sooner." Caden's lips quivered at the weak words. She'd said she was sorry, and she'd felt it, meant it. Caden let out a shaky breath, feeling her composure slip. She wasn't supposed to be sorry or sweet, but maybe being those things didn't hurt her as much as she thought it did.

"Ouch," Gabriel said. Caden looked down at their hands. Her nails were digging into the soft flesh near his knuckles.

"Sorry." She winced and quickly loosened her grip.

"Last time you said sorry this much was the day we met."

"I'm pretty sure we met at a party." She attempted to arch an eyebrow, unsure if it worked. "Like a year ago."

"Really? I wish I would have noticed you then."

Caden's heart fluttered in her chest. "Why?"

He shrugged. "Just would have been nice." He became quiet, as if unsure of what to say. "I probably would have put on a lot of weight though, with all your cooking."

"Take that back!" Her hand came up to slap his arm playfully.

Gabriel swerved lightly, as if the slap had caused it. It made Caden grab hold of the handle above the door. "Well, I might have died sooner too." He cleared his voice. "Please keep slapping outside of the vehicle at all times."

"You swerved on purpose."

"Well, I had to prove a point, plus it's true. We've practically made a habit of running people off the road. Okay, let me correct that: your friends have run us off the road. Wow, you really are a dangerous girl." His voice hummed playfully through the air.

Caden laughed. "And if I met you any sooner, I'd be dead from lack of sleep."

The car got quiet. Gabriel's mouth formed a hard line. "For a second I almost forgot about him." He sounded distant, almost wistful.

Caden chewed at the inside of her mouth nervously, wanting to get on his good side. "Well, at least you don't have to deal with him." She rolled her eyes, hoping to convey the message that if it were up to her, she wouldn't want Tom around. Though even thinking it hurt. She *did* want Tom around. He was her friend.

"I don't know, you seem pretty taken with this other side of me." His voice sounded lighter, but his face kept its stone expression. "Just the way you say his name…" His knuckles began to turn white around the steering wheel as the speedometer crept higher.

"Tom needs that kind of praise." She shut her eyes, willing the words forward. "He's a *child*, Gabriel."

"What do you mean, 'He's a child?'" His eyes stayed on the

road, but Caden watched the muscles in his back tighten. The car went faster.

"Gabriel, while you grew up, he didn't. He couldn't have. He had nothing to direct him. He's scared and alone and he just wants someone to spend time with." The words seemed to rot the inside of her mouth, as if saying them out loud made the truth sink in. She didn't want to believe it; she wanted them to be the same person. Tom was safe and happy, but she couldn't deny that a bigger part of her felt drawn toward Gabriel. "Look, let's talk about this later. We'll figure it out. I'm not going anywhere." As soon as the words streamed from her mouth, the speedometer's numbers lessened. His expression remained grim, but his mouth no longer looked hard and out of place. His hand even seemed to loosen on the wheel.

He took another corner, and the beach appeared. Endless blue. Infinite. She wasn't sure if it was talking to Gabriel or the sight of the ocean that made her problems seem small. She let out a breath, readying herself for a gulp of ocean air. The salty smell was so strong it awakened all of her senses.

Gabriel pulled the car into the dirt lot and turned it off. She watched as he opened the door and got out to stretch. She took off her sandals, leaving them on top of the old muddy stain she'd left that rainy day. The car made a repetitive little dinging sound as she got out and slammed the door shut. Her hair whipped across her face.

"Are you any good at running?"

"Am I any good at running?" Her hand came to her face, shading her eyes so she could look at him. For a second she almost thought he would remember the game of tag she'd played with Tom, as maybe another dream. "I bet you want to find out?" A giddy grin spread across her lips as she took off in a run into the sand.

"Hey, not fair, I wasn't ready!"

She looked back as Gabriel hurried to close the car door and ran after her. The sun burned her eyes, and the brisk wind traveled through her skirt, making it ripple like the waves. *Oh, thank you for not raining.* The warm sand pushed in between her toes with each footfall. It almost felt as if the sand held her feet each time, hardly releasing her to let her continue. She looked back at Gabriel closing in. When he laughed, it changed his features so much that for a split second he looked like Tom. Her heart skipped, feeling a little more whole.

"I'm going to get you."

"Will not." Caden giggled as she found a new energy. The sand lightened up into rocks, and she slowed down, being more careful where her bare feet fell.

"Get back here."

She looked back once again at Gabriel, who was tiptoeing across the rock, wincing every few feet. "A little farther. It breaks up again over here!" she yelled back.

"Where are we going?"

"You'll see." The rocks began to fall away, and soon her feet were sinking into deep sand once again. She went closer to the water, running on the wet sand that propelled her faster.

"I'm coming!" Gabriel yelled. Caden screamed as he leapt, tackling her into the sand.

Her body stopped struggling at his touch; his hands were warm against her skin. Gently, he brushed off the sand on her cheek. His head blocked the sun, creating a halo of light around his face. The laughing in the air died down as their eyes began to search one another's. Gabriel's irises didn't seem copper but more of a brown. Caden blinked up at him, Tom's name on her lips. *Can he see me? Will he remember today as just a dream?* She waited, her chest rising and falling, wishing he'd lower himself down against her. His lips were so close, so kissable. She wanted all of him.

"So, now where?" Gabriel asked, breaking their gaze and getting to his feet, his arm outstretched.

"Just a little farther." Caden looked out into the ocean, breathing deeply. Disappointment filled her. She faked a smile and let him help her up. Her heartbeat accelerated when his hand found hers. He wasn't looking at her; instead his eyes traveled out into the distance, far away.

They walked along the shore together. For the first time, Gabriel felt content. He knew it was because of Caden. She stopped walking and it took him a moment to look away from her and towards the water. Haystack rocks towered out of the ocean like a small city.

Gabriel let his fingers squeeze around hers for a second before letting go. She sat in the sand, rocking back and forth to get comfortable. He lowered himself down beside her, looking at the sand trapped in her hair. A patch of sand was still stuck to her forehead. He realized he must have missed it when he was staring at her eyes. Gabriel clenched his fists again. *Don't get attached, don't you dare get attached. She'll leave you. They all leave you.*

"It's nice here." He pushed the words out with a stiff expression, wondering if she could sense the pain thrumming through him.

"Yeah, I like it. I remember coming here as a kid. My sister Reese and I would make sand castles, and I guess one day I got bored. There's no swimming here, you know? 'Cause of the unpredictable tides. Still, I managed to get out there unnoticed."

"Out there?" Gabriel pointed to one of the haystack rocks.

"Not that one, the closer one. I got to the base and had to call for help."

He nodded as he looked at the rock he thought she was pointing toward. There were too many to know for sure. "What happened?"

"My dad came and got me, and afterward they got my sister ice cream for not following after me." She laughed, a sad tone underlying the happiness. "Where did you go when you came here?"

Gabriel leaned back onto his elbows, wanting to hold his breath. He didn't have any good memories here; he wasn't sure what had made him come today. It had been a long drive. He figured he'd done it so she wouldn't leave, so he could keep her a little longer. "Heck, I stayed in the car," he admitted in a rush as he lifted an arm out of the sand, letting his fingers run through his hair, bits of sand falling off onto his shoulders.

"What? Why? You afraid of the water or something?"

"Nah." He put his hand in the sand, drawing a line and then another. "I think my babysitter met her boyfriend out here or something. We drove out here a couple of times and she told me to stay in the car."

"You listened?"

"She wasn't the nicest babysitter." *She wasn't the meanest either.*

"Were any of them nice?"

Gabriel picked up a shell, running his nail around the edge. "Not really." He chucked the shell at the waves, watched it disappear into the never-ending blue. "Every summer they found some poor schmuck, told them they could live in a condo free of charge for the season if they took me. I was always spending those summer months in another state with another stranger."

"You're lying. There's no way that is legal." He watched

Caden swallow, trying to close her mouth and not reveal the shock.

He figured he shouldn't tell her about Christmas or any of the other holidays. "Like I said, they really had no need for a child. Plus most of the babysitters never paid me any attention; a few just locked me in my room. One guy used to have a lot of parties; that's how I started drinking." *Others just beat the shit out of me until I stopped talking for a year.*

"What did you do?"

I pretended that one day I'd have a friend, and all the shit would finally stop. Gabriel shook his head, picking up another rock. He didn't want to talk about the past. "Have you ever skipped rocks on the ocean?"

"Nope."

"Come on then." Gabriel got up, brushed the sand off his pants, and grabbed her hand. If there was one thing he knew how to do, it was skip stones. His whole life he had flocked to water; it calmed the pull inside of him, assuaged the unease of so many years of being alone. One of these days he'd get a boat and sit there, letting it rock him to sleep in the warmth of the sun. He closed his eyes and took in a deep breath. If he could, he'd live on the beach.

"Pick up all the rocks that are really flat and smooth and kind of heavy. There are a lot here." Gabriel bent down to pick up a thick, round rock about the size of his palm. "Here, like this one." The weight felt just right. "Now get to the water's edge and put your index finger against the edge of the rock." He watched as Caden fidgeted with her own rock. "No, like this." He could feel the irritation in his voice, the years of being alone and being ignored surfacing. He pushed down the feeling and looked up at her, smiling. "Like this," he said again, but with a calm, even voice. "With your thumb on one side and your index finger on the other."

His hands felt rough in comparison to hers as he moved her fingers into the right position. "Great, now stand with your feet shoulder-width apart, facing the water sideways." He did his best to act it out, and Caden rocked back and forth awkwardly as she watched him. "Squat down close to the water when you throw it." Gabriel let his go, the rock sliding against the water, flying up, and skidding again. "Five, six, seven," he counted as the rock skipped and then sank down into the calm ocean water far in the distance.

Caden stood up. "I can't do that."

"Sure you can. Get back in your squat." She tried to bend her knees, though she looked awkward and off-balance. He couldn't help smiling. "Alright now, the trick is to flick the rock across the surface, so you want to do a sharp movement with your—"

Caden let out a little scream as she released her rock too early and sent it backward toward Gabriel. He took a step to the side as the rock came toward him, skimming across his arm. "Hey. Watch it. You let go at the end."

"Sorry, sorry, did it get you? I swear I threw it that way." Caden pointed her empty hand to the ocean, her face beet red. "Oh, my gosh." Her hands flew up to her mouth. "Did my rock hit you?" She giggled. "I'm sorry. Are you okay?"

Gabriel felt the anger leaving him, her lightheartedness disarming him. "Let's try again, okay? I'll stand farther back."

"Or maybe you could stand behind me, and guide my hand?" She grinned.

Gabriel felt his cheeks grow hot. He shrugged, hoping she wouldn't notice the happiness inside him, the completeness he felt at being near her. He couldn't help but think he'd shrugged too much. Constantly trying to pretend she didn't affect him was the most difficult thing he'd ever done.

Caden looked over at Gabriel. They were almost back at the condo. The clock on the dash read 6:10 p.m. It had taken Gabriel nearly an hour to show her how to skip a rock. She managed it just fine when he was the one in control of her wrist flick, but as soon as he stepped away, her rocks all sank. That was until her last one; it skipped three times, resulting in her jumping up and down, again and again. She hadn't even noticed the time. Nikolai was supposed to pick her up at the library at six.

Caden's hands fumbled with one another, picking at her nails, biting them. Would Nikolai wait for her? Would he be mad?

"What's your problem?" Gabriel's eyes were bright copper, his lips drawn into a hard line. "I thought we had fun today."

"We did." The car now carried the heavy scent of salt from the ocean with a hint of cinnamon.

She looked back out the window as they passed the town.

"I'm just running late. I'm getting picked up at six."

Gabriel looked over at the clock. "It's past six already."

"I know. I hope he just waits," she mumbled.

"Wait, *he*?" Gabriel repositioned himself in his seat. "You're staying with a guy? Gosh, Caden, I hope you're not doing anything stupid."

"I'm fine," she whispered. "I can take care of myself." It wasn't any of his business. Gabriel most likely didn't even know Angelica and Nikolai were siblings. He probably had no idea they lived with their mom.

"Psshh. That's why you stayed with me? Because you can take care of yourself?"

"Yes, actually, I can." She bobbed her knees up and down restlessly waiting for the car to stop. The clock glowed 6:15. If she ran, she could get there in half the time.

Gabriel pulled into his parking space and turned off the engine. "Look, Caden."

"I gotta go. I'm so late." She opened the door and took off into the forest.

"Wait, Caden? Can I see you tomorrow?"

Caden waved over her shoulder without looking back. He would just have to wait and find out. She pushed harder, the branches slapping unforgivingly at her face as she leapt into the air to avoid fallen branches. The forest filled her lungs with the smell of moist dirt and pine needles. In the last stretch she could see the library in the distance. Nikolai sat with his back to her. She slowed to a walk, panting. Her lungs stung furiously.

"Nikolai!" she called, her voice heaving.

"Caden?" He turned around to see her, sunlight streaming over his face.

"You called me Caden." A smile spread across her lips. "It has a ring to it."

"Well, that is your name. Where have you been? I was worried about you."

Worried? About me? Never had a boy actually said those words to her. "Sorry. I, umm, I went for a run. The library gets so stuffy."

"That's a long run. I came here at four. I thought we could spend some time together, but I think it's almost seven." His face had a puzzled look to it, as if he was trying to believe that her run literally took three hours, which of course it hadn't.

Caden placed her hand on her head, still breathing deeply. She didn't like lying, but telling him that she had been with Gabriel wasn't an option. "I'm so sorry."

"Since when do you apologize all the time? Look, it's not a big deal. I sent a text to my mom and told her we were still out having fun so she isn't too upset about ordering pizza for dinner."

Caden grabbed at her stomach as pain laced through it. Shame tended to make her physically sick.

"Are you okay, Lucky Charms?" He put his hand on her shoulder, his touch gentle and kind.

"I think I'm okay." *Just feeling like I got kicked in the gut.*

Why are you being so nice?

"Look, I figured we still have time to get ice cream on the way home. That is, if you're up to it. I don't mind cold pizza, but if you aren't feeling well…"

"No, no. I'll survive, and cold pizza sounds great." She attempted to let go of her stomach and straighten.

"Here." Nikolai put a hand around her back and lifted her up into his arms.

"What are you doing?"

"I'm carrying a beautiful girl to my car, of course. I heard you were in need of a knight?" He grinned, his eyes locked on hers. "Anything for a girl who will eat cold pizza." He lifted his eyebrows dramatically, as if challenging her to disagree.

What have I done? How can I let him know I'm not the girl for him? She wrapped her arms around his neck, the pain subsiding in her chest as the heat from his body eased into her. He put her down in front of the car and opened her door.

The ice cream shop wasn't far from the library. Nikolai got a triple scoop of pistachio, Neapolitan, and orange sorbet while Caden settled for a kid's scoop of vanilla.

"So what did you do all day? Besides run?" Nikolai licked the stacked ice cream so that each flavor would be included.

Caden laughed, "Not very much. Just reading stuff." She could already feel the pain building up again from the lie.

"Do you think I could come tomorrow? Maybe read with you?"

Caden twirled her baby spoon in the center of the ice cream. "It's pretty boring." *Shit, I hate it when a lie comes true. What are we going to do at the library all day?*

"I can make it fun." A smile filled his face.

"I don't know. I have a lot to get done."

"Oh, really? Summer studying? It's okay, I get it. You don't want me there distracting you. You probably wouldn't even look at any of the books because you'd be so busy looking at the face."

Caden giggled as she took a bite of ice cream. The cold burned against the heat in her mouth, melting around her tongue. "It isn't that."

"Are you sure? I'm told I'm ruggedly handsome."

Caden tapped the side of the cup with her spoon. "Look, Nikolai, you don't want me." *I'm a horrible person.* "I tend to go for guys who are really messed up and make my life complicated."

"One of those, huh? Angelica's like that too. You know how I told you she was dating Gabriel last summer?" He took a bite of his ice cream, orange dripping down his chin. "That guy really messed her up, could have ruined our family if you ask me."

"Why did you go to his party then?"

"A party's a party. Got to find something to do in this small town. Plus he can be a cool guy. I wouldn't recommend him to a girl, but guy-to-guy he's okay. Enough about him. Come on, let's go home."

271

Once in the car, Caden leaned back into the seat and closed her eyes. She tried to tell herself she wasn't making Angelica's mistake, that once she figured out the butterfly wings, Gabriel could be a stable boyfriend. She just hoped she was right.

—Night—

Tom opened his eyes. Darkness surrounded him, closing in like a cage. He could still feel Caden, the dream of them on the beach, being in the sand, him on top of her. Tom gulped, feeling the lump in his throat like a brick. Pulling back the covers, he sat on the side of the bed, his head in his hands. Caden, Caden, Caden. The emptiness of the room had used to comfort him, but now it trapped him. The dead bolts glistened in the hovering light from outside. A thick, heavy feeling surrounded him like blankets, pulling him under. It felt hot, worse than hot. Tom inhaled, grabbing at his throat as the air refused to come.

He had pushed her away, told her not to come back. Now he just felt empty and alone; he regretted every moment without her. Tom fell back against the bed, wanting to open the window Caden had climbed through to see him. Instead he shut his eyes and tried to picture her. He saw her hair tangled with the ocean breeze, her smile as he chased her, her feet digging into the sand and leaving footsteps for him to follow.

"I'm coming..." he had yelled. She screamed playfully as he tackled her into the sand. His hands were on her body, all over her. Tom squeezed his eyes shut, trying to forget the dream. It refused to leave his mind. He could feel himself leaning over her, watching her beneath him. He could still feel his arms around her, the warmth of her skin.

It's just a dream.

He could remember lifting his hand from the sand, wanting to skim it across the smooth surface of her lips, wanting to kiss her. Instead his hand went to her cheek, the sand falling away at his touch. He could see his face reflected in her eyes, blinking up at him, his shadow only large enough to cover her beneath him. The laughter in his throat died down into a hum. He hadn't even realized he was laughing, smiling, enjoying her like he had that night in the rain when they played tag. It felt different though, calmer, her face somehow clearer. Tom pushed his palms into his eyes, willing the images to go, to leave him in peace. Instead he remembered her chest, rising and falling, timed with the sound of the waves rushing in and out. A tingling sensation ran through him at the thought of her.

Rolling out of bed, Tom got on his hands and knees. His hand fumbled on the underside of the bed frame until the tip of his finger felt a smooth surface; he pulled. He placed the small pieces of butterfly wing in his hand and gripped them tightly. They were his safety, and they protected him.

The butterfly was something he had always had, a gift from his parents. At night he'd stare into its lifeless body trapped within the glass. His eyes would drift over the orange veins in its wings, wishing he could touch it. The night he had broken it had been a mistake.

He had only wished to free the butterfly. Even though he ended up smashing it to pieces, that moment had brought him Caden, his only friend. He hadn't known she would become so important to him. He also hadn't known that her throwing away the broken pieces of butterfly would make him so distraught. Without the butterfly, he'd felt as though he would disappear.

The night he and Caden searched for the car keys, he'd found his opportunity to take the butterfly back. When she went outside without him, he had grabbed the largest piece out of the trash. He hadn't minded that it was broken, because he felt better the second it rested in his hand. It felt like it gave him control.

Tom slid the two pieces together between his fingers. He couldn't let them out of his sight again. He closed his eyes, thinking of Caden and what she had done. She'd stolen them from him. She wanted them for herself. Tom could feel the ache in his chest as he walked toward the window and pulled it open. The night air streamed though, filling his lungs with a sharp sting.

—Day—

"Boo!" Nikolai peeked through the books on the other side of the shelf.

"Stop it." She smiled. "I thought you said you were helping me?"

"I am helping. Helping distract you, that is."

Caden rolled her eyes playfully as she grabbed the few books on museums she'd collected and sat beside him at the table. "So you really think it might be in here?"

"No clue, but we ran out of butterfly books an hour ago."

It was true; the library had a short supply of butterfly books, but it was a start. She wanted to find out more about Tom Gabriel's butterfly, and she needed to make sure Nikolai didn't get suspicious. She couldn't imagine he would be okay with her going to Gabriel's every day when she was supposed to be reading.

When she'd mentioned her butterfly search, Nikolai had suggested art books. He said his mother was a fan of butterfly art and it could be helpful. They moved to those when the butterfly books came to a dead end. Caden flipped the pages open and ran her finger down the index of the first book, looking for anything about butterflies, only to close it and try again with the next one. A pile of books sat beside each of them. The librarian was going to hate them if she didn't already.

"So after we're done here, you want to go get lunch?"

"I told you, I can't."

"Yes, but you didn't say why."

Caden fidgeted with the page, her palms feeling hot with sweat. She had already missed the morning with Gabriel. She told herself she didn't really need to see him, and that she needed to find the butterfly wings. She missed him though, and she missed Tom. She still couldn't believe that Tom had pushed her away because of some stupid resin wings. It made her heart ache, but it also reinforced their importance. They couldn't just be butterfly wings; they had to be something far more important than that.

After closing the tenth art-museum book without a single lead, hopelessness settled into her. Her frustration was another matter entirely. Nikolai had ventured off a few minutes before, and now the time was dragging without his company. Caden got up from the table, unsure of where to go next.

"May I help you, young lady?" A woman came out from behind a row of books, wearing her glasses low on her crooked nose. She didn't look like a typical librarian; her glasses were too small for her face, and her grey hair flowed down over her shoulders in two braids that nearly hit the floor.

"Well, I…" Caden wasn't sure what to ask about; though she wanted to ask about something other than butterflies, she was afraid Nikolai might overhear and make the connection with Gabriel. He had known about Tom, but whether he knew Tom was a totally different person, she didn't want to find out. As the lady began to tap her foot, a pile of books in her arms, Caden quickly added, "I'm doing a paper, trying to correlate bugs with, I don't know, medical stuff." The lie tasted bitter on her tongue.

"Bugs?" The lady moved her face a little closer, eyeing her from under the glasses.

"Yeah, like, maybe just something on like split-personality disorder."

"It's called dissociative identity disorder nowadays, darling, better get that right in that paper of yours. Follow me." The lady turned and walked into the back of the library, passing bookshelf after bookshelf. Caden watched as her long gray braids swung back and forth, hitting the occasional shelf and flying the other way.

When they reached their destination, they were in the old wing of the library, one Caden hadn't ventured to. The lady went behind the desk, grabbed some keys and turned around to a glass case on the back wall.

"Now you be careful with this book I'm giving you, and bring it back when you're done. It isn't rentable. Been here as long as I have." She laughed. "Alright, it's a little older. Now, I probably wouldn't be using it as a reference because, like I said, names for disorders have changed, but it will get you started. From there you can go onto our database and see if anything recent corresponds with it. Work from the old to the new, I always say." Caden watched as the lady tipped her head back and looked up at the books lined up in front of her. Her finger ran across their bindings, stopping at the largest volume. "Ah, here we are."

The book was huge. "You sure that isn't a dictionary or bible or something?" It looked as if it concealed all the secrets of the world. She was counting on it holding at least one. She guessed it was five inches thick and probably a foot long. The cover and binding were covered in fabric that was eaten away at the edges and three shades lighter from sun damage. The smell of dust sat on the paper, and there were imprints from past fingers that had thumbed through its pages.

"No, darling, not a bible." She pushed her glasses up over her eyes and read, "*Malady or Myth: Disorders and the Myths that Have Carried Them through Time.*" It took both hands for her to lift it and bring it to her; she was hardly able to move it away from her body, it was so heavy.

Caden took it from her, assuming the difficulty had come from the woman's age, but her hands dropped with the weight the second the woman let go. "Thanks."

"Remember, it's part of the library's permanent collection. Bring it back when you're done." Caden nodded her head in thanks and headed back out of the old wing, a chill running through her.

When she got back to the table where they had been sitting all morning, it looked like multiple book buildings were forming a small city across it. Caden pushed a pile aside and plopped the tome down.

Specks of dust levitated from its pages. Her fingers griped its edges, pulling it toward her as she sat down. She turned it over and opened the back in search of the index. The book let out a series of cracking sounds as it refused to be opened any further. Tilting her head to the side, she read the index at a strange angle. "Multiple Personality Disorder, p. 1089."

She flipped the book open to the middle and attempted to sift through the pages. Each page refused to move as her fingers fussed with the corners. She lifted her index finger to her lips, grimacing before licking and then began flicking through the pages. 1086, 1087, 1088, 1089.

Chapter 48 Multiple Personality Disorder

Multiple Personality Disorder (MPD) patients have suffered extreme experiences of neglect and intrusive abuse at the hands of caregivers. To create this section of Malady or Myth, the author worked closely with therapists around the world to better understand MPD and how myths have carried this disorder through time.

Though these myths seem to validate the result of an alter ego, it is proven that the myths have no factual grounding. In order to understand any disorder and the myth attached to it, it is important to examine the circumstances from the first recorded symptoms. Early remedies for this disorder generally included the application of charms, herbal medicine, and spell casting...

Caden glanced over the rest of the page before flipping to the next page and the next; it just kept going. Her eyes searched for something she could use, something maybe about butterflies. Instead she stopped at "Object Relationships."

It is assumed that the myth of the Sunnifa (as stated above) was the result of object relationships. MPD victims will often associate a personality with a transitional object that may be associated or otherwise joined with the trauma. It is unclear of whether the object in question in the Sunnifa myth was beneficial (in helping her deal with the trauma) or detrimental (a constant reminder of the trauma). Beneficial objects may in some circumstances be substituted for people who are deemed trustworthy and reliable. Detrimental objects can manifest as a person who is associated with the trauma or a negative emotion, such as fear. It is important to note that not all MPD patients will obtain an object, material or person, but if they do, it is because the host and alter ego can safely love the object without risk to either—

"Hey, did you find something?" Nikolai's hands were empty.

"Nope, just killing time." Caden slapped the book closed, wondering too late if she should have read the Sunnifa myth. "I don't think I can take any more for today."

They left the library without another word, and Caden realized how the old books had filled the air with the smell of touched pages and dust. Nikolai asked again if she was hungry, his last attempt at taking her to a very late lunch.

Excuses weaved through her head like crochet needles forming loops for her to get lost in. Instead she asked for a rain check and said she would be waiting for him at 6:00 p.m. in front of the library doors.

Nikolai took the rain check and left her in front of the double doors of the library. She could smell the books as the door opened and closed behind her. Caden waved as Nikolai drove from the parking lot. His face looked solemn even from a distance.

It smelled like a storm. Purple clouds were growing dense and covering the sun. Her mind went back to the old book and the object relationships it talked about, wondering if the butterfly wings would classify as a beneficial or detrimental object. It all basically broke down to "good" or "bad," if she thought about it, but where did that put her?

She walked to Gabriel's condo. When door twenty-five was finally in front of her, she knocked softly.

The door opened. Gabriel's lips were tight, and his bright eyes shifted over her as if he wasn't sure he wanted her inside or outside of the door. Caden stared back at him; she felt as though she should explain why she hadn't come sooner, but she didn't know why. She hadn't told him when she would show up in the first place. Lifting her chin to meet his gaze, she felt her knees weaken.

"It's about time." He looked past her and at the stormy sky, as if he hadn't expected it to be so dark. "You up for cooking?" He smiled sweetly, and it made her think of Tom. "I thought we could make dinner."

Her heartbeat quickened. "I'd like that."

"Great, I put the prime rib in a little over an hour ago. Should be done around five o'clock, then it needs to sit for an hour in foil. I wasn't planning on doing it myself, but…" He shrugged, his face reddening. "Now we just need to make everything else."

Her head tilted to the side as she examined him, her eyes trained on his. Copper ribbons danced through his irises with the temperament of his other half, without the childish nature. "I had no idea you could prepare a roast." It was the only thing she could think to say. She couldn't possibly ask why he seemed so calm; it contrasted with the Gabriel she perceived him to be. It made her wonder if the beach had changed him, lifting a burden by revealing his past.

"I can't prepare a roast. I tried though."

"I'm sure it will be delicious. What else are we making?" Caden asked as she followed him to the kitchen.

"I think I got everything for mashed potatoes, and I got some of the stuff you had on an old list before because I didn't know what you would need to make gravy."

He'd kept the first grocery list she made? "Do you have a peeler? A whisk for the gravy?"

"Yeah, I'll get them."

A cabinet door closed as another opened, and Gabriel cursed with each failed attempt to find the peeler and the whisk. He didn't have to tell her why; she had seen the kitchen torn apart when she had snuck in to see Tom. Obviously he had cleaned up in a hurry and put nothing back where it was before.

"I just don't cook much," Gabriel offered when he turned to her with neither item.

Caden shrugged, grabbing a pot to boil the potatoes in and a saucepan for the gravy. "That's okay. It gives us options." They would just include the skin; maybe make them scalloped. They were cooking in no time. It seemed like only minutes passed before the buzzer was singing through the steam and heat of the kitchen. Their bodies synchronized as though in a dance as they cooked beside one another. They were weaving in and out between the stove and the island, stirring vegetables and dumping out scalding water. Gabriel whirled around with the dish of scalloped potatoes as his foot closed the oven door with a crash. Caden's fingers threw in pinches of spices as she shook herbs over the butter sauce for the artichokes until the smell satisfied her.

When Gabriel finished setting the table, they went toward the roast, which had sat wrapped in foil while they cooked. His bare fingers tested the edge of the foil. She watched as he tugged back an edge.

"It smells delicious." She handed him a fork, and he used it to drag away more of the foil. Caden could tell they were both sweating. The heat from the food warmed the condo as the air caught the flavors and carried the smell. She took in a breath, recognizing that they had worked together to create this. This time it wasn't *her* cooking, it was *their* cooking; she liked the sound of it much better. It excited her. She'd had other people in the kitchen with her before, following instructions, but she had never really cooked *with* anyone.

They filled their plates with more food than they could possibly eat, but the smells that had teased them for over an hour had their stomachs doing backflips. They sat beside one another. The storm clouds outside stubbornly kept their place, blocking the sun. One solitary light shone above the table, casting unusual shadows.

The roast melted in her mouth. Her butter sauce smothered it and ran down the sides with each cut. A bowl sat between them, filled with extra sauce swirling invitingly. They sat silently, enjoying each mouthful.

"So what do you do all day?" Gabriel asked while he dipped an artichoke leaf in the butter.

She could ask him the same question. Summer months tended to be dull, often with nothing to do unless you had friends. Even though Gabriel threw parties, she believed he was as friendless as she was.

"I've been spending time at the library." She coughed a little as she swallowed. The table was barren of drinks.

"Damn it, sorry, I forgot the drinks." Gabriel pushed back his chair as he headed for the kitchen. "Cola or water?"

"Water." The word sounded painful as it hit the air, her throat still blocked. She attempted to push the food down again as she waited. Her mind felt dizzy after his simple word: sorry. The water sloshed back and forth as it reached the table.

She gulped greedily, feeling the food slip down her throat. "Thank you."

He took her glass to refill it and got one for himself. "So what are you reading at the library?"

"Oh, no, the library. What time is it?"

"Almost six thirty, but I thought—"

"Shit. I can't believe I did it again." It sounded like a sword fight as her fork hit the plate, shoveling the delicious food into her mouth. The ease she'd felt moments before was gone. She'd forgotten about Nikolai. *Again.* Guilt and panic hit her like a freight train. It took her a moment to swallow as she glanced at Gabriel, water still in his hand, a questioning look creeping into his face. "Gabriel, will you drop me off at the library?"

"Ah, sure, but can I at least eat first?"

She stopped, flustered. "I'll just run, it's okay. I'll run. I'll get there in like twenty minutes, it will be fine." Her voice rang out frantically as she attempted to calm herself while simultaneously scrambling for her shoes. Twenty minutes longer wouldn't ruin things too terribly.

"Did you see those storm clouds when you got here? It might start raining on your way and it's probably cold. I'll drive you. Come on."

Caden couldn't understand his willingness to leave their dinner. It wasn't like him, but she couldn't argue, needing to leave, and fast. They left the condo, plates abandoned on the table.

When the car door was shut behind her and the Saab backed out, a patter of rain began thrumming against the roof. Even though the last few days without rain had been enjoyable, hearing the rain made her glad. Her mind focused on the tones of the beating drops of water instead of her racing thoughts.

Within a matter of minutes the parking lot came into view. In the distance she could see the warm light shining from the glass doors of the library. The clouds blocked all evidence of the sun, making it dark as night.

A solitary figure stood in front of them under the protection of an awning, waiting patiently. She knew it was Nikolai. Caden dug her nails into the soft flesh of her stomach, distracting herself from the guilt that threatened to make her heave up her dinner.

"You can drop me off here."

"No way, I'll take you to the awning."

Caden rotated in her seat, unclicking her seat belt. With any luck she hoped she could leave the car before they saw each other. As the car stopped, she could see the passenger-side mirror swinging back and forth in the rain, tapping the car door repetitively. Nikolai's silhouette was a blur behind the speckled droplets of rain lining the window. She watched him take a tentative step toward the car.

"Thank you." She turned to Gabriel.

His eyes met hers, and for a moment she thought he would whisper for her to stay with him. Then his eyes shifted toward the figure, and in that moment, it was as if he could no longer see her. "What's Face doing here?"

Nikolai was already moving toward the car. He clearly recognized it. She could only imagine what was going through his mind. He'd told her to stay away from Gabriel, and instead she'd lied and chosen to spend her days with him. Nikolai's family was taking care of her, and this was how she'd repaid them: by going behind their backs.

"He's…my ride."

"What?" Gabriel roared.

The explosion of his voice pushed her back against the door. It opened behind her, cold drops of water sprinkling her head as Nikolai held his hand out toward her.

"Come on, Caden, let's get out of here."

Caden didn't move; she couldn't when it looked like at any moment Gabriel would explode. The fear inside her kept her in place. After a moment she felt Nikolai's hands pulling her out of the car. Her feet dragged on the ground as Nikolai hauled her by her armpits. The fog crept back, blinding her momentarily, but when her vision returned, Gabriel's eyes were smoldering. His neck bulged with veins, and his teeth were clenched shut. She struggled against Nikolai, trying to stand, her shoes slipping out from under her with each attempt. Caden's head lifted as raindrops targeted her eyes; she blinked them away until she could see Nikolai.

"It's okay, I'll get you out of here. Can you stand? Did he hurt you?" Nikolai attempted to put her down.

Every part of her was watching Gabriel, waiting for his next move. Would he come after her? Or would he just drive away? She could still see his shining copper eyes as he stared at her from the driver's seat, and then he got out of the car. Long strides closed the distance between them. They sat there, Caden on the ground and Nikolai crouched above her, his hands still under her armpits. Nikolai couldn't move fast enough to avoid the punch Gabriel threw at his jaw. As if trapped in an endless tunnel, Caden heard the echo of her scream as Nikolai's hands were ripped away from her body.

"Wat ta fuk?" His lip hung loose as he held his jaw, and she could tell the jumbled sentence had been a painful one.

Gabriel came at him again, and this time Caden's hand darted out, grabbing his pant leg. He stumbled forward and landed on his hands. He turned his head toward her, his eyes flaming. "What are you doing, Caden?" A flicker of betrayal curved his brow.

"Let me explain, Nikolai didn't do anything."

"Who the fuck is Nikolai?" The small drops of rain doubled in size, breaking apart into fine particles as they burst on the pavement.

"Face. Face is Nikolai, I'm staying with him. Why are you acting like this? He took me in. I had nowhere to go." *You even suggested that I stay with him that day in the car.*

"What about me, Caden?"

"You?" Her hair felt heavy around her shoulders, wrapping around her neck like a noose. "You kicked me out. I had nowhere to go."

With a swift movement his hand was on hers, lifting it away from his pant leg as he stood up. Nikolai was already tossing his arm forward in an arc; he caught Gabriel between the eyes. The light from the library doors shone in the gray sky. As a few people passed, they witnessed the odd spectacle of silhouettes, their fists clenched, punches flying and hands grabbing one another. Rain shattered off their shoulders, catching the light before falling into the shadows below and rolling into the gutter. In seconds, a dozen punches had been shared. Caden pushed herself up to her feet.

"You guys, stop." Her hand came out to push them apart, and she felt a deep sting spread into her face; hit in the crossfire.

"Caden! Are you—" Nikolai couldn't finish his sentence as another punch hit him. He toppled in her direction, his body's momentum too quick and powerful for her to avoid.

A sharp, painful jab went up her spine as she landed on her tailbone with Nikolai on top of her. The wet ground was painted with designs in red as his blood mingled with the clear liquid, dispersing into pink.

"Get off her!" Gabriel yelled into the rain as he pulled Nikolai, still dazed from the punch, up. He hit him again.

"Gabriel!" Caden cried. Pain and frustration enveloped her and she once again felt powerless, but she couldn't even blame Rebecca this time; it was her own fault.

A man stood nearby, a bundle of books hugged close to his body with one arm, his other hand grasping an umbrella that shielded him from the weather. He seemed to be contemplating where he could put his books if he decided to intervene. She watched as he searched the awning for a dry piece of pavement, but eventually he gave up. The library doors swung open as he called inside.

Nikolai fell to the ground after receiving a punch to the gut. His nose was a mess of blood, and his lip was cut down the middle. Caden could no longer feel the coldness of the rain as numbness crept into her body. She crawled toward them, yelling for them to stop. Her fingers felt the crushing weight of a shoe as one of them stepped on her hand. A scream escaped her lips, but not even that stopped the boys.

The library doors swung open once more, and the man who'd once held the bundle of books approached with caution. Other silhouettes stood behind him, their bodies forming a cage around the spectacle. He yelled out to the boys, but his words were lost in the water plummeting from the gray sky. His hands reached out and were soon accompanied by more pairs of hands; more and more began to grab at the two brawlers, reaching at them from every direction. Caden's screams echoed as her ears rang with the roar of water falling around her. More men, more hands. Hands were everywhere, pulling them apart. Gabriel spat blood onto the pavement; Nikolai attempted to push away the strangers without success.

The fog cleared inside of Caden, and she could feel her legs once more. Her hands dragged across the pavement until they were under her, pushing her up. Her knees wobbled as she stood. Then she realized she should have run all along; it only seemed right for her to run now. Blinking into the stormy sky, she knew she couldn't go back to Nikolai's. She couldn't laugh at a table with his family and pretend things were as they should be. The hands holding Nikolai and Gabriel stopped moving, and then heads turned to her and stared.

My fault, this is my fault. Her legs grew more anxious until they were moving beneath her, taking her far away, into the dark. Alone.

19

—Night—

Gabriel's head rested against the steering wheel of his car, his breathing still deep and ragged. Drops of scarlet trickled down the length of his face, plummeting into the beige carpet. He imagined the fight had looked worse than it was. In the end they would both have bruises and a few cuts, but nothing worth a hospital visit. He had been lucky no one called the cops, and Nikolai had told him to leave before someone did.

He clenched his fist into a ball, pain shooting up his arm. With every moment, his distress grew. The image of Caden running into the rain played in his head. If she had looked back, just once, he told himself, she would have stopped. Just one look. He would have taken her back with him. She could have stayed with him like before.

Though he knew he didn't want things to be like before. At the beach he'd felt something inside of him open. A hidden past was haunting him, locked away without his consent. Some part of him knew she was the key to that lock.

Groaning in pain, he moved back into the seat, his head

against the headrest. The metallic taste in his mouth made his stomach turn, though it wasn't as potent as the thought of the two plates of cold dinner back in the condo.

Facing the inside of his condo was unavoidable; the car was getting colder by the minute. His teeth chattered as he opened the door. The folds of his wet clothes dragged across his body, and each movement made him colder. He was sure his heated seats were ruined. This time though, he couldn't bring himself to care. It actually comforted him somewhat, like it was some kind of punishment he deserved. Closing the door behind him, he walked out from the carport to the sidewalk. His wet clothes felt warm compared to the new specks of rain falling across his shoulders and his hair.

It was truly dark now, and the moon was covered by the ever-present rain clouds; he could hardly see a thing. The light on the side of the building was on, illuminating about four feet of wall and nothing else. The lamppost near the carport stood dark, probably broken again. At the path leading into the condos, Gabriel followed the small garden lights to his door.

His thoughts flickered back to Face pulling Caden from the car, her expression frozen with fear. He had given her that fear, not Face. For years, he had felt the rage inside him was justified; it spilled from him as easily as letting out a breath of air. Until recently, the anger had kept him at ease, made him powerful in a world outside of his control. He fought it and sometimes he won. Though tonight, he couldn't understand what had conjured his anger. He assumed it was fear of what losing Caden would do to him.

———————————

Caden knew if she waited any longer, the wind would continue to stiffen her clothing until she could no longer move. She had been hiding behind the carport for nearly an hour, just waiting for Gabriel to get out of his car. The minutes ticked by as she watched the car, wondering what he could be thinking. Finally, she heard him open the car door and looked up to see him dragging his feet toward the light of the building.

He looked horrible. Old blood washed away from his features and clothes as rain trickled down the length of his face. She told herself she could have broken up the fight if only she had tried harder. Caden put a hand to her face, wincing. It would bruise, that was for sure; and as for her tailbone, running with the injury had been the worst physical experience of pain she'd ever endured. When she got back to a normal life, she would have a new respect for the ass-kicking heroines she saw in movies. She also knew that she could never be one. The whole week had been a series of mess-ups, but now she understood what she could handle.

Without Gabriel, she wouldn't have survived the week. If she hadn't starved, she would have frozen to death. It wasn't below freezing, but the moisture picked at her bones and the wet clothes on her back kept her teeth chattering. Her long black hair might as well have been strings of iron chains; her head felt its weight keeping her down.

When Gabriel rounded the corner to his condo, she moved quickly, crouching low as she went for the car. She hoped the hidden key would still be hidden beneath the carport shelves. The fluorescent bulb above her flickered as moths launched their bodies at it, avoiding the rain and seeking the heat. For a moment she wished she were that small, so that the bulb would warm her in the same way.

The hand that had been stepped on couldn't help much, and the discomfort gnawed at her with each movement. Instead she used her left hand, awkwardly feeling along the underside of the shelf. The hard edges of the key were a relief. She unlocked the Saab and climbed into the back, closing the door behind her. Even after several minutes of being sheltered from the rain, she couldn't control the shaking. Rain no longer sounded so wonderful; she wished she hadn't missed it while it was away. She stripped off her wet clothes, unable to get warm as they moistened her skin. The T-shirt from the first day Gabriel had picked her up was still in the back, crinkled from getting wet when she had used it to protect his heated seats. She slipped the T-shirt over her head, and it covered her like a dress.

The tips of her fingers were stinging; she cupped them close to her face, breathing into them. Her body shook violently from the cold, but without the wet clothes surrounding her, she felt better. The safety of the car and carport roof were simple comforts; she hoped she would have as much the next night. If she could escape unnoticed by morning, she could live in the car each night as Tom sat locked away in Gabriel's room.

Hot tears streamed from her eyes when she thought of Gabriel.

She couldn't stop picturing the first punch Gabriel threw toward Nikolai. She didn't understand what had caused the fight, what strange tension had snapped between them after only a glimpse of one another. It probably had something to do with Angelica, though she doubted Gabriel had any idea she was Face's sister. They had told her that they didn't tell people about their personal lives. It kept them safe, Angelica had said, and boys didn't wander too close if Nikolai was there. They didn't mind what people thought as long as they protected one another. It made her think of her sister, Reese, and she wondered if she was okay staying with their father and his new girlfriend.

When the tears finally stopped, Caden drifted off, her chattering teeth no longer able to keep her eyes open.

—Day—

White light spread across the room as the rattle of blinds jarred Caden from her sleep. His silhouette revealed his broad shoulders, and when he turned, his square chin and toned chest became visible. Her eyes fluttered again as the smell of eggs and sausage drifted to her nose. Her dry mouth instantly filled with saliva as her tongue ran across her cracked lips.

"Where am I?"

"Home."

The word startled her. Home. Where was home? A car, a floor, a couch, a room she no longer belonged in? The word hurt; it didn't belong with her. She'd made a decision to give it up when she trusted herself to defy her mother and live with Sean.

"How did I get here?" Her fingers touched the side of her face, pulling away when they both began to throb. Her eyes were out of focus, and her senses were thrown off by the smells in the kitchen.

"You ready to come eat?"

"Gabriel?" Once his voice finally registered, she hurried to stand up only to fall back down on the couch. His arms were instantly around her, helping her back to her feet.

"Yeah, it's me. I made you breakfast."

Caden fell back against him once more. "You what?" It seemed impossible that Gabriel would do such a thing, though the night of them cooking had been a surprise as well.

"It's not special, the way you make it, but you need to eat." His gentle touch surprised her as he pulled out the chair and led her to a sitting position.

She didn't know if she could look at him, not after last night. Instead she looked down at her bare legs, and the realization of only having a T-shirt on hit her. She pulled at the edges, attempting to cover more of her thighs. "How did I get in here?"

Gabriel passed her a plate, the sausage links rolling back and forth.

"Thanks," she whispered, still hoping he would answer her question. Still hoping she wouldn't have to look at him. He was being quiet, and very calm. She was only afraid that it was the calm before the storm.

"Can I get you anything else?"

She shook her head as she picked up the sausage link with her fingers and dropped it, the burning too much for her tender fingertips. "Umm, maybe a fork."

"Right, forks," he mumbled. His face went scarlet as he turned from her to get the forks.

Awkwardness surrounded them, all too similar to their first day together. She inconspicuously watched him as they ate. Her eyes darted to the bright red numbers on the microwave; two in the afternoon. It bothered her how long she'd slept. Her eyes left the red numbers, traveling to the purple-and-blue skin on his face. Bruises trailed around his eye and down the side of his cheekbone. The apprehension within her deepen.

"So, am I missing something?" Caden asked as she pushed the eggs around on her plate without looking up at him. Part of her couldn't stand the splotches of color on his skin.

When she finally looked up, Gabriel was eyeing her plate.

"I said it wasn't anything special. I didn't want to leave you here alone to get hash browns." He let out a frustrated sigh. "I didn't know when you would wake up, and I didn't want you to wake up if I wasn't here. I thought you might…leave."

It felt as if the air would choke her. "I'm not talking about the food, Gabriel."

"You're not?"

Caden shook her head, looking up with a small, nervous smile. She was afraid it might be more of a grimace. She didn't feel hungry anymore, maybe because she'd eaten almost everything on her plate except a small pile of cold scrambled eggs. "What is this? Why are you acting this way?"

"What way?" Gabriel asked as he leaned over and grabbed her plate to bring it into the kitchen. He stood there looking dejected, the line of his mouth hard and unmoving.

"Well, you aren't exactly like this all the time. You're normally—" Caden stopped herself, afraid the words would result in a plate being hurled across the room into a wall.

"More angry?"

"And you're normally hotheaded," she added.

He seemed to think about this for a moment before nodding.

Caden felt relieved after finally letting the words out; part of her didn't want to stop. He'd screamed at her, and he had hurt Nikolai. He was a jerk, self-centered and arrogant. "You have to be in control all the time or everyone else suffers."

His hand came up, signaling her to pause. "Look, Caden. Last night, I…" his mouth twitched lightly as he adjusted himself for the words. "I really messed up. There, happy? I freaked out."

"No, I'm not happy." Caden tried to hide her face in her hands, but it hurt too much. Everything on her body throbbed. "You should have let me explain."

"You didn't need to. I shouldn't have done it. I get that now. He was just so flirtatious with you at the party; I wanted to wring his neck then. I didn't know you were still spending time with him. It just shocked me, I don't know." He furiously ran his hand through his hair, causing it to stick out in different directions. "And your face." His voice trembled. He raised a hand to rub his jaw as he stole a look at her.

"What about my face?"

"It looks like it hurts. You shouldn't have tried to come in between us."

You shouldn't have started the fight. Caden wanted to stick up for Nikolai, to tell Gabriel that he had never yelled at her or kicked her out; he made her feel special and coined her first real nickname. However, it didn't seem like telling him this would fix the problem.

"I want to try and be good for you, Caden. I—I know I'm no good for you now." She watched as his eyes went glossy, and he finally dropped his hand from his jaw. "I'm a horrible person without you." He turned back toward the sink, hanging his head low once again.

"You're not a *horrible* person, Gabriel." Caden got up from the table and rested her hand on his back. "You just have a lot of…stuff you need to work through, and I don't know if I can handle it all." *I have enough of my own problems to work through.*

His hands released the countertop and pulled at his hair as a low growl escaped his perfect lips. Instinctively she took a step back from him, unsure of what to expect.

"I'll stop. I'll make myself stop. I have to. Caden, I need you."

I need you. The words caught in her ears, and she blocked out the rest. It wasn't the *I love you* Sean had offered the night he had taken everything from her, but the way the words hung in the air, tightening around her delicate throat, said enough. Part of her didn't trust him. Whether that was a result of her past or the time she'd spent with him over the last week, she didn't want to know. She half expected him to run toward his room and slam the door shut, then ignore her for the day. The last thing she'd expected to hear was *I need you.*

Gabriel didn't move. Instead he leaned up against the sink next to the dirty dishes. His eyes were fixed on the floor beside her feet.

"So." Caden cleared her throat. "You going to tell me how I got here?"

His shoulders curved into his back as he straightened. From her angle, she could just see the hint of a grin spread across his lips. That simple turn of his mouth set her lungs on fire, her cheeks stinging with anticipation. She once again remembered her lack of clothing, his simple T-shirt hanging loosely around her frame. Her hands moved to the bottom of the shirt, awkwardly pulling it down at the sides again as she got up to bring her empty glass to the sink.

When he turned to face her, his face showed the Gabriel she knew. His confidence made him seem taller, and his presence grew around her until she felt small and helpless. He cleared his throat. "I woke up early to go find you. Only thing was, when I got to my car there was a very distractingly beautiful girl unconscious in my backseat. That, and I couldn't find my car key."

His eyes met hers, and she quickly looked down at her feet, feeling more like her shy old self again. The chill of the kitchen tiles seeped into her toes as she wiggled them back and forth.

"Anyway. I carried her here."

"Carried?" Her voice squeaked the word, causing her to gulp. She didn't know what made her so nervous about the idea.

He reached for her hand, squeezing it once before letting it drop.

I want to trust you, Gabriel, but who are you? What happens if tomorrow you don't want me anymore? She knew that whether or not he would be there, she would still be better off than where she started. The last week had made her realize something more important than her feelings for him: her true

303

self. She wouldn't die without him; she would miss him, sure, but it wouldn't change who she had become.

"She didn't wake up?" Caden attempted a look of suspicion as she crossed her arms, but she ended up uncrossing them to pull at the shirt once more.

"You don't remember?"

"No, what? Remember what?" Her heartbeat drowned out any feeling, only the constant thrum keeping her attention. "Gabriel, remember what?"

"That is just so weird." He leaned casually against the counter. "You were talking and flirting and, well, we had a really great time. You sure you don't remember?"

Caden could feel the dryness surrounding her mouth before she realized it hung open in shock. "You've got to be kidding me." *I'm fine, Rebecca is gone, I swear she wasn't real to begin with.* The thrum of her heartbeat made her nauseous.

Gabriel stared at her with a straight face, watching her. "Relax. Relax, I'm kidding, Caden. You sleep like a rock. I could have dropped you and you wouldn't have woken up."

Her fist flew through the air, landing hard on his shoulder.

"Ouch." They both shouted in unison.

"I can't believe you. Jerk." She meant it as an insult, but the smile still crept up her lips as she shook out her hand. A napkin on the kitchen counter got her attention, and she tossed it at him.

"I'm sorry." The words were hardly audible between his laughs. "I'm sorry, I'm sorry. I couldn't resist."

"I bet you couldn't resist." She took another napkin, the one draped over her breakfast plate, and threw it. She gasped as the cold scrambled eggs bounced off his bruised cheekbone and onto his shirt.

"Oh, food fight is it?" he asked as the eggs fell from his shirt onto the floor.

"No," Caden laughed. The sore, bruised muscles in her cheeks ached from the movement as she playfully backed away.

"Tickle fight?"

"Definitely not." She stopped giggling when he approached. "Gabriel, no. I'm…I'm not ticklish." Caden began to turn toward the couch, already feeling his fingers brush her skin.

"Get back here." She could hear Gabriel's smile through the words.

For a moment she felt like a child again, playing games, being happy, laughing. His hands wrapped around her waist as the two of them fell to the floor. Every part of her body hurt but it didn't seem to matter; she couldn't stop the laughter from flowing out.

"I'm not ticklish!" she screamed, but she couldn't tell if he could hear through the laughing. Her fingers reached out to find him, searching for a rib or armpit to return the favor. He winced in pain before laughing as they rolled across the floor giggling. Her body stopped moving the moment she felt his warm hand on her thigh. Not even a second passed before he pulled away, as if burned.

"I forgot, I didn't mean—I wasn't trying anything—I just—uhh, shit." He rolled off her to the side and stared up toward the ceiling, eyes wide. A blush stained his cheeks.

It wasn't that kind of touch, she knew. Still, she hadn't ever been that clothes-less with a boy aside from Sean. She tried to remind herself she'd been in a single T-shirt all morning. Somehow it felt different now. Caden turned her head to the side; he didn't look at her, his eyes closed as if he was embarrassed.

"So…my clothes?" She remembered taking them off the night before, completely rain-soaked.

"Washed them early this morning, they're folded in the main bathroom."

"I assume you saw the—"

"Yep."

"And the—"

"Yep, that too," Gabriel said, opening his eyes but not looking away from the ceiling. "I like owls, but I've never really been a fan of polka dots. I can't believe girls can get glow-in-the-dark underwear. Why isn't this made available to guys? Gender bias, if you ask me."

Caden hissed through her teeth, wishing she hadn't worn the "You're a Hoot" owl underwear with glowing eyes. The ratty polka-dot bra said, "Want Some Dots," "Bra-tastic" and "Gotta

Get Some," in each colored circle. Well, it was comfortable, but still embarrassing. She'd never made the switch to "adult" underwear, figuring she could wait for college.

"Did you put the polka-dot bra in the dryer?" It was all she could think to ask. She couldn't handle the silence.

"Yeah." He turned his head to look at her. "That a bad thing?"

"Pretty bad. You're not supposed to dry them."

"I'll get you a new bra."

Caden thought about this for a moment as they lay across from each other. "No, that's weird. Plus that bra is way more special than a dozen bras put together."

"Why?" Gabriel turned on his side and propped himself up with his elbow.

"You serious? Haven't you ever found the perfect jeans, and you wear them 'til they fall off? Same for a bra. Hard to find and irreplaceable. Most comfortable after breaking 'em in." Irreplaceable. The word seemed strange when used for a bra. She doubted Gabriel could understand. It wasn't so much the bra itself as the day she'd bought it, and she figured that even if it had gotten ruined in the dryer, she wouldn't throw it away. She remembered her mom with her that day they had gone shopping, vibrant with happiness. They hadn't found out yet that her dad was a two-timer. The memory turned her stomach; maybe she didn't want the bra after all. Her mother had never gone bra shopping with her after the divorce.

"What's wrong? We can find you another bra. Oh, gosh, Cade, don't cry. I'm sorry."

She hadn't even realized she had let the emotion through for him to see. "It isn't about the bra." A laugh followed, though it sounded hard and forced.

"You want to talk about it? You can borrow some pajama bottoms if you want to stay in the T-shirt."

She nodded. After he got the pajama pants for her, she put them on and met him in the bedroom, where they propped up pillows and leaned into the headboard.

She wanted to tell Gabriel that her real name was Rebecca, and she wanted to tell him about her new self, who was strong and forceful but also had a quiet side. Caden could finally accept all her actions as her own, and she wanted to share that with him but she couldn't. The words wouldn't form, so they sat there quietly. Gabriel took her hand and didn't pry, didn't ask why she wasn't actually telling him anything.

He ran his thumb back and forth on the side of her hand, their fingers still tightly linked.

Caden began to fidget. Summer would be over soon. The fact that he would leave and she would return to school unsettled her. She didn't want it to be over, not yet; part of her felt like it was just beginning. "Gabriel, what about the summer?"

"What about it?"

"Well... Don't you leave at the end of summer?" She wondered if he would ask who had told her; telling him it had been Nikolai seemed risky.

One by one, Gabriel began to unthread their fingers. Caden attempted to fight the pull of each finger as he wedged his hand free. "Caden," he whispered, his breath hot on her neck as he rotated toward her on the bed.

She hadn't noticed their closeness before, or the fact that they were on a bed. A bed was where Sean had told her she was worthless.

"What's wrong, Caden?" Gabriel leaned away, causing the bed to rock like a ship on stormy waters. "Look, I'm sorry I pushed myself on you before. I can change. We don't have to do anything. I just…" He sighed, looking away from her. "I just want to kiss you," he finished lamely.

The weight inside of her lessened as Gabriel got off the bed and walked toward the window. It felt as if she would never catch her breath as old memories continued to linger. Sean. He had ruined her. She doubted she would ever be able to trust effortlessly again, but she could at least try.

There was nothing that would bring back the past, and there were no do-overs in real life. Sean would always lurk in the shadows, waiting to ruin her life with those buried memories. She pushed herself to the edge of the bed, the sheets bunching up around her. The bed squeaked as she got to her feet.

At the window, Caden stood behind Gabriel, close enough

to feel the heat of his body. Their shadows stretched out on the floor as the room glowed with warm light. Her hands trembled as she brought them around him and pushed her body up against his back. The closeness sent chills through her as she took her other hand and ran it across the waist of his pants, her finger caressing his skin. He spoke her name in a moan, his voice rich and deep. Then he turned around in her arms, and with an urgency and desperation that both surprised and thrilled her, he cupped her face and brought his lips to hers. Her fingers wound tightly in his shirt as her body yearned to be closer. When he finally pulled away, too soon, she looked up at him breathless, the feeling of his lips lingering on hers. This was right. This was what she had wanted.

"You have no idea how much I wanted to do that." He released his hands from her face, running them down her sides and around her waist, pulling her in once more.

Hesitantly, she leaned back in to kiss him. She didn't want to stop, not yet. With each kiss she breathed in his air, making herself dizzy as their kisses deepened. Her hands slipped under his shirt, the softness of his skin weakening her knees. Her mouth searched for his lower lip, lightly biting and pulling as she ran her hands across his chest. When their lips released, he stepped back to pull off his shirt.

Caden looked down, feeling self-conscious. He was so beautiful; it didn't seem like he would ever like her. She wasn't beautiful like Angelica. The thought of Angelica's mouth on his soured the moment. It had been easy to be with Sean—he'd never been with anyone before. At least he said he hadn't.

"What's wrong, butterfly?" Gabriel lifted her chin, the warm sunlight seeping around the edges of his shoulders. It was so much like the day at the beach.

Caden turned her head, confused. She tried to look into his eyes, but the brightness from the window formed a halo of light around him; she couldn't even see the copper in his eyes. She wondered if maybe she was hearing things. "What did you say?"

He shrugged, his default shrug that she'd dedicated to memory. "I call you butterfly sometimes." Gabriel ran a hand through his hair, attempting an innocent smile. "I thought it suited you, you know, beautiful and whatnot." He looked over his shoulder, back out the window.

"Just because it's beautiful?" The words caught in her throat. She didn't feel beautiful, but it wasn't only that; Gabriel seemed like he was hiding something. His unease was apparent. "Come on, Gabriel." She nudged him a little, hoping she wasn't going to push her luck and snap him in half. "Anything else?"

He turned back to her, attempting to steal a kiss, but she pulled away, and crossed her arms defiantly over her chest.

"Alright, alright. So when we were in the car and I had that butterfly wing in my pocket. You said you broke it. I was furious at first." He paused for a moment. "This is going to sound so stupid." Gabriel ran a hand through his hair again. He let out a breath, and she waited patiently for him to continue. "It's the only thing my parents ever bought me. Sure, they gave me tons of money, but it was my only actual present. My mom—" he laughed nervously, as if embarrassed by the memory, "—she told me she actually picked it out for me on one of their trips across the world.

"I remember thinking to myself, *I'm not invisible. She actually misses me when she's gone.* I found out a few months later that my nanny had picked it up from a flea market and made fifty bucks selling it to my dad. They'd forgotten my birthday, and my nanny came to the rescue." He laughed again, rubbing his neck. "It's dumb, but when I was younger, I used to cry at night looking at those stupid iridescent wings, hoping my nanny had lied and that the butterfly really had been handpicked for me."

"That's horrible, Gabriel." Caden took a step closer to him. "What happened?"

"Nothing. Still don't know. Then you broke it and I swear just holding it broken in my hand changed something in me. It had held me in place for so long, anchoring me to my past. Anyway, it's stupid but I feel like you replaced the butterfly. You care about me, all of me. I can feel it, I think you're the only one who ever has." He took a step forward, closing the space between them, and tentatively stroked her bruised cheek before stealing a quick kiss.

"I don't want to be your butterfly," Caden whispered against his lips as their mouths parted.

Gabriel pulled his head back abruptly. "That bad of a nickname, huh?"

"No." Caden looked down at the floor, not wanting to see his eyes, suddenly remembering Tom. She didn't want to think about Tom, not right now. "I just want to be a new memory, something free of your past. Just you and me."

He pulled her in closer. "Fine, be that way. I'll just have to call you something else." He ran his fingers through her hair, then down the front of her chest. She gasped at the contact. "Sorry—" he grinned, "—got carried away."

"Sure you did." Her fingers dove for his ribs before she remembered the bruises.

"Ouch, stop that, it hurts. Caden's revenge; tickling bruises." He laughed as he pivoted and grabbed her waist, throwing her over his shoulder and spinning her around the room before tossing her down on the bed. Her body bounced lightly before settling.

Her laughing subsided as he bent down to her, crawling on the bed. When he was directly on top of her, he asked, "Could I call you omelet?"

"No. *That's* a horrible nickname."

Gabriel grinned, lowering his lips to hers softly before closing the space between their bodies.

—Night—

Only once before had he woken up in a cold sweat, the heat around him stifling. He attempted to roll, hoping to find a cold pillow, but he couldn't move. Tom grunted, feeling the sleep begin to wear off. His eyelids fluttered open. The first thing he noticed was the light threading in from downstairs.

The door to his room stood open.

A fog in his mind hovered as he attempted to move again. Nothing; he was too heavy. The sweat on his body made him feel nauseated. His hand moved across his wet chest. His eyes widened, alert; he had only woken up shirtless a few times before. His hand traveled down to his waist, and he let out a breath when he felt the edge of his pants, glad he wasn't naked this time.

Tom tried to sit up without success. Everything hurt. His eyes still hadn't adjusted to the dark, but he assumed his arm had gone numb. It felt different though, heavy. Rolling over, he put his hand out but recoiled at the touch of skin. Tom went still as he attempted to stop breathing. Listening.

He pulled back when he heard someone breathing right beside him. Someone was in his bed. Tom jerked and twisted as if the person touching him would melt him away. A delicate murmur drifted through the air as the bed squeaked.

"Gabriel?"

Tom's heart stopped. At least he thought it did; he would know Caden's voice anywhere. He pushed off the side of the bed, falling to the floor and scurrying back until the wall stopped him. His legs continued to move, trying to push him back farther.

"Shit," Caden hissed, suddenly sounding awake. "Tom?"

"Get away from me."

"Damn it. Where's the light?" He could hear the room come alive with her in it, the sounds of everything moving and shuffling filling the space as she searched. After a moment a *click* filled the room with light.

Tom blinked against it. His eyes stung from the brightness. "Turn it off." He didn't want to see her face. When she didn't respond, he looked up from his hands, blinking heavily until she came into view. Her black hair sat pulled to one side, the tangles making it seem shorter. A gray T-shirt fanned out around her body, and as his eyes traveled down her, he noticed her long naked legs. She pulled at the ends of the T-shirt, stretching it out.

"That's my T-shirt," Tom said as he put his hand to his mouth and bit down on his fingernail nervously. Why did Caden have his shirt on? He also wanted to know why she'd called him Gabriel. He was stricken by the idea of her being in his bed like the last girl, and the girl before that. They all called out for Gabriel.

"Sorry," she whispered, though he didn't know if he heard her correctly. It was such a small noise, like a squeak from a mouse.

"What are you doing here? I told you not to come here anymore. Did you come through the window?" He looked at the closed window. "Did you come to see me?" He looked down at the carpet, the answer somehow already clear in his mind. Clear and unclear; he couldn't really make sense of it.

"Tom." His name sounded like a plea. She bit her lip. "You're just a boy, Tom, I can't explain it to you." She ran her hands over her arms as she leaned back against the opposite wall. "We can get through this, it's just going to take time."

What was she talking about? The memory of her lips pressed against his made him uneasy. He wanted to kiss her again, but he didn't remember how. But more than that he wanted to play a game. He wanted to sit with her for hours so they could ask each other questions. He wanted the friendship he always craved, the one she had given him the first night they met.

She tapped her foot. "Sorry about taking your butterfly wings, by the way."

Tom looked up, suddenly feeling the need to touch the

butterfly wings, to hold on to them. The butterfly wings kept him whole, made him safe. "I won't let you have them."

Caden brought up her hands, "Okay, okay. I won't push."

They sat staring at one another for a few minutes before Tom couldn't take it any longer. "I don't want you here anymore. Why don't you go?" It wasn't true; he wanted her, in more ways than he could understand. He could feel the pleasure stream through him, the happiness of just being in the same room as her, and it terrified him.

"I'm not going anywhere, Tom."

Caden could feel the lump building in her throat as she watched Tom in the corner. Gabriel, Tom, Gabriel, Tom. He—they—worried her, and what did it mean for him and for her? She didn't want to leave; she wanted to wake up in Gabriel's arms as if the night had gone by without interruption, as if Tom wasn't really there. The guilt latched onto her; what was she thinking? Tom was part of him. She couldn't have one without the other, unless… Unless the butterfly wings were Tom's anchor, his object. If Tom was the little boy looking for his parents' compassion, holding out for love and acceptance, then maybe the butterfly wings were keeping the hurtful memories in place. Perhaps the wings were only a symbol of the betrayal of a parent, a lie, a reminder of the love that was never there.

"Tom?" Caden looked up from the floor to the man curled

in the corner. He looked like a caged animal, beaten into submission. She lowered herself onto one knee, hoping to seem less intimidating. "Where are the butterfly wings?"

Tom's eyes narrowed, his irises blacker than a crow's wing. "No, can't have them."

"Just let me see them, Tom. Please." She waited. Tom didn't move. "Okay, let's play a game."

Tom's shoulders eased out of their protective curled position, though he continued to look at her suspiciously. "What kind of game?"

"Well…" Caden pulled a hand through her knots of curls, her fingers snagging and staying there. "I'll walk around the room and you say 'cold' if I'm far away from the butterfly wings and 'hot' if I'm close. But you can't lie." She pointed fiercely in his direction. "You can't say cold when it's hot, get it?"

"But I don't want you to find them. They're mine. You'll just steal them again."

"Ugh. I never stole them, Tom." The wings had been on the floor that night. Caden kicked at the carpet, crossing her arms over her chest. The wings were definitely the object anchoring Tom, they had to be. If she got rid of them, things could change.

Tom crawled forward, grabbed a navy blue shirt off the floor and pulled it up over his head, crossing his arms over his chest once it concealed him. His dark eyes followed her as she casually walked around the room. She didn't glance up at him, purposely looking anywhere else. She wondered if she would miss him once he was gone and Gabriel took his place in-definitely. *Tom isn't real,* she reminded herself. *He is just a part of Gabriel. They will become one, like they should have been all along.*

Deciding that he couldn't pass on playing the game, Tom continued to say "cold" as she wandered from the closed blinds, stopping at the desk and opening the drawers. When she looked up at him, she saw his nervous eyes glance at the bed. The sweat on Tom's brow glistened in the light as she took a step closer to it.

"Tom? Am I warm?" She already knew she was, and she wondered what she would do when she found the wings.

His eye twitched as she took another step toward the bed and ran her hand across the edge where she'd slept minutes be-fore. Caden pushed her fingers between the mattress and the bed springs. Nothing.

"Stop, Caden. Stop. Don't find them," Tom pleaded.

She looked up at the boy in the corner, his fingers spread wide across his face, peeking at her through his hands.

His plea went unheeded as the hunger to find the wings overcame her. The solution was suddenly within her grasp. Her hand gripped the bottom of the bed as her fingers ran across the edge of the frame and the box spring.

Caden's body went still as she felt the soft edge brush her finger. The two broken pieces of wing slid on top of one anoth-er, like silk rubbing between her fingers.

"No." Tom leapt to his feet, and Caden looked at him, his

courage startling her. His dark eyes lightened into a rich brown. "Give them back."

Caden placed the wings on the bedside table, lifted up the old bulky alarm clock, and brought it down with all of her force. The wings crumbled at impact, the hard plastic shattering them with the weight of Caden's push. She lifted the mechanism again and slammed it against the table repeatedly. The loud banging of plastic on wood filled the room. The fragments of iridescence broke into finer pieces.

I'm sorry; this is for your own good.

Tom's legs buckled, and he landed on his knees near Caden's feet. His hands grabbed at her arms in an attempt to stop her. She didn't resist his pull; they both knew it was too late. The iridescent pieces were nothing but dust, reflecting bits of light.

Caden lowered herself to her knees beside him. She looked at him, expecting his eyes to brighten to copper, but instead she watched the dark brown fog over into black. Tom's soft, sad features turned hard as stone.

"How could you?" he screamed. "I hate you, I hate you Caden!" His hands cupped his face as he collapsed into himself.

Caden's arms opened as he fell into her chest, his head nestled in the crook of her neck. He cried. Tears ran into the T-shirt, some running past the neckline down onto her bare chest. She remembered when she'd held him after the party.

I'm so sorry, Tom, forgive me.

She ran fingers through his black hair as she lightly rocked him back and forth in an attempt to calm him. He had given her a feeling of safety when she had needed it, and what had she done for him? Aside from destroy his little world?

"Hush, Tom," she whispered in his ear. "You don't need the butterfly anymore. Tom, you have me. I'm not going anywhere." *Gabriel will be back in the morning. Everything will be fine. Things will finally be normal.*

Tom's body stiffened, and she stopped the rocking in her shoulders. The room was deathly quiet. The night made it a silent, empty space that sent a chill down her back.

Tom pushed at her chest as he attempted to break away from her hold. "I don't want *you*." Caden loosened her arms. The black eyes staring back at her were void of love. "*He* doesn't want you either."

"What?" Caden asked, startled.

"Gabriel," he snarled. "Gabriel doesn't want you either."

"You don't mean that. You don't know anything about him. You're different people. He isn't like you." She pushed herself up off the floor and walked out of the open bedroom door and down the stairs. Caden went into the main bathroom and slammed the door, locking it behind her.

Her hands shook as she grabbed the sink's edge, her stomach lurching and spinning, making her gag. Bile teased her throat, but she pushed it down. The circular lights above the mirror weren't bright enough, and they cast a soothing yet eerie glow. Caden turned toward the cabinet, opening it to find her clean clothes folded nicely on top of one another, just like Gabriel had said. She grabbed them hastily and pulled them on one at a time, attempting to ignore the tremors of her body.

Outside of the door she could hear Tom mumbling to himself. She didn't want to see him. Her thumbs hooked around the belt loops of her pants as she pulled them up over her hips. Her fingers ached and trembled as she pushed the button through the small hole. She was surprised to feel that her anger was stronger than the sadness.

The touch of Gabriel's hands lingered on her skin as if fresh, but she could also feel the trail of Tom's tears, which had rolled down her chest, drying over her heart. Her hand rested on the door handle, and she let out a breath. She'd come back in the morning, she decided. It was for the best. Gabriel would understand why she couldn't stay. Though talking to him openly about Tom scared her. They'd avoided the subject for the most part. Now she could finally tell him it was over for good. Tom would be gone after tonight. Her fingers fumbled for the lock in the dim bathroom. She opened it and walked past Tom. He started to follow her.

"Tom, don't. Stay here." Caden hesitated as she remembered the bedroom. It had been locked for the past few nights, hadn't it? Had Gabriel simply forgotten to lock the door because she had distracted him? Or had Tom been behaving? When Tom sat back down on the couch, Caden felt satisfied he wouldn't leave.

Her eyes glanced once at the kitchen, a memory of Tom and another of Gabriel seeping into her thoughts. Caden closed her eyes and counted to three before she opened the door. The night air woke her senses and she took in a deep breath before closing the door behind her. Her feet carried her down the path to the dark carport. Gabriel had told her that the lantern posts were all on the same circuit and tended to malfunction. It was just her luck that they were out tonight. She couldn't see a damn thing. Everything that had happened in the last fifteen minutes had put her on edge.

Caden took a deep breath as she walked across the pavement to the car. Rage sang in her blood, the displeasure burning through her fingertips. She could see Gabriel's car, barely visible in the dim light of the carport's ceiling. She would take his car for a spin. The desire to feel her foot push down on the gas pedal was overwhelming. She wanted the dirt roads to fly by while she let her hand hang out the open window. The thought felt exhilarating, and she couldn't wait to taste the reality.

Her fingers slid under the shelf until the key was in her hand.

The car smelled different than it had the first time she had been inside of it. It now smelled of mold. The leather and cinnamon was nearly imperceptible. She pushed the key into the ignition and turned it, the car coming to life around her. Her hands ran over the steering wheel, and she felt in control, savoring the power the small car brought to the tips of her fingers. She sat there in the running car for a few moments, thinking of where she should go.

Just drive. Get away from here, she told herself.

She took in a breath, taking a moment to collect herself before pulling the stick into reverse and whipping the car around with a screech. Caden put the car into drive, the road ahead too dark to see. She pushed her foot to the floor. The car protested for a second before shooting forward as she fumbled for the headlights. They flickered on, revealing Tom as he ran out in front of the speeding car.

21

The second she saw him, she hit the brake. It didn't stop the car from running straight into him and flipping his body over it. Caden sat with her hands on the wheel, looking into the empty parking lot, Tom's body somewhere behind the car. Dread gripped her as if physically tying her down to the seat.

It had never occurred to her that Tom would come after her, not after she told him to stay. If she hadn't stayed the night, if she hadn't kissed Gabriel that one last time, maybe they wouldn't have fallen asleep. Maybe Gabriel would have remembered to lock the door. *Gabriel.* Her hand brushed over her arm, remembering his touch, begging her to get out of the car and make sure he was alive. Caden closed her eyes and counted to three before opening the car door. Only seconds had passed…

Her body collapsed to the pavement at the sight of Tom sprawled-out in the red of the taillights. Sobs escaped her lips as she hurried over to him on wobbly knees.

"Tom." Her voice scratched the surface of the air as the tears came more willingly.

"Caden?" He moved up onto his elbows, and Caden let her hands hover around his neck.

"You shouldn't move."

His shaky arms gave out, and Caden's hands caught his head, lowering it back down.

"Tom?" She wished she had been more careful with him, the boy in a man's body, a deceiving trick of the eye. "Tom?" Her fingers pushed into his neck, and she held her breath, waiting for a pulse. It was there, just under the surface, and when she pushed her fingers deeper into him, it pounded willingly and strong. Caden let out a thankful cry as she collapsed onto Tom's body. His neck wasn't broken. He'd be okay. She looked up toward the condominium, the windows all black. The hum of the engine filled the night air. Caden searched for the moon in the sky, but it hid behind dark clouds. The lanterns jeered at her in the darkness as the moist air filled her lungs. It would rain before morning; she could feel it.

Caden put her arms around Tom, struggling to pull him up without success. She needed to get him an ambulance, but her voice refused to scream for help. The thought that something so horrible could happen and the night could stay so quiet upset her. What if she had killed him? A sob wrenched from her throat, making it hard for her to breathe. She gripped him in an attempt to keep her body from shaking.

"Tom. Wake up, Tom."

Where were the neighbors? Why didn't they wake up? She

didn't want the decision to rest on her shoulders—a decision that seemed to equal a mental hospital, not an ER. And what about her? Could she go to jail? She couldn't tell anyone about Tom, but how else could she explain the accident?

"Tom. Wake up!"

The idea of dragging his already-damaged body all the way to door twenty-five seemed ridiculous, but the longer she sat there with Tom's body in her arms, the more she feared to call attention to the situation.

Caden cursed as she tried again to lift his shoulders off the ground and drag him toward the lit pathway. Every part of her hurt. By the time she made it to the door, with Tom half dragging behind her, it felt like an hour had passed. An hour of horror, an hour of her heart racing at the thought of someone opening a door, of someone asking her if he was okay.

She pushed the door open and continued to drag Tom in. Unable to get him on the couch, she brought a pillow from the bed and placed it under his head before checking his heartbeat again. Satisfied, she ran outside to move the car.

When Caden came back inside, she turned on all the lights and sat beside the unconscious body. As he lay on the ground in front of her, she felt as though she had made the wrong decision. After cleaning his cuts, she stroked his bruised face with the back of her hand, wondering what she would do if he didn't wake up in the morning.

—Day—

Restless, Caden watched the sun come up. By the time the oranges and pinks seeped in over the horizon, she had begun searching the kitchen. It seemed silly, but she hoped that if she cooked something, the smell would wake him. He had stirred a few times, though he still hadn't opened his bright copper eyes. She told herself that it was a good sign. Her chest felt tight as she paced the kitchen, worrying about him. She wanted to tell Gabriel about everything that had happened, but mostly she wanted him to be okay and awake.

After searching, she found the baking powder in the back of a cabinet and the waffle machine. Days before, she had bought coconut milk and coconut flakes for a curry recipe that she never got a chance to make. So instead she mixed them with butter and flour and the last two eggs and made coconut waffles. The smell filled the air as she poured the mixture into the hot, greased waffle maker. The pop and sizzle filled the kitchen like a song as she closed the lid and counted down the minutes. By the time she set the table, warm light spilled through the windows. A stack of waffles sat in the middle, leaning ever so slightly to the left. Not having any syrup, she dissolved brown sugar in water, letting it boil and adding a tinge of vanilla flavoring.

Gabriel still hadn't woken up, so Caden grabbed an orange from the bowl of fruit on the table and cut it into perfect thin slices to garnish the plate. Now she had no choice but to try and wake him.

"Gabriel," she whispered. "Wake up." She gently touched his shoulder.

He moaned, touching his head, pulling his hand away from the pain. "Where am I?" He turned over on his side and opened his eyes.

"Home," Caden said, as she kneeled on the floor, pushing him up from the shoulders. "I made you breakfast." The words felt strange, almost like a lie. She didn't want to start with the truth, the fiasco that had developed once they had fallen asleep. "I made waffles."

"Waffles?"

His voice sounded different. Caden leaned over toward Gabriel. She tried to convince herself that this small change came from the bump on his head until she looked in his eyes. Dark irises looked back at her. The warm light from the window disappeared into their blackness.

"Tom?" Caden pulled back, letting go of his shoulders.

He straightened. "Caden?" He looked up at her, and she wondered if he could see the fear in her eyes. "What happened? My head really hurts." She watched him wince again as he touched the back of his head.

Caden felt the lump develop in her throat. *Don't cry, don't you dare cry.* She put out a hand to help him up. "It's daytime." *Where is Gabriel?*

—Day—

One week later.

"Don't forget you can't drive. Make up some excuse. You just aren't ready."

"I thought I was pretty good."

Caden smiled. "Pretty horrible."

Tom pushed a folded shirt into his suitcase. She handed him another and another until the shirts stacked so high they had to stop. She'd told Tom all she knew about Gabriel, which wasn't much.

It had been a long week full of tears. Every part of her felt completely sapped of strength. The bruises on her face were now an ugly shade of yellow but were not as noticeable as before. Still, because of them she had avoided her mother, and she was glad Laura hadn't come looking for her.

Caden didn't tell Tom that every night she woke up from the couch to check on him and how every night had been a disappointment. Tom slept soundly. The last two nights she had sat by the door watching him sleep through the whole night, hoping something would break and Gabriel would come back.

He hadn't.

Tom seemed to be there every second, morning and night. During the first few days of the change she'd found Gabriel's phone, and inside it was a return address and home phone number in case the phone was ever lost. After some fake soliciting calls to the number, she talked to a lady named Janice who clarified the address. It took some convincing, but soon she had Tom call and let Janice know to expect his return home and that he needed someone to pick him up at the airport when he arrived in Southern California. Janice hadn't asked any questions and arranged the flight for him.

"I'll come back next summer." Tom pushed the top of his suitcase down and Caden helped him pull at the zipper.

She didn't know what to say. So she smiled and told him she hoped he would. Tom leaned over and kissed her cheek, blushing after. Her smile wavered, but he didn't notice, consumed by his own embarrassment.

"How will I reach you again?"

"The address to your condo is in the top zipper of your bag, write to me." She would be going back to her mother after she dropped him off at the airport, but the chances of her getting her cell phone back were slim to none. She hoped her mother would forgive her. Caden needed her now more than ever.

Tom opened the door, suitcase in hand. The sun poured over him, and he lit up with happiness. He told her every second how much he loved the daytime. He wanted to play at the park every day and so they had. They played tag, rolled in the grass and found shapes in the clouds. She'd hoped if she satisfied his requests he would grow less hungry for the world and return to the night, but he seemed too happy where he was.

On the way to the airport, they passed the bridge where

Gabriel had picked her up weeks before. Tom bounced to the music, his face glued to the window, oblivious to the bridge where she had sat alone in the rain. That rainy day when Gabriel had come into her life seemed far away now; Caden could no longer remember a time without him. A tear trailed down her face, and she wiped it away.

As they passed the bridge, Caden regained control, and she warned Tom about the plane. She told him how his ears would probably pop, and she had given him a pack of gum. After he ate one with the wrapper, she explained not to swallow the gum and to take off the wrapper on the next one.

She paid attention to the road and attempted to ignore the numbness inside of her. The sun didn't seem as bright, and her cooking no longer brought her the same joy. After the accident, Tom told her he had followed her that night to ask her to stay. He told her he forgave her for hitting him with the car, but he never mentioned anything about what he'd said about Gabriel. She didn't bring it up either.

Caden swerved to the side as the terminal came into view. "Remember, Tom—" she leaned over, unbuckling his seat belt as they came to a stop, "—if anyone asks, your name is Gabriel."

Tom grunted disappointedly. "I don't want to be Gabriel, I hate that name."

"Tom. Tom? Look at me." Caden watched as Tom continued to bounce in his seat, distracted by the people passing by. "This is important, Tom. No one can know except for me.

I want you to tell your parents you need to see a doctor, alone. I found a specialist in the area and her name is Dr. Norman. Call her when you get there. Her number is on the same piece of paper with the address where you can send me letters, in the top pouch." Caden pointed to the spot on the suitcase. "You can tell her that your name is Tom. Okay?"

"Okay, okay." Tom let out a whine and looked back out the window. "Caden? Can you come with me?"

"No, Tom. I have to figure my own stuff out. Write to me." She put out a hand to ruffle his hair and smiled when he turned to her. "Go." She gently nudged her head in the direction of the door. Her heart broke with every movement. Part of her wanted him to stay. She would be lonely without him, but it was Gabriel she would really miss. "If you get lost, ask for gate 324A."

Tom nodded, his hand finding hers and squeezing it lightly before letting go and leaving her in the car alone.

Epilogue

Three months later.

"Ha, there you are, you little devil." Caden plucked the jar of mayonnaise off the shelf. She had gone down four aisles at the grocery store before she found it. Of course her mother wanted mayonnaise, of all things.

The jar flew out of her hands as a passerby bumped her shoulder. Caden rushed to catch it, elbows flying, but couldn't. Its plastic container hit the ground with a little bounce.

"Ouch."

Caden winced, wondering where her elbow had landed on the stranger. "I'm so sorry, I—Nikolai?" Her face felt hot, and her chest became tight. "I, uh, umm… Shit. I'm sorry."

Nikolai grinned. "Seeing how I bumped into you on purpose, I suppose I had it coming." He held the side of his face. "I thought you might run the other way if I called out your name."

Damn it. She hadn't seen him since the night of the fight with Gabriel. She'd done the cowardly thing and hadn't called to check up on him. At the time it had seemed like the better plan. "How are you?" *You probably think I'm a huge bitch.*

"I'm good. Aside from the obvious bump that might be growing on my face." Caden started laughing as he gestured playfully at his head and pretended to throw an elbow at a make-believe shopper. "It's throw-an-elbow day because, you know, the mayonnaise is on sale and you have to fend off all the competition."

Caden was bent over laughing, watching the onlookers give them strange looks. She hadn't felt this happy in a long time.

"I'm glad I ran into you, Caden, literally." He gave her a little nudge.

"Oh, Nikolai, why are you being so nice to me?" She rubbed her hands over her face. "I never even called to see if you were okay. I thought you hated me."

"Hate is a strong word; plus you promised me a rain check on that late lunch date. Remember?"

"You want to see me again?"

"Yes, let's just not tell Angelica quite yet."

They talked for a while longer and exchanged phone numbers. She explained how she had just gotten off restriction a few days before and that her mother had new rules, which included interrogating anyone new face-to-face. He seemed excited by the notion and mentioned something about impressing her with his obvious charm. The topic led him to his own mother, Cassandra, who he said missed her cooking and had no idea Caden had had any involvement in the fight with Gabriel. Caden didn't mention that she hadn't been cooking much other than when she was in school.

When Caden got to the parking lot, mayonnaise in hand, she climbed into Gabriel's Saab. Duct tape now held the passenger mirror in place. A pine-needle air freshener masked the smell of leather and cinnamon. The moldy smell had vanished after she'd scrubbed the seats with wet wipes. The heated seats didn't work any longer, and the scratches from where the branches had dug into the paint on their getaway from Sean had started to rust. She sat in the car for a moment, thinking of Nikolai. He had lifted a weight off her shoulders, and she wanted to see him again. She needed a friend.

After starting up the car, she began to drive over to Gabriel's condo. Over the past months it had become a sort of second home. At first she had told herself she would use it to cook, but she hadn't been cooking. Her cooking classes had gotten harder this year, and her motivation hadn't been as strong without someone to cook for. The first weeks after Tom had left, she had tried to cook, but it had only resulted in lonely meals full of tears. Now a spark seemed to have returned. The idea of seeing Nikolai again, and maybe even Cassandra, filled her with hope. If Caden could avoid Angelica, it would be even better.

She had thought about Nikolai's family often over the past few months, wondering if Cassandra had been right and Caden's family would be strong once again like theirs. It seemed possible; things had already gotten better. Reese was back for the year, and Laura had taken them shopping. Caden had gone back to wearing black, and as part of her *restriction,* she'd had to join the book club her mother held once a week. They were even reading *Pollyanna,* per Keira's suggestion, though she knew her mother had already read it several times. Things were coming back together, slowly. Now, with Nikolai, it seemed that things were better than she'd previously thought.

Her foot lightly hit the brake as she pulled into the parking area of Gabriel's condo, parking in spot twenty-five. She would probably leave the car there tonight. She didn't want to push her luck and have her mom find out she had been using a car that wasn't under her name and was likely not insured.

Caden sat in the car for a moment, eyeing the community mailbox in the rearview mirror. She had heard from Tom once. He had talked about the house he lived in. He wrote of birds singing outside the window in the morning. Surprisingly, he had even told her he missed her. The worst part of it all was that she didn't want Tom; she only wanted Gabriel. She wondered if there would be another letter. She almost wished there wouldn't be.

Caden opened the door of the Saab, the crisp air entering her lungs and pushing her hair back off her shoulders. She stared at the keys, picking out a tiny silver one for mailbox twenty-five. Caden let the key slide in and turn. The door opened, revealing a single letter.

Her hand grabbed the letter, pushed it into her jacket pocket, and closed the mailbox. She followed the small path to the dark gray door, opened it, locked it, and then fell onto the couch. She still hadn't told her mother about the condo. It had become her place to think, her place to dream of Gabriel without interruption. Maybe she didn't need it anymore. What would Nikolai think if he knew she spent her time here? Caden looked at the ceiling for a moment before she brought the letter up in the air. She turned it over, running her finger along the edge. She unfolded the lined paper, the light from above shining through it.

Caden,

What the heck happened? I'm only awake at night. I need answers. I need you.
—Gabriel

Her fingers fumbled nervously for the envelope. Hoping to find more, her hand reached in and pulled out a plane ticket, scheduled to leave at midnight that night and arrive in Southern California at 2:00 a.m.

Caden let out a heavy breath and closed her eyes,

counting to three. Opening her eyes again, she glanced back down at the short letter. She held it up with a trembling hand. *Five hours.* She didn't have that much time to pack.

Thank you for reading *Sleeping Tom*!

Continue the series with *Waking Gabriel*. For updates sign up for my newsletter email list by visiting my website **fairfall.com**

I appreciate all reviews—they help readers find my book. Please take a moment to leave a review on **Goodreads** or **Amazon**.

Acknowledgments

I'd like to thank my editing team and life support, Michelle Rimlinger, Ara Grigorian, and Jeff Seymour, for making Sleeping Tom a reality. I appreciate your direction and your willingness to read my book over and over again. Ara and Michelle, a special thank you for always having so much faith in Gabriel and encouraging his sweeter side. Thank you for helping me get back up during the difficult editing weeks/months. To my beta readers, KelleyAnn Thai, Cindie O., Judie Roderick, Tiffany York, Emily Bradley-Dorman and Nyx(Mony): you are all so wonderful. Thank you! To Elijah Girgis for talking to me about culinary school. To my husband, whose crazy sleepwalking/sleep-talking—and my lack of sleep in response to it—gave me the idea for the book in the first place. To my family for your support. And to anyone who has had a less than easy life, I hope this book is a comfort, reminding you that you aren't alone in your struggles and that slowly, things do get better.

About the Author

The hunger is encompassing, so she feeds the beast books. But the hunger never settles... so she writes. E.V. Fairfall has an itch that drives her to the world of story telling. With several published short stories, and soon several books (fingers crossed), she explores the topics of humanity and hardship.

During the daylight hours, a book is always within reach. She spends her nights reading with her husband, surrounded by towers of tomes and three furry children curled in close. If she isn't reading, she is browsing bookstores or hiking, but always awaiting her next adventure.

Fairfall.com